BLEEDING LIKE ME
Riley Parks

JACKIE,
 I CAN'T THANK YOU ENOUGH FOR YOUR CONTINUED SUPPORT. YOUR COMMENTS AND COMPLIMENTS HAVE BRIGHTENED MY DAYS IMMENSELY & I WILL BE FOREVER GRATEFUL FOR YOU.
 LOVE
 Riley Parks

www.BOROUGHSPUBLISHINGGROUP.com

PUBLISHER'S NOTE: This is a work of fiction. Names, characters, places and incidents either are the product of the author's imagination or are used fictitiously. Any resemblance to actual events, locales, business establishments or persons, living or dead, is coincidental. Boroughs Publishing Group does not have any control over and does not assume responsibility for author or third-party websites, blogs or critiques or their content.

BLEEDING LIKE ME
Copyright © 2017 Riley Parks

All rights reserved. Unless specifically noted, no part of this publication may be reproduced, scanned, stored in a retrieval system or transmitted in any form or by any means, electronic, mechanical, photocopying, recording, or otherwise, known or hereinafter invented, without the express written permission of Boroughs Publishing Group. The scanning, uploading and distribution of this book via the Internet or by any other means without the permission of Boroughs Publishing Group is illegal and punishable by law. Participation in the piracy of copyrighted materials violates the author's rights.

ISBN 978-1-979932-14-1

*To those who dare to love even in the wake of seemingly insurmountable obstacles,
this one is for you.*

ACKNOWLEDGEMENTS

Thank you to my family who always support me, even when I get stuck in my head, lost in the stories I need to tell.

A special thank you to Jill, for her honesty and insight.

Thank you to all my friends who believed in me.

BLEEDING LIKE ME

1

Three minutes. That's all it took for the course of his life to diverge, his ambitions and priorities to shift in a different direction. It wasn't as though he hadn't been groomed for this. He was South Side after all. Kids in his neighborhood grew up ready to piss their potential away at the hands of drugs and crime. He'd been an eager participant in too many objectionable acts to count, so he figured he may as well man the fuck up and get paid for it. It wasn't that he was unaware that it was stupid as hell to be standing in the middle of a dilapidated building with four men squared up around him; it was just that Evan didn't care.

"Only jumped me in with two," Kane said, making sure the disapproval could be heard in his voice, but careful that it wasn't too loud.

"Yeah, well, you're always talking up how tough the fucker is, G. We going to find out if it's true," Cedric replied with a wry smile. "You bad, Red? Hmm?" he questioned, the challenge evident on his face.

Kane threw an apologetic look toward Evan, but he was too busy staring down Cedric to acknowledge it.

"Guess we'll find out," Evan stated flatly.

One of the bangers standing behind him cracking his knuckles obnoxiously caused adrenaline to flood Evan's veins and made his fists clench tight. He'd been in plenty of fights. From typical scrapping with classmates when he was younger to angry ass beatings and some fight club shit, he'd never felt like he'd been bested.

As cocky as he was, he wasn't delusional. If he'd been brawling four guys who were smaller than him, he would've worried about his chances. Taking on four guys who were around his size had him focusing on survival rather than victory.

Either way, he wasn't going to complain. Not in this situation or any other. Bitching was for bitches, and he wasn't a fucking bitch. He'd learned at an early age that nobody gave a shit about what he said, and they gave even less of a shit when he griped, so he didn't.

"Guess we will," Cedric agreed. "Got the timer ready?" he asked, turning to Kane and Jamal, who were sitting on upside-down milk crates. "Keep him honest."

"Know me better than that," Kane huffed, clearly insulted by the implication that he would fuck around with the time. As much as he didn't want Evan to endure more than he had to, he'd told his brother earlier, he wasn't going to cut it short. Evan was a big boy and knew what he was getting himself into, he knew the score.

"Blood is blood," Cedric stated with a click of his tongue, "right?"

"Blood is Klown Killerz," the younger Goodwyn shot back, earning him a satisfied nod from Cedric, an appreciative pat on his back from his friend beside him, and nothing from the man standing inside the circle of wolves; not that he'd expected anything from him anyway.

Malted beer had always been thicker than blood in their family; it's why Kane had joined up in the first place. He wanted to feel like he was a part of something, loved, special. He'd told Evan he would benefit from the camaraderie, too. Kane had always been a loner, more difficult to understand than the rest of Evan's siblings who spouted off their issues like a busted fire hydrant. It wasn't that Kane didn't love Evan. He did. It was more that he didn't really know him.

Evan wondered if anyone ever had.

"What're your favorite colors?" Trent barked out. "Hurry the fuck up. I wanna get this shit over. I got shit to do for a couple of the O-Gs."

"Maroon, blue, and white," Evan rattled off, feeling his body vibrate with anticipation of what was about to go down.

Cedric nodded. "We about to make that white body bleed maroon and bruise blue. Make you prove you're worthy of wearing those colors."

Three minutes. It was incredible how short a minute felt when Evan sprayed graffiti or got lost in his drawings. Hours turned to seconds, which was particularly problematic when he was tagging. Too many times, he'd found himself so wrapped up in his piece that he forgot that his brand of art wasn't appreciated by the cops. The only benefit he'd derived from his propensity for distraction was that it had conditioned him to run fast and hurdle high. He was well aware neither of those skills was going to come in handy in his current situation. It seemed a tolerance for pain and an outpouring of suppressed anger were going to be his most valuable tools.

He was cognizant that he needed to focus on Cedric and Trent, because getting hit from behind was too much of a pussy move for the KKz.

Though he knew it was coming, the first punch took him by surprise. He had been expecting the blow to be delivered by Cedric, but it was a jab from Trent directly in Evan's right jaw that started the clock. He admonished himself for letting them get one in, but shook it off when he remembered how unrealistic it would've been for them not to. When Trent went for a second jab, Evan blocked him and gave the dude an uppercut that had his head spinning as he fell back. Evan's survival instincts had heightened his senses, allowing him to tune into every sound and detect from where the next threat was coming.

"Strong," Cedric grumbled, signaling for the two guys behind Evan to restrain him so that he could whale on him. "But that ain't really the point, man."

They didn't hold Evan there for long, but it was enough time for Cedric to fuck him up pretty good. Without the ability to defend himself, punch after punch clobbered his body from his head to his stomach and back up again. The pain was so intense and widespread that he could barely focus on which parts were affected. When his arms were dropped, his body went slack, but it took him a second to comprehend what the lack of support indicated. Upon realization, he implored his wobbly knees to hold him upright, knowing he'd be worse off on the ground. As he bobbed he felt warmth pouring from his nose and mouth, the unmistakable taste of iron on his tongue.

With four men coming at him in unison, his attempts at landing hits were futile, but he kept swinging anyway, refusing to fall until he received a brutal uppercut from the man he'd given one to moments before, and Evan went down. He felt his eyes rolling back in his head as feet pounded into his body; the several kicks his stomach and balls received had him gasping for air. He curled up in the eye of the storm of aggression as agony rained down upon him. Just when he thought he couldn't take any more, it stopped. As quickly as it had escalated, it subsided, hands reaching for his to pull him up to a seated position and pats on his back congratulating him for his new status.

"Put up a good fucking fight," Trent complimented, rubbing his jaw as he looked down at the battered man Evan had become.

Evan nodded and turned his head to the side a bit so he could spit out a wad of blood. Tracing his tongue over the upper and lower rows of his teeth, he checked that they were all still there, relieved when he felt that they were.

"Told you he was hard," Kane boasted, leaning down to hug his brother, who grimaced at the touch but still managed to lift his aching arms to hug Kane back. "Blood in, man."

"Blood in," Evan muttered, spitting again and watching as it splatted across the concrete ground.

"Not going to lie, tough as a motherfucker," Cedric commended, tossing Evan a blue bandana to clean up his face with. "But I don't think they're going to put him on the war crew, he's definitely party."

Evan looked up at them skeptically as he wiped off the blood. Kane had given him the rundown of as much of the Klown Killers' activities as he could, but he hadn't told Evan anything about a party crew. He enjoyed getting faded, probably more than he should have, but parties weren't his thing. "I tag," he informed him with a sputtering cough. "Could do that."

"They'll have you tag turf, no doubt, man. But that ain't going to bring in any money. War crew does that physical shit. Protects our turf, drive-bys, extortion, robbery, kidnapping, homicide, peddling the product, you know, all that," Trent explained. "They put the pretty boys on party crew."

"Should I be insulted?" Kane joked, lighting a cigarette, "Because I'm pretty fucking insulted."

"Shut the fuck up, cuz. You pull more pussy than any of us." Jamal grinned, pounding his friend's knuckle with his own.

"Speak for yourself." Cedric smirked.

"If I'm not doing any of that, what am I doing?" Evan asked, uninterested with hearing how much tail the guys were pulling.

"You deal with hoes and parties. Dress up real nice, go around to the clubs and get hot, rich bitches to be down with Klown Killerz," stated one of the members who had participated in holding him back so Cedric could beat the shit out of him.

"So, getting guys fucked?" Evan questioned, unimpressed. Dealing with women was incredibly low on his list of shit he wanted to do in his life.

"Some of that, but we get the bitches to do shit for us. We use their cars for drive-bys, have them run drugs, give us shit from where they work at, come to our parties so we can sell more beer cups, sometimes we get them into whoring," Cedric clarified. "A few of the O-Gs will let you know more tomorrow. Sleep this shit it off, a'ight man? Don't worry about anything. You going to be good to walk?" He extended Evan a hand, which he took, allowing himself to be pulled to his feet. A wave of nausea immediately had his stomach flipping, causing him to bend over and dry heave. It was the first time he was thankful that he hadn't had anything to eat for the past two days.

"I got him," Kane assured the rest of the guys as they fist pounded and half-hugged their good-byes.

"Party crew?" Evan lifted his eyebrows and pursed his lips at his brother. "You never told me anything about that."

"Figured you'd roll with me, I guess," Kane said with a shrug. "It's pretty cool though. Don't got to worry too much about doing serious time if you get popped by the cops."

Evan let out a light laugh, which he instantly regretted, holding on to his side and groaning at the stabbing pain in his rib. "I don't know, three squares and some fresh suburban air doesn't sound that bad right now." Neither did the never-ending rotation of "gay for the stay" ass he could fuck, but he certainly wasn't going to add that.

"You're saying that now because you're all fucked up," Kane teased with a toothy smile. "You'll feel better in the morning. You find a place to stay yet?"

"Nah, but got a spot at the shelter last night, so it was a'ight." Evan hoped he'd get a bed tonight too. The summer day was scorching and sleeping on the ground would be brutal on his bruised body.

"Crash with me and the boys," Kane offered. "You're affiliated now, not going to be a problem."

"You sure?" Typically, Evan didn't like to take any favors, but in his current state he was willing to make an exception.

"Yeah, man. Skizzo got thrown in the can for racketeering, so there's an extra room and a bed. All that shit. We even got air."

"That's awesome." Evan nodded his approval. "Thanks."

"Not awesome for Skizzo," Kane stated with a smirk.

"Plus they call him Skizzo, so that kinda sucks to begin with." Evan chuckled then grasped his side and sighed out of the laugh. "You have hot water?"

"Yup."

And just like that, three minutes had changed his whole life.

2

Jackson didn't jump people in. Not anymore. That was kid shit and he was too busy moving bricks to worry about the next round of young motherfuckers who were going to end up in body bags. He hardly remembered life before Dem Demonz. It had been ten years since he was on the receiving end of the beatdown that changed lives. He wished he could say that he would have made a different decision now than his thirteen-year-old self did then, but he didn't fucking lie to himself or to anyone else. Except cops. Those pigs didn't deserve the truth.

Evidently the set had come up short-handed and needed to push this new guy through. As usual, when a favor was needed, they turned to the member who they knew would always come through. Jackson didn't jump people in, until his gang needed him to, and when they did, he was there whether he was above that shit or not.

"Well look who the fuck showed up," Aiden greeted excitedly, shaking Jackson's hand and pulling him in for a hug before doing the same with Luke. "How's this asshole unlucky enough to get two Jablonics?" Aiden questioned, giving the skinny recruit standing on the pitcher's mound an exaggerated grimace. "You're fucked, brother."

"Don't know, but I ain't happy about it," Jackson grunted, knocking the side of his nose with the pad of his finger and glaring at the boy who looked like he was about to wet himself. "Got better shit to do than snap a fucking twig in half."

It wasn't the kid's size or the fact that he seemed like a halfwit that would send him to prison or the grave within his first two years with the Dem Demonz; it was simply the realities of street life.

Jackson did his first stint at fourteen. He and Aiden were told to knock over a shitty little convenience store called The Stop. After they emptied the register, Jackson's cocky ass decided to hang around and go grocery shopping when he should've just fucked off with Aiden. The owner, who appeared ready to shit himself prior, grabbed his balls and popped Jackson in the thigh before calling the police. He served a year that time and when he got out he was right back to banging.

He'd lost count of the number of times he'd been behind bars. The last decade had felt like a revolving door of incarcerations. Though he was ready to be done with the cycle, he knew it was just a matter of time until he got thrown back in. Having a rap sheet like his kept him on the cops' radar, and that type of attention didn't bode well for discreet operations.

"C'mon, Jack," Luke poked with a grin, "you're throwing it back old school today. A little reminder of what it's like to be on the bottom."

Jackson knew all about being on the bottom. Though he was more than all right with it in some aspects of his life, there was no way he was interested in falling down the hierarchy of Dem Demonz. He'd busted his ass to get where he was, and as far as he was concerned there was no going backward.

"You worry about staying on the bottom, faggot," Jackson shot back with a sniff. He wasn't in the mood for any bullshit, even Luke's typical brand. "You going to at least fight back, motherfucker?" he questioned the recruit, who seemed to be doing his best scared puppy impression. "Make it worth it for me to give up three minutes of my day?"

The kid nodded quickly.

"He asked you a fucking question, Terrence," Aiden barked, giving Jackson a sly wink. "Do like they tell you to do in kindergarten and use your goddamn words."

"I'm going to fight," Terrence answered, clearing his throat and balling his fists. Jackson tried to stifle his laughter, deciding that this might be fun after all. It had been a while since he scrapped. He had a reputation that made anyone with half a brain keep their distance. The problems Jackson had to deal with were more homicide level than a kick in the balls.

"What're your favorite colors?" Luke questioned, knowing his brother wasn't one for formalities.

"Black, gray, and white," the recruit answered quickly, as if he was proud that he'd studied up. Jackson smirked, knowing how much more he had to learn.

"Don't matter if you're black or white, you betray Dem Demonz, you end up gray," Luke rattled off, signaling for Aiden to start the timer. He glanced at Jackson, who was already bored with the process but was approaching the kid anyway.

"Get off the dirt," Jackson directed, waving Terrence toward him. "Not going to get my shoes dirty."

The recruit did as he was told, standing on the grass of the diamond for a second before falling on it in the next as Jackson coldcocked him.

"You got to be shittin' me." Jackson shook his head and punched out an aggravated exhale. "Is he fucking serious right now?" he asked Aiden, who was laughing hysterically. "Holy shit, we're letting pussies in?" He leaned over so he could pick Terrence up by his collar. "Stand the fuck up. Stand. The. Fuck. Up," he demanded louder. The boy struggled to plant his feet, and as soon as he did, Jackson laid him out again.

In any other circumstance, Jackson would've given him one good kick, spit in his face, and rolled out, knowing there was no pride in an unfair fight, but it was a jump-in and he owed it to his colors to fuck the kid up for the full three minutes.

"Think you're going to have to sit this one out, huh, Luke?" Jackson said, scratching his head as he watched Terrence climb to his feet, looking like a baby deer testing his legs for the first time.

"Yup," Luke replied, lighting up a cigarette and taking a seat on the patchy turf next to Aiden.

"Get one in, man. C'mon," Jackson practically pleaded, moving closer to the kid, who was sporting a hell of a bloody nose. "Hit me."

Terrence narrowed his eyes and appeared skeptical that it was some sort of test he was about to fail. But it wasn't. There was something about the feeling of a fist pounding into his bone that drove Jackson crazy: an almost sexual release of tension that brought him to another plane of consciousness. Every so often he craved pain as much as he did pleasure. Sometimes he fantasized about having both simultaneously, but there wasn't much time for rough play or bondage behind the bushes in a park.

"You fucking stupid? I said hit me, bitch," Jackson growled, sighing when he felt the punch crack against his jaw. He laughed and licked his lip, satisfied that the guy could jab better than he took one. "Again."

"Jack," Aiden warned, "you got to wreck him, not play punching bag."

"I'll take care of him." Jackson shot Aiden a look that screamed *shut the fuck up* before turning back to Terrence and raising his eyebrows. "Again."

The younger man delivered another blow to the side of Jackson's face, causing him to hum "Like that" quietly. Knowing that he had to get down to business, Jackson placed his hands on either side of the kid's face and bashed their foreheads together. As soon as Terrence crumpled to the ground, Jackson started to go off on him, kicking him harder each time he drew his foot back. The final blow was a brutal punt to the underside of the kid's chin that had him lying motionless with his mouth hanging open.

Jackson nudged the thin body with the toe of his boot until the new member was on his side. Squatting down, Jackson slid his hand into the back pocket of Terrence's jeans and pulled out his wallet. He opened it and tsked. "Dumbass ain't strapped and he brought two hundred dollars to the fucking hood. We really gonna let him in?" He turned to Aiden and Luke, who shook their heads at the news.

"Got to have the idiots to put on the front lines." Aiden shrugged. "If we don't take them the fucking faggot-ass KKz will. They're growing quick. Our Halstead boys said they're starting to tag our corners. We got to have some disposable foot soldiers to sacrifice."

"Yeah, all right," Jackson mumbled, rubbing his forehead in irritation. "I don't want him working my product, though. I need higher functioning people peddling the good shit."

"You know that ain't my decision. I recruit them. That's all. Talk to Isaiah," Aiden suggested with a yawn. "I got to take a fucking nap. This shit took a lot out of me."

"What took a lot out of you?" Luke chuckled. "The two blocks you had to drag your fat ass to get here? A little exercise ain't going to hurt you, Tubs. Promise you that."

"Fuck you, Mop Top," Aiden huffed, giving his friend a hard shove. "Help me up."

Luke rose to his feet, brushing off the back of his jeans, and then tugged on the heavier man's arms to assist him.

"I'll talk to Isiah then," Jackson decided, shoving the bills into his wallet and standing up. He climbed over Terrence so that he could prod him over to the other side. Reaching into his second pocket, he pulled out a flattened pack of cigarettes with a grin. "Deserve to get paid for taking time away from the shit I got to do to take care of his scrawny ass."

"By shit you got to do, are you talking about Tamara?" Aiden teased. "Because it ain't right to talk about your girl that way."

"That's why I fucking wasn't." Jackson grinned, lighting up one of Terrence's cigarettes and throwing the rest of the pack on his feeble form.

"Am I going to see you guys at Lyle's tomorrow night? I'll buy you a cup," Aiden volunteered, looking at Jackson so it was clear that the offer was for him.

"Me too?" Luke questioned as they all walked away from Terrence, who Jackson figured would come to in the next hour or so.

"Not fucking happening," Aiden scoffed. "You're a nasty little shit making fun of my weight."

"Don't be so sensitive, man. If you don't want people to talk about your lard ass, lose some weight," Luke suggested. "Then you won't have to get butt hurt."

"You guys ever shut the fuck up?" Jackson groaned as he took a drag and blew the smoke into the hazy summer air.

"Sometimes, but it ain't as fun when I do," Aiden replied with a proud smile. "You going to come, Jack? Tomorrow night? C'mon. You don't come out enough. Bring the girls."

"You still trying to get with Amy?" Luke asked, while Jackson pointedly ignored Aiden's questions and focused on enjoying his smoke. "Because that's never going to happen. She's still fucking with Isaiah and when he's done with her she's off limits."

"Don't talk about my sister that way," Jackson warned, glaring at Luke out of the corner of his eye. "She ain't one of his hoes."

"She's my sister, too," Luke reminded him.

"Yeah? Then act like it, prick." He rolled his tongue under his bottom lip and huffed out a sigh, hoping he didn't have to teach Luke a lesson on respect soon.

"Sorry, Jack."

Jackson nodded as they approached his street. He slapped Aiden on the back and said, "I'll see you tomorrow night, fatass."

"Can't wait, brother. It's going to be a rager, I promise."

Jackson didn't really party. Not anymore. He didn't party until his friend asked him to, and then he showed up.

3

It didn't take long for Evan to get settled in his new room. He only had as much as he could shove into his backpack, so setup consisted of dumping that shit on the floor and lying down on the stained mattress to rest his head. Though there were no sheets on the bed and his body was sore, it was the most comfortable night's sleep he'd had in a while.

He'd never had his own room. When he was younger, he'd shared with his brothers and after he got kicked out of the house he'd crashed wherever he could: friends' couches, with people he fucked, or shelters in the winter, and the banks of the lake or park benches in the summer if he couldn't get a bed at the Mission. He regretted not listening to Kane and joining the KKz years ago. He had to remind himself to keep control and not fuck it up.

He wasn't sure how long he'd slept, but there was sunlight streaming past the kinked blinds when his rumbling stomach woke him, insistent that he put something in it. Groaning as he stretched his achy limbs, he climbed out of bed and headed into the kitchen to see if there was anything to eat. He was surprised to find Kane, Jamal, and a guy he didn't know sitting at the table playing cards and smoking blunts.

"Breakfast of Champions?" he asked with a smirk, nodding when Kane passed him a blunt. He took a deep inhale, cringing when his side reminded him that he'd gotten rocked the day before.

"It's noon, cracker." Jamal laughed as Evan looked to Kane for confirmation. His brother nodded and patted him on his bare hipbone.

"Doesn't look so bad," he stated, gesturing to the bruises on Evan's torso.

"All good," Evan assured, glancing at the guy he didn't know. "I'm Evan."

"Luis," the dude said as he reached out his hand to shake Evan's. "There are some burritos in the fridge if you want one."

"Yeah?" Evan asked, raising his eyebrows eagerly.

"Mmmhmm."

He didn't waste any time grabbing one and tossing it into the microwave. He could hardly wait the minute it took to heat it up, digging in as soon as he pulled it out. The guys watched as he scarfed it down with fervor.

"Look pretty thin, man," Kane observed, taking in Evan's boxer-clad form. "You not eating enough?"

"Don't worry about it," Evan mumbled, his mouth full of Mexican food.

Kane tapped his cards against the table and sighed, deciding not to push the issue.

"You and I got a date today, Red," Luis informed him, taking a sip of his forty.

"Not on that faggot shit." Evan grinned around the burrito he was still shoving into his mouth.

"Good, 'cause I wouldn't want to fuck a bitch without an ass anyway," Luis teased back, drawing a laugh from Evan, who was in a pretty fucking good mood with his belly full of food and his head getting a nice buzz off the Kush. "Nah, man, I'm not typically on party but I'm doing my boy Micah a favor and training you tonight. We got to go out and get you some clothes, a razor, and shit like that this afternoon."

"Don't got any money," Evan stated plainly.

"You're a Klown Killer now, cracks," Jamal told him. "We take care of our own."

"When you start bringing in some dough, you'll get us back. We collect money for the house once a week. You know, for groceries, alcohol, and weed. Enough to cover the necessities," Luis explained.

Evan nodded and noticed the look of warning he was getting from his brother. He didn't blame him for the nonverbal reminder. He'd spent enough time fucking up in the past to know that the concern was warranted, but his brother had put his own reputation on the line to bring Evan in and there was no way he was going to screw that up.

Of all the things he'd done that he regretted, and there were a lot of them, stealing from the family's shoebox savings was tops. The first time he did it, he'd intended to pay it back but got himself into some heat with a local dealer and wasn't able to make it happen. The second time he hadn't given it a thought. He was desperate for a hit and knew there was a can of money sitting idly in the kitchen. He should've shown more remorse when he was caught, but he hadn't; his mind was too overtaken by the drugs he was flooding it with to give a shit.

Mom and Pops had bolted so his older sister, Emma, and brother, Paul, had taken over running the family. When they'd had enough, they'd kicked him out, fed up with his habit and his propensity to gank shit to feed it. At seventeen he was on his own and now, four years later, he wasn't going to make the same mistakes again. It meant something to him that Kane had offered him a bed, even though he was well aware of his history. He wanted to do right by his bro and, selfishly, wanted to enjoy having his own room for as long as possible.

"Go throw on some clothes and we'll hit up the Goodwill for some club clothes. We're heading up to the North Side tonight to pick up some daddy's girls."

"Or girls that'll call you daddy," Kane corrected with a cocky head nod.

"What do you know about that?" Evan belched loudly and tossed the aluminum foil that used to hold the burrito into the trash.

"Bitches have been calling me 'daddy' since elementary school." Kane smirked. "Don't act like you don't remember that shit."

"I remember you got caught fucking that Gracie chick under the bleachers in seventh grade," Evan reminded Kane. "Emma was pissed as fuck, but Paul and I smoked you up that night to celebrate."

"Fuck, those were the good old days," Kane sighed, seeming to get lost in the memories.

Evan was glad he never got caught doing the same with Ryan Spellman. He would've had a lot more explaining to do than Kane ever had, and Evan was sure his brother Paul wouldn't have gifted him with weed after the revelation.

He felt a stir in his boxers and quickly excused himself to take a shower before he started tenting them. He knew it had been too long since he'd gotten laid if thoughts of his middle school sex life were turning him on.

Since he was going to be on the North Side later, he knew exactly where he was going to go to get fucked. He couldn't wait to be done with whatever bullshit he had to take care of so he was free to find some dude's ass to rail.

X

The Drexel was everything Evan hated about the North Side and people in general. It was packed with girls who were fake as fuck from their tans to their hair, tits, and personalities. The guys weren't much better, wearing douchey pink Polo shirts and talking about their cars, boats, and latest business deals. Evan was pretty sure he and Luis stood out like sore thumbs, despite having picked collared shirts and dark wash jeans especially for the occasion.

"Remember what you're going to say about your eye," Luis prompted, studying Evan's face to see if his black eye would be noticeable in the lighting, which he knew it was. "Rugby."

"Have no idea how the game works," Evan informed him. "What if they ask me some questions I can't answer?"

"You find a way to answer them, Red," Luke laid it down. "Don't use rugby. I don't give a fuck. Just come up with something that sounds rich."

Evan nodded. He knew the plan. Luis had decided to start small and teach him their credit card fraud tricks since the whole party scene wasn't really his area of expertise. Though the training wasn't extensive, Evan felt confident that he'd be able to get the job done, and the thought of indulging in the spoils was amazing. As he approached a busty blonde, he kept repeating the items that he intended to buy with her credit card number. It made talking to her a more palatable exercise. It had only taken a few seconds for her to notice, before she began to flirt mercilessly.

"Can I buy you a drink, doll?" he crooned, giving her the widest smile he could muster.

"Only if you tell me where you got that black eye, handsome," she flirted, resting her hand high on Evan's thigh. "Love my men rough."

He cleared his throat, attempting to steel himself for the onslaught of questions he was sure she'd ask.

"Got in a fight over some dumb shit." The lie rolled off his tongue, and yeah, he was well aware that he was going off script.

"Sexy," she sighed in reply, tossing her blonde locks over her shoulder and licking her lips suggestively.

"Lemme buy you a drink?" He did the man-beg as he made a show of staring at her cannonball tits even though they disgusted him.

"I'd love that." She giggled, shimmying her chest slightly in order to entice him even further, not realizing she was barking up the wrong tree.

Luis had busied himself with another desperate bitch as Evan and blondie requested their drinks from the bartender. When it came time to pay, Evan made a show of pulling out his wallet like he was supposed to and sighed as he feigned his disappointment when he realized his nonexistent credit card wasn't there.

The girl took the bait, immediately waving off Evan's faux protests as she pulled out her own card and laid it down on the mahogany surface of the bar. He forced a smile as she placed a hand on his freshly shaven face and then let it drag down the front of his maroon button-down to the waist of his jeans. She looked away as she let her hand move down to the crotch of his pants, while she took a sip of her Amaretto Sour.

He discreetly reached into his pocket and took out the burner that Luis had given him. As the blonde attempted to play it coy, he snuck a picture of her credit card before the bartender had the chance to slide it off the bar top to run it. Within seconds of Evan completing his task, her coquettish act had given way to a more direct tactic. She leaned in close and whispered, "You ever fuck on cocaine?"

Chugging his full beer bottle until it was empty, he raised his eyebrows and followed her as she sauntered toward the bathroom. All of a sudden the club wasn't as shitty a place to be as it had been moments before.

The women's lavatory was crowded, but nobody seemed to bat an eye when he entered or when blondie started cutting lines on the brushed metal countertop. It had been so long since he'd had the opportunity to bump the good stuff. He'd had to settle for whatever he had been able to get his hands on and he could feel his mouth begin to water with want as he watched her roll up a Benjamin. Leaning over, she snorted two long lines in practiced succession before handing the money over and gesturing for him to hit the other two lines she'd cut. He did so enthusiastically, licking his lips and closing his eyes when he felt the delicious rush.

When the coke was all inhaled, he left the bathroom wordlessly, hearing her shrill voice call after him over the pounding beat of the hip-hop music that was thumping in the club. He planned to fuck on cocaine, but it wasn't going to be her who he was banging.

4

Lyle's basement was packed with sweaty, drunk revelers by the time Jackson, Tamara, Luke, and Amy rolled up. At twenty-three years old, Jackson felt like a fossil in a crowd that consisted mostly of unaffiliated neighborhood kids who had overpaid for their cups, and the younger generation of DDz. Since Aiden was in charge of recruitment, he was always throwing house parties. Jackson rarely came though, much more interested in chilling with O-Gs rather than the KinderKids, but occasionally he made an exception if he was feeling particularly generous. He knew that his reputation held a certain appeal for guys looking to make a name for themselves in the streets, so his presence was good for the bottom line.

Most of the air had been sucked out of the space, and what was left reeked of weed, cigarette smoke, stale beer, and body odor. Bodies bobbing to the bumping beat looked like a human wave, undulating with the rhythm, alive with energy.

"Smells like high school," Amy stated, sticking out her tongue and cringing.

"I love it." Luke grinned, taking in the scene. "Lots of cuties here."

"They're pretty much all jailbait, perv," his sister tsked, shooting an unimpressed look toward Jackson, who sighed and shook his head in reply.

"It's so humid in here," Tamara groused, raking her perfectly manicured fingernails through her thick black hair, making a show of it. "I literally just went to Janelle for a blowout today, baby. I don't want it to get poofy."

"Ain't going to be here long," Jackson promised, draping an arm over her shoulders and giving her a reassuring shake. "Just making an appearance."

"I told Kylie we'd be over by eleven," she reminded him, blue eyes giving fair warning that she wouldn't be pleased if they were late. "So we need to be."

"Heard you the first twenty times you told me, Tams," he replied with pursed lips, removing his arm as quickly as he'd put it there.

It wasn't that he didn't try with Tamara. He did. He'd spent years trying, but he could never make himself fall in love with her, want her, or be attracted to her. She was a woman after all, and he'd known early on that women didn't do it for him.

When he was growing up, he remembered chilling with his brothers and viewing porn where a girl got fucked. They all made a big deal about her tits and pussy, but he'd never understood the appeal. Watching a man take cock was much more exciting to him. Like most adolescent boys, he'd jerked off like a fiend, always discovering new ways to please himself. His hand on his dick never felt like enough. He experimented with his fingers first, learning how to stretch himself by mimicking the men on his screen. He relished the feeling of being breached. Craving more, he moved on to dildos and butt plugs before venturing out for the real thing.

He lost his virginity when he was thirteen to some whore the O-Gs gifted him with after a bunch of recruits had been jumped in. They were all sitting around in Isaiah's living room, smoking weed and drinking beer, when three skanky girls were brought in. They were already naked, rolling on E or some other cocktail of drugs the bangers had gotten them high on. One of the older guys had tossed condoms to the kids, and Jackson remembered watching as the rest of the new members dropped trou to slide them on. The sight of the women didn't do it for him, but the visual of all the ready cocks helped him get it up and preserve his pride. He fucked girls after that, but never found it as satisfying as fucking himself.

In his later teen years, he started to hit up Humboldt Park. It was on the West Side, a safe distance from his hood and his life. There was still some level of risk involved, but the more he got fucked by guys there, the more he knew he needed it and decided that it was safe enough. He was never with the same guy twice. There seemed to be a never-ending rotation of new cocks, and Jackson didn't see any reason to get too connected to one. Besides, it was around that time he'd found himself in a relationship, and that was taking up a shit ton of his energy.

Tamara was a neighborhood girl who was used to getting what she wanted, and she'd made it abundantly clear that Jackson was it. At first, he'd tried to resist her advances, but he quickly realized the more he turned her away, the more suspicious his boys were becoming. They all wanted Tammy and found it unfathomable that he wouldn't, so he pretended he did.

Early on he discovered that if he got drunk or high enough, he could fuck her more convincingly. He learned how to give her orgasms and fake his own. After they were together for about a year, she began pouting that he never went down on her. He'd told her flat out he didn't do that shit, and if she wanted it done she'd have to go ahead and find herself a dude who did. She never asked for it again. As time passed, they had less and less sex. Jackson was always coming up with excuses and Tammy always accepted them. Six years later, she mostly gave him head and he fucked her if he got wasted enough to not see straight. He knew she deserved better, but like so many other girls in their neighborhood, she didn't realize it.

He kept her happy enough, always making sure she had money to get her nails done, waxing, blowouts, facials, new shoes, purses, jewelry and whatever the fuck else she decided she needed at the time. Bankrolling Tamara was more expensive than the rent he paid for the apartment they lived in with Amy.

Jackson often found himself wishing that Tam would cheat on him or give him some legit reason to get rid of her, but she wasn't stupid. She knew Jackson's influence on the streets and what doing wrong by him would mean for her. Though he would happily pack her fucking bags if she found somebody else, his boys wouldn't do the same. He thought about ending it with her often, but figured there was no fucking point, since he'd probably end up having to fuck around with another girl to maintain his cred.

"You never come around my girls and I want you to know that it's important to me," Tamara whined, deliberately interlocking her slim fingers with Jackson's when she saw a few of the younger girls eyeing him down. "Want me to gouge your fucking eyeballs out, you dollar store bitches?" Tammy snapped, drawing a laugh from Amy and a look of horror from the girls who quickly turned away.

Jackson didn't say anything. He was painfully used to Tammy's jealous outbursts. He knew he got a fair amount of attention from the chicks, but his girlfriend's temper shined a spotlight on it.

"That's right, you better not look at my man," Tammy sneered, calming down as she turned to Jackson and gave him a sweet kiss on his cheek. "Can't take you anywhere. Get the girls too riled up."

"Why do you get so fucking pressed by sluts? Hmm?" Jackson questioned, licking his lips. "Told you that you don't got to worry about any other girl." Technically it was the truth. He hated to lie.

"Just hate hungry hoes," she replied.

"I fucking love them," Luke chimed in, giving his brother a wink. "Speaking of hungry, what's up, cuz?" he shouted as Aiden approached with a stack of red Solo cups in his hands.

"I'm going to ignore that 'cause I'm in a good mood." Aiden lifted his chin at Jackson.

"This shit got anything to do with it?" Jackson questioned, taking the new chain that was hanging around Aiden's neck between his fingers. It was seemed to be about twice the weight as Jackson's and had him wondering how his friend was able to afford it. Aiden had a few customers he sold powder to, but even if he'd moved all the product Jackson had given him, it wouldn't cover the cost of his new piece. "You sell all the eight balls?"

"Nah, Jack, I got a little side hustle goin' on."

"That right?" Jackson raised his eyebrows with curiosity. "Why don't you tell me about it?" He turned to Tammy. "We got some business to discuss, take care of Amy and I'll come get you when I'm done."

"I can take care of myself," Amy snarked with an eye roll.

"Well then fuck me for giving a shit," Jackson huffed, throwing his hands up as if he wasn't sure why he tried to be nice in the first place.

"No later than ten forty-five," Tammy warned.

"You don't give me terms or curfews, Tams," Jackson snarled, ice dripping from his voice. "If I'm not done, fuck off yourself to Kylie's."

Tammy looked like she was going to protest, but his face had turned to stone, and she knew she better not start shit. Instead, she allowed herself to get led to the keg by Amy, while Jackson, Luke, and Aiden went out to the front porch.

It was 10:55 when Tammy emerged from the house. "You ready to go?" She crossed her arms over her ample chest.

"Not going to make it tonight. Got some shit to handle," Jackson replied coolly.

"Are you serious right now?" she hissed. "I gave it 'til the last possible minute, Jack. Now I'm going to be late."

"Didn't fucking tell you to stay," he reminded her, taking a drag from his cigarette and exhaling, focusing on the way the smoke billowed in the air rather than his girlfriend's eyes.

"Asshole," she muttered, making her way down the steep porch steps in her five-inch heels.

"If I had pussy like that, I'd run after her everywhere she went," Aiden mused, taking a swig of his beer.

"Yeah and that's why you don't got pussy like that," Jackson poked with a tilt of his head and a smirk.

"That's the trick, huh? Be a dickhead?"

"It's always worked for Jack. Been a dickhead since the day he was born. Swear this motherfucker came out of Mom's vag telling her to go make him a fucking sandwich," Luke joked, dodging the beer can that his brother had lobbed at his head. "What kinda shit do we got to take care of anyway?" he questioned.

"Eh, it's on me," Jackson replied, staying as nonchalant as possible. "You don't got to worry about it."

"Don't need us to get your back?" Aiden asked.

Jackson shook his head. "Nah. Don't need any backup."

He was planning to back it up all on his own.

5

When Evan told Luis he got what they needed and was going to meet up with a fuck buddy, his new friend threw him the peace sign, and seemed more than happy to roll solo at The Drexel surrounded by beautiful women.

Evan made his way down the bustling North Side block that was filled with Chicago's elite, club kids, and the rest of the late-night set: different groups of people, all seeking the same magic that could only be found in a perfect moment, one that defined the evening and created a memory that would dance through their minds for years to come. Evan knew the feeling they were chasing. He felt it when he got lost in a painting. It had been so long since he'd been able to sweep acrylic across a canvas, and he couldn't help but smile knowing that the activities of the night had enabled him to have a paintbrush in his hand soon.

Luis had informed him earlier that they'd most likely be able to use the credit card for twenty-one days. That was how long it took before the typical victim got their bill and realized there was fraudulent spending. In Luis's experience, the rich ones sometimes didn't even notice when they received their statement. They simply paid it, not concerned that it was higher than usual. Luis's eyes lit up when he told Evan he'd once used a card for nineteen months before it was cancelled. The crew still talked about it as it grew to legendary status among the gang. Luis filled Evan in on all the tips and tricks, everything from how to purchase the goods to where to have them shipped. It all seemed surprisingly easy and Evan chided himself for not thinking of it on his own.

As he rode the bus to the West Side, he was more invigorated than he'd been in years. He wasn't sure if it was the Fire pulsing through his body, his belly being full, the fact that he had his own bedroom, or access to a credit card. Whatever, or all the above, he felt invincible. He stared out the window at the city lights blurring by, thinking that the city looked as alive as he was.

He rarely took it all in and acknowledged that though his life was mostly shit, he was surrounded by immense beauty; he just had to recognize it. Throwing his head back and laughing wildly at his flowery thoughts, he drew perplexed looks from fellow passengers. He couldn't help but grin when he realized it was definitely the coke. Everything was more magnificent when there were snowstorms in summer.

"You've never seen somebody happy?" he asked the woman in the seat next to him.

She nodded, surveying the bus as if she was looking for another place to sit.

"I'm in love," Evan confessed, licking his lips and leaning in closer to her with cocaine, Klown Killerz, his bedroom, and food fueling his sociability.

"Congratulations," she muttered, scooting as far to the edge of the seat as she could get without falling off. He pondered if she would've been as scared years ago, when he was an unassuming freckle-faced kid with puppy dog eyes. Though physically that boy had disappeared, on his best days Evan still felt like him on the inside.

She hurried to get off at the next stop and he wondered if she had planned to or if his boisterousness had caused her to run. Either way, he was thankful for the extra space.

He turned so his back was leaning against the window and stretched his legs across the empty seat. It had been a good day. All he needed to make it better was a warm mouth around his cock and then a tight ass to bury it in, preferably belonging to the same person.

He'd never been to Humboldt Park before, but he heard it had a pretty good scene. When he was unaffiliated, he could get away with going to the gay spots on the South Side, but now that he was with the KKz, he had to be more careful. He disembarked and walked the short distance to the big rock where guys supposedly met. Sitting down on a bench, he pulled out a cigarette he had bummed off Luis and watched as a couple of queens made a connection and disappeared into the wooded area a few feet behind the boulder. He let the filter rest between his lips as he leaned back to stare up at the moon. It was a waxing crescent that barely glowed against the black expanse of the sky, making the already poorly lit park even darker.

He peered down at a man who took a seat on the bench next to him. They sat quietly, Evan's head still thrown back and the guy smoking his cigarette as if he hadn't just propositioned him.

"Nice night," Evan threw out as if he was telling the moon rather than the guy beside him.

"Are you looking to chitchat or are you trying to fuck?" When Evan finally dropped his head, he noticed that the guy was peering at him with raised eyebrows. They stared for a moment, and without a doubt, a spark arced between them.

"Depends what you're into I guess," Evan replied, noticing that the man had a perfectly plump pout. He wanted to see what those lips looked like wrapped around his cock. "I'm not going to bend over."

"Wouldn't want you to," the guy replied with a sniff, blue eyes dropping to momentarily study the grass before returning to Evan's.

"That right?" he questioned, moderately surprised. Mr. Ready To Hook Up seemed to be tough as fuck, with his sleeve tattoos and muscular biceps that were perfectly displayed in his gray sleeveless shirt. Evan knew it was a stereotype that men who exclusively took cock were soft, but in his experience, more often than not, they had been. He'd fucked a variety of guys, and there was always some negotiating between him and a dude who was versatile. This hot motherfucker was clearly a power bottom, a fact that had Evan's cock standing up to take notice.

"Need me to spell it out for you, Daywalker?" he huffed, eyebrows raised in challenge.

Evan shook his head and self-consciously ran his fingers through his red hair. "So you want to go—" he began.

The guy interrupted by saying, "Show me what you got."

Without wasting another second, Evan tossed his cigarette to the ground and unzipped the fly of his jeans, arching his back enough to shimmy them, along with his boxer briefs, down his thighs so his hard cock could spring out. Instinctively, he moved a hand down to the shaft and started to pump it.

Blue eyes observed every stroke as full lips smacked subconsciously. "Yeah, I want to fuck," the guy stated, seemingly impressed by what Evan was working with. Wordlessly, the hot-as-shit motherfucker stood up and started walking, leaving Evan scrambling to get his pants up so he could follow.

The guy strode like he owned the park, the ground, the city, demonstrating more swagger than one person had the right to have. He was the same height as Evan, but somehow his presence made him appear even taller than six feet.

When they reached the edge of the wooded area, and obscured from view by a thick tree trunk, Hot Shit demanded that Evan take his "fucking shirt off." He complied, unbuttoning the maroon collared shirt and tossing it to the ground, slightly puzzled when the guy kicked it rather aggressively through the dirt. Evan gave a mental shrug then yanked off his wife-beater and tugged down his jeans, pleased to see the guy taking off his own pants and dropping to his knees.

The guy sucked dick like he was made for it, working Evan fervently until he felt like he was going to tumble over the edge, and then slowing it down to lap him up. Evan held back the moans that were desperate to escape his mouth, leaving only the sound of slurping to fill the air.

He watched as the man with the talented tongue reached beside him to pull a lube packet out of his wallet, which was in the pocket of his discarded pants.

"Holy shit," Evan breathed, tilting his head to the side so he could take in how the man was prepping himself as he gave him head. He was impressed by the skill level and efficiency. It was clear Hot Shit was well practiced in the art of park fucking, and Evan regretted not venturing over to the West Side years ago.

"Put on a rubber," the guy directed as he rose to his feet, rested his hands on the tree, and presented his ass to Evan.

That ass. It was firm, thick, and fucking perfect; the definition of a bubble butt. Evan had to hold himself back from leaning down and biting one of the fleshy mounds. That ass was the ultimate confirmation that he was having a phenomenal day.

"Don't have one," he stated, grabbing onto his hips with one hand and lining his cock up to his ass with the other.

"Ain't going to fuck me without a condom," Hot Shit scoffed, glaring over his shoulder and giving Evan a look that made him feel like a complete imbecile. Shaking his head with aggravation, Hot

Shit bent down to take a condom out of his wallet. It was shoved in there deep, far from anyone's peeking eyes. Evan wondered if the guy was married, but noticed he didn't have a ring on his finger.

Hot Shit tossed Evan the condom, and he quickly ripped open the foil and struggled to slide it over his cock. Once he rolled it down the best he could, he repositioned himself to breach that incredible ass. Though the pleasure of his cocaine high had waned, his body was falling into an even more addictive feeling.

The guy let out the sexiest breathy grunts as Evan bottomed out. As he began to roll his hips, he couldn't get his mind off how tight the condom was. Uncomfortably tight. So tight that he thought he was losing blood flow to his dick. "I need a magnum. This thing is strangling me." He pulled out abruptly, causing the other man to groan at the loss, while he sighed in relief at the release of pressure when he took the condom off. "Do you have one?"

"Do I look like a fucking drugstore to you?" Hot Shit snapped, hastily pulling up his pants, muttering something about Evan being a "waste of a big fucking dick."

"I can give you head," Evan offered, moderately embarrassed by his performance or lack thereof.

The guy eyed him down as if he was unsure if he wanted to find a guy who could actually fuck him or if he was all right with blowing his load on Evan. "Fine," Hot Shit relented, pulling down his pants again, which prompted Evan to get on his knees.

He sucked him good while he fingered his ready asshole, wishing it was his cock shoved in there instead. With his free hand he tugged on his own dick, thinking that both of his highs had now gotten away from him. When he hooked his fingers and jabbed against Hot Shit's prostate, the guy spasmed in Evan's mouth and poured a truckload of jizz down his throat. As Evan licked the guy's cock soft, Evan shot his own come into the dirt.

They got dressed quietly, Evan attempting to brush the dirt off his shirt before putting it on.

"Bring a fucking condom next time," the guy ordered before walking away.

Next time.

6

Jackson should have been annoyed that he'd gone all the way out to Humboldt to get fucked and didn't get the full cock ride in his ass. It should have turned him off that the redhead was clearly a dumbass, showing up to a fuck spot without a condom for his huge dick. Jackson should have been doing what he always did: fuck and forget. But for some reason he couldn't. There was something about the Daywalker that had Jackson not giving a shit about his should-haves and thinking more about what-ifs.

The last thing he needed was to get involved with some closeted North Side twink who wore maroon collared shirts like it wasn't a fucking insult, not to mention those goddamn skinny jeans. Dude was probably the male version of Tamara: too good-looking for his own good and needy as hell.

The fact that Jackson was even considering what the redhead's personality was like was blowing his mind. Maybe he was hypnotized by that dick. It was perfect: as thick as it was long and straight as an arrow. He loved the way it had lain full and heavy on his tongue while he was giving head and how deliciously it had stretched him during the nanosecond it was in his ass.

Jackson had never been with a guy so big. As soon as the redhead bottomed out, the tip of his cock had brushed against Jack's prostate, sending electric shocks through his body. Imagining what it would be like to get thoroughly fucked by that dick was mind-blowing. It had to be the reason why he couldn't get the dude out of his head. Once they properly fucked, Jackson would be able to move past it the way he had with so many men before. He was sure that it was the anticipation of the fuck that never happened that had him all messed up. So much so, he found all he could focus on, as the L made its way back to the South Side, was the stupid rich kid he had almost banged.

Of all the shit that went down, the maroon shirt should've bothered him the most. On the South Side, if he ran into a guy wearing that color, he'd assume he was a Klown Killer and fuck him up. He wouldn't give a shit how incredible his cock was. Those motherfuckers were bottom feeders, scavenging around to pick up scraps that Dem Demonz left behind.

Though the guy had a black eye and some bruises on his torso that made him look like he could've been about that life, Jackson was sure he was a college student or a trust fund kid. He'd probably fucked up his daddy's boat and got a fist to the face or got whacked by a pansy named Thurston in a polo match.

Jackson had never had respect for people who were born with money, not after he hustled to get where he was.

Maybe the guy had to keep up appearances and had a girlfriend like Jack did, social pressure forcing him to be somebody he wasn't. Jackson knew that shit too well. It was how his ass got stuck with Tammy. He sighed at the thought of her and hoped she'd be asleep by the time he got home. Unfortunately, he wasn't that lucky.

"It's late. Where were you?" she hissed from the couch in the dimly lit living room. Her hair was pulled up in a sloppy topknot and she was wearing one of Jackson's sleeveless tops, a gesture that he may have found endearing, if he was endeared by her.

"Why are you wearing my shit?" he grunted, pulling his wallet out of his pocket and placing it on the kitchen counter.

"Why am I wearing your shit?" she scoffed, shaking her head in disbelief. "Where were you, Jackson?"

"We've been together for six years, Tams, and I haven't answered that question once," he stated coolly, looking directly into her glassy eyes. He could tell she was drunk, and he knew that their conversation was seconds away from escalating.

"Well maybe you should start fucking answering it then," she screeched, throwing the blanket that was lying over her lap onto the ground before crossing the room and getting into his face. "Where the fuck were you?" she demanded, standing too close to Jackson for his liking. Her warm breath fanned over his skin, getting him more heated by the moment.

"Back the fuck up, Tamara," he warned. "I'm not playing with you right now, you better get out of my fucking face."

"Or...?" she taunted, closing the mere inches between them so their noses were practically touching. "You going to hit me, Jack? Fucking hit me then. It would hurt less than all the other bullshit you put me through."

Jackson closed his eyes and clenched his fists, attempting to steel himself. He'd never hit a woman, but fuck if he didn't want to sometimes. Tamara knew how to push every single one of his buttons, and though she was often careful not to provoke him, when she was drunk her self-control got away from her. As far as he was concerned she was difficult enough to deal with when she was sober and nearly impossible when she was under the influence.

"Do you know how badly it embarrasses me when I tell people you'll be coming through and you never fucking do?" The spray of her spit misted his skin as she grew louder. "Hmm?"

"People probably think I'm fucking pathetic to stay with a guy who clearly doesn't give a shit about me. Maybe I am. Maybe I'm fucking pathetic." She let out a wry laugh and rubbed her forehead. "Am I, Jack? Am I pathetic to stay with you? I mean, you won't tell me you love me. Six fucking years and you've never said the words." She kept ranting, not noticing that a sleepy Amy had exited her room and was standing by her door, arms crossed over her chest. "We never fuck, like at all, and you can hardly get it up for me to suck your dick." She let out a sputtering sigh. "I am. I'm pathetic."

"Don't tell them I'm going to come through," he suggested, lifting his brows, determined to ignore the rest of her outburst. "Solves the problem, right? Don't tell them."

Tammy's spray-tanned skin flushed an angry red. "You're a fucking piece of shit," she screeched louder, putting both hands on his chest and shoving him back as hard as she could. As soon as she heard the thud of his body hitting the granite counter, the realization of what she'd done shifted her temperament from furious to alarmed. "I'm..."

"Get out." His voice became low and deadly. Almost anyone else in the DDz would've whaled on the bitch by now, but Jackson had some morals. Not many, but not hitting women was one of them.

"Jackson, I'm..." She backed away, legs shaking and lips quivering as tears sprung from her terrified eyes. "I shouldn't have..."

Standing off in the corner, Amy seemed completely taken aback by the way the scene had unfolded. She was used to being woken by their fighting, but this was the first time Tam had taken it too far. But Amy knew Jackson. He would never lay hands on a woman. She approached him and rested a grounding hand on his shoulder.

He barely glanced down at his sister before turning to Tammy. "Get your shit and get the fuck out," he demanded, rage coursing through his veins and hardening his heart as Tammy dropped to her knees in front of him, her face flooded with the evidence of her remorse.

"Please," she cried, "I'm sorry. I never should have..."

Jackson growled, "Did I slur my fucking words?"

"Where am I supposed to go?" she wailed, running after him as he stormed into the bedroom they shared. He pulled a duffel holding some of his cocaine out of the closet and dumped the baggies onto the floor so he could start throwing Tammy's shit into it. As she sobbed, he emptied her drawers, shoving some of the contents into the bag that was clearly too small to hold much and tossing the rest into the corner of the room. "It's the middle of the night."

"Should've thought of that before you started acting like a goddamn psychopath, Tamara," Jackson derided, yanking dresses off hangers and adding them to the pile. "Amy, get me a few garbage bags. Got to take the fucking trash out."

Amy did as she was told. She knew Jackson well enough to see he wasn't going turn back from this long overdue decision. By the time she returned seconds later, Tamara was face down on the bed whimpering and Jackson was in their bathroom tossing all her expensive beauty products into the trash in the bedroom. She looked up when she heard Amy reenter and shrieked at the sight of Jackson unplugging her hair dryer and straightener.

"Don't break my SinglePass," she howled as Jackson took the iron into his hand. "That was three hundred dollars, Jackson."

He turned slowly and narrowed his eyes at the mess of a woman crumpled up on the bed. "Excuse me?"

She rolled her lips in as guilt overtook her face.

"You spent three hundred dollars on a fucking flatiron?" He balked, pulling his head back and raising his eyebrows in disbelief.

"It's a really good one," Amy stated softly. "They're hard to find, so they're pretty expensive."

"Want it?" He held the coveted item out to his sister, while Tammy bawled.

Amy looked at Tamara and then at Jackson before she took the flatiron from his hand as Tammy yelled, "Bitch."

"You know what?" Jackson looked at Amy then began rubbing his knuckle against his nostril as he drew in an aggravated inhale. "You're going to keep all this shit. It's all mine anyway. Ain't no reason for Rocky over here to have it." He dumped all the items out of the duffel, deciding to fill it more strategically with Tamara's bras, underwear, a few T-shirts, and a pair of shorts. When he moved toward Tammy, she cowered in fear, but he leaned over anyway and carefully removed the oversized gold hoops from her ears and the diamond necklace from her neck.

"Really, Jackson?" she wept. "One mistake. I made one mistake."

"Nah, Tams. I made the mistake. Should've done this a long fucking time ago," he stated, hoisting the bag up and gesturing for Tammy to follow him. "Put on your pants and shoes."

She did as she was told, still sobbing as she pulled on jeans and tied her sneakers.

Jackson opened the front door and tossed the bag into the middle of the hallway, waving for Tammy to follow it.

"Where am I supposed to go?" she whispered, looking at him with pleading blue eyes.

Jackson shrugged. "Maybe go stay with those friends that are so concerned about our fucking relationship." He chuckled. "I don't know though, might look pathetic."

He slammed the door once she exited and turned to his sister, who had an astonished expression on her face.

"Want some pizza?" he asked, as if the last half hour hadn't happened. "I'm fucking starving."

7

It had been a week since Evan had become the proud owner of somebody else's credit card number and he had put it to good use. His bed was now covered in sheets and a comforter, his closet was full of clothes, and the new easel in the corner of his room was holding a canvas that had vibrant acrylic paint brushed across it. With Luis's guidance, Evan had purchased items with the intention of reselling them for a cheaper price, thus padding his pockets with cash. He used most of his earnings for drugs, remaining loyal to his brother for weed, but going to a few of the Klown Killerz who were higher up in the hierarchy for his coke. He'd learned the hard way that Kane's shit was cut with baby laxatives. Now that he was able to spend money that wasn't his own, he'd decided to spring for the good shit.

During the day he mostly chilled with Luis, Kane, and Jamal, playing video games and getting high, or he hid in his room, lost in the abstract landscapes he created on canvas. Through his art, he constructed a world full of happiness and love, a place so contradictory to what he knew. His paintings allowed him to live unapologetically. To walk down the streets into structures he built, knowing that they'd keep him safe; a dream that had yet to be realized anywhere but in his imagination. He wondered if years of not having a home had inspired him to develop sanctuaries that could hold him, even if only through the paintbrush in his hand.

Evenings were spent targeting women who were desperate or stupid enough to do things for the set. He'd been able to lock down two girls who, according to the information that was passed down to him from the O-Gs, had already proved to be invaluable. He'd been sent out to tag turf only once, and wielding that can of spray paint had felt like a homecoming.

With everything else there had been a learning curve, but cloaking himself in the darkness of night and spraying graffiti came easy to him. He was as precise as he was fast, both qualities needed to get the message across without ending up in prison. When he was younger, he'd made the mistake of becoming too wrapped up in the work and not cognizant enough of the ticking clock that began counting down as soon as the paint hit concrete. He'd gotten himself thrown in juvie quite a few times as a kid, but only ended up in jail twice as an adult, which he figured was growth, all things considered.

Every night after his KKz responsibilities, he made his way to Humboldt Park with several gold foil condoms in his wallet. He sat on the same bench, looking at the same rock, hoping that the same man with the pale blue eyes would show up. He didn't. Evan regretted not working out a date for their next rendezvous or at least getting the guy's phone number.

Evan had never asked a guy for his digits before. Even the concept of doing it seemed incredibly weird and unnatural. The men he'd been with in the past had all chased him. He wasn't used to having to put in work, and yet he found the anticipation and nervous energy to be quite the aphrodisiac.

Assuming that he actually saw Blue Eyes again, Evan knew that the sex was going to be amazing, not just because the man was hot as fuck, but because Evan had been thinking about how goddamn sexy he was for the past week. It wasn't out of the ordinary for Evan to be horny as fuck, day in and day out. After all, he was a twenty-one-year-old guy. Wanting to bang all the time was pretty much par for the course. But at thought of plowing Hot Shit's ass, Evan had found he was even more worked up than usual. It felt like he had a perpetual case of blue balls from constantly wondering what could have been if he hadn't been such an idiot and brought some fucking condoms.

He was about to jack off for the second time that day, his inspiration seemingly never-ending thanks to the mystery man, when he heard a knock on his bedroom door.

"Come in," he called, zipping his fly and quickly scooting into a sitting position on his bed.

"Ready to roll?" Kane asked, coming into the room and looking around. "You have like three more paintings than you had this morning," he mused, surveying the pieces that were leaning against the wall.

"I keep starting things and deciding that I need to move onto something else," Evan stated with a shrug. "I think it's the excitement of finally painting again. Too much shit in my head that's trying to get out. It's hard to focus, I guess."

"Well, lucky for you all you got to focus on now is getting a shirt on and coming to Cedric's. The new member parties are always lit as fuck. I think I'm still drunk from mine."

"That was two years ago." Evan shook his head with a laugh as he pulled on his cobalt blue t-shirt. It was strange to have a wardrobe that only consisted of maroon, blue, and white, but he was getting used to it.

"I know," he replied with a smirk. "Can that shirt get any tighter, man?" he questioned as Evan leaned over to tie his shoes. He took a break from tying his laces long enough to give Kane the finger. "It almost looks like you're getting some of your muscles back."

"Never lost them." He macked before following Kane out of the room.

"You were looking pretty skinny, man," his brother informed him, "leaner than I've ever seen you."

"Wouldn't randomly bulk up in a week," Evan tsked. "Doesn't make any sense."

"Whatever. Can't you take a fucking compliment? You're looking good, a'ight? Healthy even."

"Shit, I wouldn't go that far." Evan laughed. They stood on the porch and smoked as they waited for Jamal and Luis to come down and join them.

Cedric's house was a few blocks away, but Evan could hear the bass from the music coming from Ced's place. It became more intense the closer they got to the party and as soon as they entered, the beat pounded through him, prompting his heart to thump at its rhythm. Evan wasn't sure if he would've had the same visceral reaction if he hadn't been high, but with cocaine navigating his system, the whole scene felt intense and he wasn't sure if it was in a good way. He knew that he didn't have much choice but to stay for at least a short period of time to show that he was thankful to be a part of the KKz.

After doing a few shots with some of the boys, he found himself sitting on a sofa in between two other guys who he guessed were new like him. He thought he was hallucinating when he saw three topless women, who looked to be the South Side's version of Vivid porn stars, enter the room, big fake tits bouncing with every step. He glanced at Kane to gauge his reaction and determine if he knew that this was going to happen, and from the goofy grin Kane gave back, it seemed he did. Evan could feel people watching him as one of the girls climbed onto his lap.

"I got lucky," she cooed in his ear, her wavy blonde hair cascading onto his cheek. "You're the hottest guy here."

He nodded, unsure of what to say in response. She proceeded to give him a filthy lap dance, shoving body parts that he wanted nothing to do with in his face and grinding her big ass against the crotch of his jeans, trying to bring some life to his flaccid cock. "Not going to work," he stated as she dropped her hand below his waistband and wrapped it around his dick. "I'm high as fuck."

She gave him an exaggerated pout. "Wanted to ride you. Feel really big."

"Guess you didn't really get lucky then." He pursed his lips as he glanced at the guy to the right of him getting his dick sucked and then to his left where one of the strippers was bouncing on the dude's bare cock. Panic began to press against chest as he surveyed the room and saw eyes looking curiously at him, wondering why he wasn't fucking the hot piece of ass on top of him.

Attempting to think on his feet, he did the only thing he could think of that would possibly allow him to save face. He told the blonde to lie face down on the dingy carpet. He proceeded to pour a long line of cocaine from the base of her neck through the crack of her ass and down her leg. He wanted to cry when he saw all the white powder leaving his possession, but he knew it was his only way out. "So many Klown Killerz have done more for me in this short period of time than I could ever fucking do in return," he began, "so this is a start."

Much to his relief, a bunch of the guys approached, shaking his hand before leaning over and bumping a portion of the line. The crowding around the girl enabled him to duck out and make his way through the packed house to the front porch where he sat on a rickety rocking chair and lit up a cigarette.

"What the fuck was that?" Kane questioned, squatting down next to Evan and looking at him skeptically.

"What was what?" Evan asked innocently.

"Not like you to give up that much of your shit. Especially not the good stuff," his brother stated, shaking his head.

"Like I said, everyone's done a lot for me." He shrugged and blew a plume of smoke into the humid air.

"Mmmhmm."

"What?"

Kane's eyes were heavy with concern. "The thing about being in a gang is that everyone's the same. We all do the same things, want the same things, and function in the same way. A fucking unit," he began. "It's not a good thing to be different. Being different gets you killed. We don't do different."

"Not sure what you're getting at," Evan evaded, feeling his defenses wrap around him like a shield.

"You know what I'm getting at," Kane replied, biting his lower lip. "I don't give a shit. Always suspected it. But those guys in there," he paused and shook his head, "they give a shit."

"I don't know what you're talking about," Evan repeated stubbornly, refusing to look down at his brother for fear that his face would admit he did.

"Whatever, Evan. Deny it to me, deny it to yourself, I don't care." Kane sighed as if he didn't want to say the next statement that was going to come out of his mouth. "But you got to learn how to fuck women." With that Kane stood up and left his brother dumbstruck in his wake.

The realization that somebody in his life suspected his deepest secret had him reeling. With all his coke gone, he needed to find something to abate his stress and there was no better way than fucking.

He prayed Hot Shit would be there to take the pounding.

8

The past week had been full of aggravation for Jackson. As relieved as he was to be done with Tamara, there were a lot of loose ends to tie up regarding their relationship. It blew his mind how intertwined their lives had become, at least financially. It took him a full day to cancel all her credit cards, remove her from his checking account, and drop her phone plan. When he wasn't dealing with that bullshit, he was dealing with her bullshit. He knew she wouldn't fuck off quietly, but it had been wearing on him how persistent her reconciliation attempts had been. She was blowing up his phone constantly and showing up randomly at the apartment. He'd refused to talk to her, but did give her some more of her stuff back, thinking that maybe she'd be less desperate if she had some more of her shit. As he suspected, the gesture slowed her down, but hadn't gotten him the radio silence he'd hoped for.

He wondered if Tammy had ever really loved him, or if she'd fooled herself into thinking she did. She'd stuck with him through everything, even when he treated her like shit, which had more to do with a lack of self-worth than her affection for him.

Outsiders would look at Tamara and think she had it all with her beautiful face and banging body, but nobody in the hood had it all. What Tammy did have was a father who was serving life for murder and a meth-head mother who looked the other way when her deadbeat boyfriends touched her kids.

Initially, he'd felt like he'd saved Tamara in the same way he'd rescued Amy. If he hadn't been expected to have romantic feelings for Tams, he may have been able to love her like he loved his sister, but it had been unrealistic to have thought there wouldn't have been pressure for him to feel more. When it came down to it, everyone had a fucking sob story on the South Side, and he wasn't going to piss his life away trying to make someone else's better.

As if Tammy's shit wasn't causing him enough stress, his suppliers out of Mexico seemed to be having a hard time getting high-end product to him, which didn't bode well for his bottom line. Jackson's clients expected the best and that was what he intended to get for them. While he could've peddled some cut bags, it wasn't his style. He'd spent years on the corner making twenty dollars here and there and giving the real money to the big dogs. He wasn't interested in falling back. Still, he had handed off some janky shit to his foot soldiers and was expecting to see a return. Just because he wasn't going to sell the low-end product himself didn't mean he was above profiting from it. He had to pay some of those motherfuckers a visit and collect. But not tonight; tonight he was finally making his way back to Humboldt Park with the hope of getting railed by that big cock that had been on his mind since the failed fuck attempt.

When he spotted the redhead on the same bench he'd sat on the last time they'd hooked up, Jackson felt his cock stiffen. He adjusted himself as he approached, standing in front of the dude rather than sitting down beside him like he had before. The guy didn't look at him; instead, he kept his head tilted back and watched as the smoke from his blunt snaked up to the sky.

"So are we going to fucking do this or what?" Jackson asked impatiently, raising his eyebrows as the man lowered his head.

A wry smile played on his pink lips before he brought the spliff between them and took a deep inhale. "Hey."

"Hey," Jackson muttered back, rolling his eyes when the man held the weed out to him and gestured for him to sit down. "Ain't interested in talking," Jack said, yet he reluctantly took a seat and then a puff.

"A'ight," he replied, seemingly unfazed by the statement.

They sat in silence, alternating hits as a foggy haze of smoke filled the space between them. Trying to be as discreet as possible, Jackson allowed his eyes to study the man beside him. Daywalker was even more attractive than Jack remembered, with a stray strand of red hair falling on his forehead and lean muscles pressing against the fabric of his tight blue t-shirt. As much as he hated the color blue, he couldn't help but think it looked pretty fucking good on

Red. Jack felt his face flush when the man caught him staring and looked directly into his eyes with a smirk.

"You can look at me. Don't have to pretend you're not."

"Wasn't," Jackson protested, rolling his eyes at the assertion. He pointedly focused on the grouping of trees in front of them, refusing to give the guy the satisfaction of catching him gazing again.

"Suck my dick," the guy directed in a voice so husky it sent chills down Jackson's spine and straight into his cock.

"Fuck off," Jack scoffed, equal parts annoyed that the redhead was telling him what the fuck to do, and taken aback by the fact that he was prompting him to give him head on a park bench that was unhidden by the trunk of a tree or the mass of a boulder. When Jackson turned to shoot him a dirty look, he was surprised to find the guy leaning back with the blunt hanging from his mouth and his hand stroking his cock slowly. Instinctively Jack licked his lips and looked around to see if anyone was within viewing distance. The only people he could find were two fags making out against the rock, too into each other to notice anything going on around them.

"C'mon," Red urged, giving Jackson a salacious grin. "Do it."

Jackson sighed, beside himself that he was actually considering it. Though he ached to be dominated, he'd never let a guy take control during sex. He'd always held himself back from going there, feeling that once he did he'd be too far gone.

"You look like a badass," the redhead commented with a shrug. "It's a'ight if you're not into it. Just figured you wouldn't be scared of shit."

That was all it took for Jackson to let himself go. He leaned over and took Red's cock into his mouth, drawing a soft moan from the man's lips as Jackson began to bob eagerly on the enormous dick.

"Mmhmm, like that," the guy crooned, digging his fingers into Jack's hair and leading his head up and down as Red gently rolled his hips into Jack's face. "Such a pretty mouth."

Jackson bristled at the compliment, but the heavy dick lying on his tongue and pushing against the back of his throat had him too turned on to pull away.

As Jackson swirled his tongue around the man's smooth shaft, Jack worried that this motherfucker already had him hooked. He moved his way up to the tip so he could lap at the pre-come beading on Red's slit before pulling off. "You bring a fucking condom this time?" Jackson didn't want to admit that he'd brought a few in case the dumbass forgot.

The redhead nodded, stubbed out his blunt, and tucked his dick into his pants.

Jackson walked toward the tree line, his body buzzing with anticipation. As expeditiously as possible, he took a packet of lube out his pocket, handed it to the redhead, and turned around to face the tree, unbuttoning his pants as he did.

"Can you toss your piece on the ground?" the guy asked, his use of a street term taking Jackson by surprise.

"Uh, yeah, sorry," he said, removing his clip. "Forgot I was packing." It was rare that he wasn't, but he typically didn't carry when he hit up the park, thinking that he could handle a bunch of queens with his fists, if necessary.

"A Glock, huh? Nice," Red stated as he traced a slick finger around Jackson's puckered hole. He was about to question what the fuck Red knew about guns when he was distracted by a long finger pushing into him. The man didn't waste any time opening him up, adding digits as soon as Jackson was ready to take them, dipping in deep and scissoring out wide.

He heard the foil tearing and felt the pressure of that big dick inching into his opening. He couldn't help but groan as the man behind him swayed his hips slightly in an attempt to stretch him out farther. "Fuck," Jackson grunted when the guy bottomed out. He'd never been so goddamn full before in his life. The girth of Red's cock was pushing against Jackson's walls in the most delicious way and his knees began shaking from the overwhelming feeling.

The redhead began fucking him gently, as if he was used to working guys in who couldn't take his size. Jackson heard a slight laugh tumble out of the guy's mouth when Jack started to push back, wanting more, "Shit, I see you," Red teased, following Jackson's lead and snapping his hips quicker and more intensely.

It was everything Jackson had hoped it would be when he'd spent the last several nights jacking off to thoughts of that huge dick. He squeezed his eyes shut and gritted his teeth as his body naturally attempted to pull away. "Goddamn," he groaned, clawing into the bark of the tree to steady himself.

"Take it so good," Red praised, punctuating his words with deep jabs.

Jackson couldn't help but cry out when the man began to properly slam the shit out of him. He could hear his breathing get heavier and his moans grow louder as a pair of weighty balls slapped against his ass with every bang. He felt the guy's arm loop tightly around his neck and pull him down farther onto his cock with every thrust. Knowing that he was close, Jackson dropped his hand down to his dick and began to tug fervently.

"You close?" the redhead asked, his voice croaking as he drilled into him.

Jackson was too far gone to reply, but found it in him to whimper when the guy knocked his hand off his dick so that he could take over jerking it. It only took a few strokes before Jackson was shooting his come all over the tree. He leaned his forehead against the rough surface as he attempted to catch his breath, letting out a satisfied sigh when he felt the warmth of the other man's release empty into the condom.

"What's your name?" the guy panted as he carefully pulled out of Jackson's ass. "Wanted to say it but I didn't know it."

He'd already broken his own rules meeting up with the guy for a second time; there was no way he was going to let things become more intimate than that. "None of your fucking business," Jackson huffed, glancing over his shoulder, amused to see a slight smile on the other man's lips.

"I'm Evan," he said with a grin. "When can I see you again, 'none of your fucking business'?"

Jackson sniffed uncomfortably as he tugged up his pants. "Not into repeat performances."

"Even when it's the best fuck of your life?" Evan asked skeptically.

This cocky motherfucker. It was, but there was no way Jackson was going to admit it to the entitled prick. He hated old money. They never had to work for shit. "Who said it was the best fuck of my life?"

Evan chuckled. "The tears coming down your face."

Jackson raised his hand to his cheek, mortified when he felt wetness. He wiped it away and gave the guy the finger in response.

"Unless you always cry when you get fucked."

"Saturday," Jackson stated, grabbing his gun and getting the fuck out of there without so much as another glance in *Evan's* direction.

On Jackson's way back to the L the only thing crossing his mind was *fuck*.

Fuck that guy.

He loved fucking that guy.

Fuck his dumb cocky ass.

Shit he'd fucked his ass good.

Fucking Saturday.

What the fuck was he thinking?

He was fucked.

9

Evan lengthened his body, stretching his arms over his head and letting out a sated groan at the pull. It wasn't often that he woke up content, but that's exactly how he felt. Soft sheets draped over him as he adjusted his position and the cool breeze from the air conditioner kissed his skin. He was sore as fuck, but it wasn't the type of discomfort he used to deal with when he was sleeping on unforgiving surfaces like benches or concrete. It was the delicious ache of being thoroughly fucked out.

He'd been with a lot of men, but he'd never had an experience like the one he'd had the night before with "none of your fucking business." The guy could take dick like a beast. Evan was used to whiny bitches who talked a big game until it came time to get it on. They'd squirm and complain, unable to accommodate his size. When he really started banging, they'd urge him to slow down and fuck them gently. An epic disappointment. He was into knockdown, drag-out hole drilling, not making love.

Other men inched away when he pulled them down farther onto his cock, but the sexy brunet had pushed back, demanding more. Evan could tell that the guy had tried to stifle the noises that poured out of his mouth, and Evan was glad the beast had been unable to. Every gasp and groan had driven Evan fucking crazy and spurred him to go even harder.

The guy was tough as fuck. It was easy to recognize that from his attitude, but his tattoos and gun were confirmation. As far as Evan was concerned, it took a badass to take a rod up his ass and enjoy the railing.

And the man was gorgeous.

Evan was sure that guy could get as much dick as he wanted. Yet there was no doubt in Evan's mind that the brunet hit up Humboldt for similar reasons as Evan: too much to lose if his proclivities saw the light of day.

Evan wanted to know more about him, starting with, but not limited to, his fucking name. It was out of the ordinary for him to think of someone for longer than the time he was with them. Shit, sometimes even then his mind would wander. With the brunet, Evan was focused. That mouth, his ass, Evan wanted to get his tongue in both. He couldn't wait to see him again.

Five more days.

He climbed out of bed and threw on his clothes, taking a moment to stare longingly at his canvases before exiting the room. As much he wanted to stay home and paint all day, he had to meet Micah and Chance at the university. They were showing him how they worked co-eds and got them to carry for the war boys.

Supposedly smart girls would do really stupid things if they were complimented enough. Evan pissed, brushed his teeth, and made his way into the kitchen to grab some Pop-Tarts and orange juice. As he was chugging from the carton and cringing at the bitterness the juice had after toothpaste, he felt a punch on his arm.

"You're fucking nasty, you know that?" Kane chided as he ganked the package of breakfast pastries out of his hand and ripped it open so he could take a bite. "Other people drink that shit."

Evan just gave him the finger and took his breakfast back.

"Where'd you fuck off to last night?" Kane questioned, regarding his brother skeptically as he leaned against the counter and peeled a banana.

"To fuck some women," Evan replied coolly, clearly not appreciative of his brother's allusions the night before. Whatever Kane thought he knew he should've kept to himself. Evan didn't like when people acted like they had any right to his life, even if those people were his family. He'd been on his own for too long to answer to anybody else.

"Oh yeah?" the younger Goodwyn smiled to indicate that the shot was well-deserved. "You have a good time?"

"The best." That part wasn't a lie.

"Good. What're you up to today?"

"You my keeper all of a sudden?" Evan asked, lifting his eyebrows in displeasure. He'd gone down this road with his family before and he wasn't interested in partaking in the trip again. "Got a lot of fucking questions."

"You know, I can always tell when you're not fucked up," Kane stated, taking a big bite of a banana. "Much nicer when you are."

Evan shrugged and took another sip of the juice before closing it up and putting it back in the refrigerator. "Going over to CSU to get some runners for you assholes."

Kane nodded and pursed his lips as if he was deciding whether to mention their brother's name. Yeah, he was. Dumb fuck. "Maybe you'll run into Paul. He's still taking classes there."

"Who?" Evan questioned, earning an eye roll from Kane. He was aware that his brother was still in touch with Paul, but Evan had told Kane long ago that didn't mean that he wanted to be too. If he'd felt like being around somebody who constantly judged his decisions, he would have tried to make things right with Emma. At least she came with a house, unlike Paul, who came with a smug, know-it-all personality and a superiority complex.

"He asks about you every time I chill with him," Kane stated. "Wants to hear you're doing well."

"Hmm," Evan hummed, crinkling up his nose at the revelation. "And what do you tell him?"

"Tell him you're the same," Kane replied with a shrug. "What am I supposed to say?"

Evan let out a wry laugh and nodded. "Nah. That's fair."

"He said his offer still stands."

"Yeah, well, he can still fuck off." Evan headed out of the house without another word. He lit a cigarette and shook his head in frustration as he walked toward Micah's place.

Paul was a pretentious piece of shit who liked to act as if he didn't grow up South Side. As soon as he'd gotten his scholarship, he'd distanced himself from the life they used to live and expected Evan to do the same. All of a sudden tagging, fighting, and coke were below him, and his family was too. Evan had put up with Paul's holier-than-thou attitude for a while, but when he had the audacity to stage an intervention, and offered to take out a loan to pay for Evan's rehab, he'd had enough. He didn't need help and he wasn't anybody's charity case, especially not someone who came from the same slum he did. Fuck that. Fuck Paul. And fuck Kane for bringing him up and ruining Evan's good mood.

When he approached the apartment building, he found Micah and Chance sitting on the stoop waiting for him.

"Wassup, man? Ready to get into some sneaky shit?" Micah greeted, standing and shaking Evan's hand before pulling him in for a half hug. Though he liked all the Klown Killerz he'd met, Micah was probably his favorite. He was funny as fuck and cool as he was handsome with his coffee-ground skin tone and chocolate eyes.

"Always," Evan replied, nodding his hello to Chance. He didn't know the tattooed blond that well yet, but he seemed a'ight enough from the few times they'd been around each other.

"We got to swing by the Circle K and pick up a package from Lo," Chance informed them, brushing off the seat of his basketball shorts as he stood up from the step.

"Let's roll then. Got to get to CSU by eleven. That's when all the fine honeybees start to swarm around the Student Union. Easy picking," Micah informed them with a grin.

As they walked the few blocks to the convenience store, Micah kept them entertained with a crazy-ass story about the threesome he'd had the night before. Evan probably wouldn't have found it nearly as interesting if anyone but Micah was telling it, but he had a way with words that cracked him up.

"You're full of shit," Chance chuckled, shaking his head in disbelief. "There's no fucking way."

"I'm telling you," Micah insisted. "She did a full split on my dick like she was trying to win a cheerleading competition. It would have been hot as fuck if she wasn't wiggling her fingertoes on my lips."

"What the fuck are fingertoes?" Evan exclaimed with a laugh.

"You've never been with a bitch with fingertoes? Long ass things, man. You're lucky."

"Fuck." Evan grimaced. "Yeah I am." He wondered what kind of toes "none of your fucking business" had. Evan suspected they were probably perfect-looking like the rest of him.

As they turned onto Pershing, Evan heard a car revving behind them. The sound wasn't out of the ordinary but the yelling that came after it was. "This is for Kaneos." Successive pops from an AK-47 had him diving to the ground to curl up in the fetal position, gasping when he heard a body drop next to him with a sickening thud. "Rest in pieces, motherfuckers."

When he heard the car speed away, Evan lifted his head, disgusted to see Chance's brain matter strewn across the blood-drenched sidewalk.

"Don't fucking puke now," Micah warned. "Wait until we get away from the scene." Without a moment's hesitation he was on his feet running, waving for Evan to follow him. "C'mon, Goodwyn, run."

"Shouldn't we call nine-one-one?" Evan asked frantically as he ran after Micah.

"He's dead, cuz," Micah replied, glancing at Evan as he caught up. Micah shook his head and grimaced. "Ain't nothing anybody can do for him now."

"Fuck." Evan had seen dead people before, but that was at wakes, not in the middle of the fucking sidewalk. He wondered if he'd ever be able to get that image out of his head. He hoped so. The sound of screams echoed behind them as traumatized people discovered the bloody body.

"Yeah, fucking Demonz. Don't know what the fuck Chance did to piss them off, but them pussy asses never miss an opportunity to light one of us up," Micah sighed. "Over here, yo." They ran down an alley and watched as police cars sped down the street, sirens blaring and horns beeping. The ambulance wasn't far behind and they both shook their heads, knowing it wasn't needed.

Evan leaned back against the warm brick wall, desperately attempting to catch the breath he'd left on Pershing. Closing his eyes, he attempted to steel himself, but immediately saw Chance's hollowed-out head. He felt his stomach flip angrily and crouched over so he could upchuck his breakfast.

"First time?" Micah asked, clearly knowing the answer. He laid a soothing hand on Evan's back as he nodded and then puked again. "It'll get easier."

10

"Ready to do this?" Luke asked as they took the stairs up to Lyle's porch by twos. Jackson could see the concern on Luke's face, the question holding more weight than it ever had before. Maybe he thought Jackson would have second thoughts, that he'd give Lyle another chance. Jackson figured his brother would have known him better than that.

"Always ready," Jackson stated evenly, unflinching at the task at hand. It wasn't the first time he had to regulate shit and he knew it wouldn't be the last. Some of the other high-status guys had the lower-level thugs take care of their dirty business, but Jackson always handled his. He wanted rats to look him in the eye as they took their last breath and know that he wasn't one to be fucked with. He'd had to teach that lesson more times than he could count.

Loyalty was everything on the street. As soon as someone breached his, they were dead to him, and then the rest of the world a short time later. There was no forgiveness for betrayal. As far as he was concerned, if a motherfucker didn't follow the South Side rules, he asked for it. It didn't matter if it was Jackson's brother, cousin, friend, or father. They had to live by the code, and if they chose not to, Jackson followed through. No mercy.

They banged on the door loud enough for Lyle to hear it in the basement.

"Motherfucker won't stop begging," Lyle informed them as he swung the door open. He shook Jackson's hand and pulled him in for a hug before doing the same to Luke. "Thinks I'm going to Underground Railroad his ass out of here or some shit."

"Sell your ass out for his?" Jackson sneered. "Sounds about right for an entitled cocksucker."

"Can't believe he did you like this, man," Lyle tsked. "After everything you've done for him. Fuck that pussy." He signaled for the Jablonic brothers to follow him down to the basement where they saw Aiden strapped to a chair with a tarp laid out underneath it.

"Jackson. Jack," Aiden began, brown eyes as wide as they were frantic. "You got it all wrong, Jack. I'd never do you like that. You know I'd never do you like that."

"Used to think you wouldn't," Jackson sniffed indifferently, nudging his nostril with his knuckle as he glared at his former friend and future victim. "But I got that shit wrong, huh?"

"Fucking low to steal from your boy," Luke chided, shaking his head in disappointment.

"I didn't," Aiden started again, but an aggravated Jackson quickly cut him off.

"So you didn't take ten eight balls of my best shit, say you were going to sell 'em for me, and then sell 'em for yourself on the low after telling me it got fucking stolen?" he asked, already knowing the answer. "'Cause it seems like that's what you fucking did, running around flaunting your new Jesus piece and AK like the pig-ass piece of shit you are."

Aiden shook his head fervently. "It ain't like that."

"What about the reports Jack got from some of the boys then, hmm? How do you explain that shit?" Luke interrupted, crossing his arms over his chest and staring down at the fat fuck traitor with disgust.

"I'll get you the money," Aiden promised, pleading for pity. "Please. I'm sorry, Jack. You know I'm fucking good for it." His legs were shaking violently against the chair as his lower lip quivered with fear. "Ten years of friendship has got to mean something, right?"

"Seems like it don't though," Jackson replied. "I mean, you taking what's mine and all." He shrugged. "Seems like it don't." He studied Aiden for a moment and then turned to Lyle. "Tarp the wall behind him, too. Motherfucker's got a big fucking melon."

The man quickly did as he was told while Aiden continued to appeal to Jackson for clemency.

"I wasn't thinking, man. I got wrapped up in the lifestyle," Aiden cried, tears streaming down his face. "Wanting to floss and shit.

Wanting to seem like I had it going on. I should have never gone there. I'm fucking sorry I did."

"You know how I feel about begging," Jackson reminded as he pulled out his Glock. He aimed the gun in Aiden's direction and prepped the trigger while the man sobbed. Without hesitation, he lined up the front sight with the center of his former friend's forehead, held the gun tight, and squeezed the trigger, sending a one-sixty-five grain bullet straight through his head. "Got to shut 'em up quick."

The room was eerily quiet as Luke untied the ropes around the corpse, allowing it to fall heavy on the tarp. All three men worked to roll Aiden up and carry his body up the stairs.

"Goddamn he's bulky as fuck," Lyle groused as they struggled to maneuver him through the doorway and into the garage. He dropped Aiden's feet and keyed open the trunk of his car so they could dump him into it.

"Not as huge as Big Mike was," Luke recalled, shaking his head. "Pulled my back out. Had to rest up for a week after getting rid of his hefty ass."

"Are we going to go on a walk down memory lane right now or are we going to go out and get a beer?" Jackson groaned, bringing the trunk door down. "You dumping him tonight?"

Lyle nodded. "Yeah, got a couple of the younger guys coming through. I'm going to show them our drop spot."

"Ah, enriching the minds of the youth of America, one thug at a time," Luke laughed, earning an annoyed glare from Jackson.

"Seriously though, are we getting a fucking drink?" Jackson repeated with a sigh.

"This one hit you hard, Jack?" Lyle questioned, draping his arm around Jackson's shoulder and giving him a companionable shake.

Jackson shook his head. "Nah, it ain't like that. Just trying to get my mind off some shit."

He didn't want to tell them that he intended to drink the days away until Saturday. The hours felt too long as he anticipated seeing Evan again. It had only been a day and a half since he'd gotten the best orgasm of his life, but it had felt like twenty. As hard as he tried, he couldn't get the Daywalker out of his head. Jack felt like a fucking pansy, pining over some dude, but redhead was so hot, and goddamn could he fuck. Even worse than the crush Jackson seemed to be stuck with was that he actually wished he had the dude's number so he could call him and meet up sooner.

He didn't get like this. Sure, he liked to get fucked, but he never gave a shit enough to know the dudes that screwed him. He wanted to get banged and go about his business. It surprised him that he was interested in learning more about the redhead; like how the fuck he knew about guns? Jackson figured the only guns Evan had been around were rifles for duck hunting or whatever the fuck rich people did. Maybe he had more edge than Jackson had originally thought.

Before their last meeting, he'd thought the guy was pretty fucking cute and a little goofy, but after the pounding he gave Jackson, and his knowledge of firearms, Jacks was thinking that he may be a badass, and that thought turned him on massively. He'd found himself getting lost in filthy fantasies about Evan owning his ass, tying him up, fucking his face—all the shit he'd wanted to try but never let himself consider due to his circumstances. With his newfound freedom from Tamara and the room to himself, he was actually contemplating bringing Evan back to his place. He'd have to tell Amy to fuck off to Isaiah's, which didn't concern him because he knew his sister was smart enough not to ask questions.

Unlike Aiden, Amy lived by the code. Though he was closer to Luke when they were growing up, he'd recognized in his teenage years that Amy had always had his back, even more than his brother had, and that was what had prompted him to have hers. He didn't understand how he'd been so blind to it for so long. Maybe he hadn't wanted to see what was right in front of him. After all, it wasn't something a kid wanted to believe about his father. It wasn't that he didn't know that his dad was an abusive asshole, he always had been. Jacks never thought he would go that far.

Everything changed the day he'd found twelve-year-old Amy bleeding on the bathroom floor. She'd told him that she was pregnant and losing the baby. Jackson hadn't been an expert in the area, but he'd known that there was too much blood for it to be considered normal and had rushed her to the hospital. He'd been aware his sister got around, that hadn't been a secret, so her being knocked up hadn't seemed like a stretch. What had taken him by surprise had been the bruising he'd seen on her belly when the nurses had lifted her shirt. Jackson had felt rage pump through his body as doctors and social workers took turns questioning Amy, trying to find out who had hurt her.

South Side rules had kept her mouth shut, but she'd opened up when they made their way home the next day. Calling the cops wasn't going to happen, so Jackson did the next best thing to putting his father away. He had gotten Amy out of that hellhole. Then he had gotten jumped into Dem Demonz two days following her miscarriage. And after a month of stealing and selling for the DDs, he had been able to pay a friend of the family for him and Amy to stay in his basement.

As soon as Jackson turned eighteen, he'd gotten an apartment for them and they were free. Luke had stuck by their father, unable to fathom that their dad could impregnate his daughter and then beat the shit out of her to abort the baby. Jackson wasn't sure in what fantasy world his dumbass brother had been living, but things had never been the same between them since, and Jackson was all right with that.

Luke rolled a tarp as well as he rolled a joint and though he pissed Jackson the fuck off sometimes, both of those skills were essential.

So that was that.

11

In approximately fifteen hours Evan was going to be fucking the hell out of the hottest guy he'd ever laid eyes on, and he couldn't wait. As he put on his basketball shorts and sleeveless top, he decided that getting in some physical activity on the court wouldn't be a horrible thing. He felt like he could use some conditioning for the amount of banging he was going to be doing in the not-so-distant future. He'd decided that he was going to ask the guy for his number that night. Though "none of your fucking business" seemed determined to keep things incredibly casual between them, Evan was pretty sure that if he fucked the shit out of the guy, he'd loosen up and make it a more regular thing.

Evan didn't want to keep trolling parks to chase his next orgasm; he wanted to have someone he could fuck on the regular, maybe get to know a little bit...normal shit. He knew that he was probably being unrealistic. If the brunet was getting with guys in the park, there was a good chance his situation wouldn't allow him to fuck around in a spot that wasn't anonymous, and there was no way in hell Evan would ever bring him back to his place. With three roommates, he'd be begging to get caught, and as much as he could hold his own, if he could avoid a fag bashing and a possible bullet to the head, he was going to go ahead and do that.

Fag. That wasn't the way he thought of himself.

He wasn't attracted to women at all. He'd fucked a few, but that was mostly to have a place to sleep for the night. For as long as he could remember he liked guys. He liked the strength of their bodies, the angles of their jaws, the tightness of their asses, the hardness of their cocks. That probably made him gay, but he wasn't about to go march in some fucking Pride Parade wearing booty shorts, waving a rainbow flag, and sucking off a twink in a pink tutu.

Sometimes he thought the guys who were so out there with their sexuality were actually tougher than the ones stuck in the closet. To be so loud, proud, and not give a shit what anybody said about it. Maybe he would've been like that if he hadn't lived the life he had…if survival hadn't always eclipsed emotions. He didn't give much of a shit. It wasn't like he desired any sort of support or acceptance; he'd never had it in any other facet of his life anyway. When it came down to it, what he wanted was an ass to stick his dick in, preferably the badass hottie's from the park, a bed to sleep in, and powder to snort.

He finished getting ready and met the rest of the guys out on the porch.

"How's it feel to be out of bed before noon, cracks?" Jamal teased, slapping Evan on the back companionably.

The rest of the guys delivered their own jokes and Evan rolled his eyes with a slight grin pulling up his lips. "Yeah, yeah, yeah laugh it up, c'mon." He had forgotten that there could be good parts about living with people. The last couple years he'd spent in his family's house had been anything but pleasurable with the near constant fighting and guilt trips. Things with the Klown Killerz were much easier. The boys didn't give a shit where he went or what he was doing as long as he brought in some money. Kane was the exception, but he'd gotten the hint after their last discussion and backed off a bit, for which Evan was thankful. He didn't want to get into it with his brother, especially if it meant putting his room at risk.

Evan was surprised that the park was relatively crowded. He couldn't believe so many people got up at the ungodly hour by choice. They walked past a bunch of families enjoying snacks on picnic blankets and flying kites. He searched his memories and tried to remember if his deadbeat parents had ever taken them for a Saturday play in the park, but wasn't surprised when the he realized they hadn't. Fuck, they were losers. Either way, he was playing in the park now, and he'd be having an even better time in a park later, so fuck them.

"They're always late," Micah groused, dribbling the ball on the black asphalt of the court before shooting it directly into the chain-link basket.

Evan scoffed at the graffiti on the backboard. Amateur shit. He was going to have a hard time focusing on his shots with that ugly scrawling. Well, that was the excuse he was going to use when he no doubt sucked ass. It wasn't that he wasn't athletic, he was, but wasn't into organized sports. He'd played on a baseball team when he was nine for one season. It had been a good year financially because his parents had been cooking meth in their basement. Once they blew the place up, the money stopped rolling in and there was no more baseball. That's when he got into street art. He started stealing spray paint from Ace Hardware and honed his craft. He loved seeing his vision come to life all over the South Side.

Thirteen years later and it still gave him the same rush.

"Off our court, motherfuckers," a voice called from behind them. Evan was too wrapped up in shooting an air ball to turn around, thinking whatever pest said it was about to get his. He did, however, wonder what kind of stupid prick would approach five guys who carried themselves like they did.

"Aw hell no. We ain't going to fuck off for some bitch-ass Demonz," Luis scoffed, prompting Evan to bristle. Dem Demonz. The same gang who killed Chance. He hadn't thought the morning was going to start with a fight, but suddenly getting up so early may have been worth it. He whipped around, shocked to see "none of your fucking business" looking at him with his jaw dropped open. His skin was paler than it seemed at night, but that may have been because he was looking at Evan like he was a ghost.

When he really thought about all the shit that had happened to him in his life, he realized he wasn't a lucky guy. He figured this was yet another example of his misfortunes.

"Don't want to have to make you," a blond guy said, cracking the knuckles on his tattooed hands.

"Didn't think you motherfuckers liked to fight. More into that pussy drive-by shit," Micah snarled, clearly seconds away from ripping somebody's head off their shoulders.

"You into that pussy shit now, Jackson? Going soft?" Kane asked with a smirk. "Ain't the hardest anymore?"

"None of your fucking business." Jackson laughed sardonically. "Still hard as fuck. Want me to prove it to your faggot ass?" He raised his eyebrows in challenge, glaring from Kane to Evan, blue eyes wild with anger.

Evan crinkled his nose at the slur. Now he knew for real what Blue Eyes situation was and why he kept shit on the low. Jackson. His name was Jackson and he was a Demon.

"You can prove it to me," Evan replied, positioning himself slightly in front of Kane. Though he said it, he wasn't sure if he was trying to defend his brother, flirt, or get some fucking contact with Jackson. Whatever had possessed him didn't impress the brunet if the fist pounding into his cheek was any indication.

Without pause he lunged at Jackson, grabbing him around the waist and tackling him to the ground. The rest of the guys were scrapping while he and Jackson rolled around the hot asphalt fighting for dominance. Evan realized he'd opened his mouth because he had wanted to touch him in any way possible. He gazed up at the man panting above him and thought that he looked more beautiful in the light of day. As soon as he felt his lips turning up in a grin, the hot-ass brunet punched it off his face.

"Fucking bitch," Jackson growled. "Klown Killerz? Pussy-ass motherfucker."

Evan had gotten beatings like this enough times to recognize it. Jackson was angry at himself more than Evan. So though he attempted to appear like he was fighting back, he let the other man have at it.

"Pigs," Jamal called out, prompting everyone to pull apart immediately. Evan watched as they scattered in all different directions, running as quickly as they could from the cops.

Grabbing Jackson's wrist tightly, he ventured to ask, "See you tonight?"

The hot-ass Demon was taken aback by the question that sounded a lot more like a statement; Evan could see it all over Jackson's face. There was no way Evan was going to give up the best fuck of his life for some gang rivalry. Maybe it was because he was new to the lifestyle, but it didn't seem like a good enough deterrent—at least not good enough not to get balls deep in that ass again.

"Fuck you," Jackson scoffed, spitting on his face. "Fucking trash."

He shook Evan off and gave him one last disgusted scowl before sprinting away.

Adrenaline and lust coursed through Evan's veins as they ran in opposite directions, wondering what the fuck they'd gotten themselves into.

12

There was no way Jackson should make the meet at Humboldt. He knew that. As if it wasn't bad enough that he fucked guys, he was now fucking one who repped the KKz. Granted, he didn't know Evan was affiliated before they'd banged, but Jackson wondered if it would have made a difference if he had. Evan turned him on like nobody ever had before. During the brief times Jack had been around him, he'd been putty in the redhead's hands. He still couldn't believe that he'd sucked that huge cock out in the open. He was in disbelief that he wanted to do it again, even knowing what he did now.

He wasn't sure what the fuck was wrong with him. He didn't get dick-whipped. He fucked them once and threw them away. But Evan had felt different from the start. Jackson wanted to believe it was his body and the way he used it, but Jacks feared it was more than that. He liked his attitude and the way he carried himself, the way his eyes shined even in the dark and how Jack realized in the light of the day that they were toffee-tinged brown. He found himself drawn to Evan's smile. Though Jackson had spent only a short time with him, he could already tell that the redhead's grins weren't easy to come by.

Jackson could relate. He didn't see much of a point faking shit. He smiled when he fucking felt like it and lately, that hadn't been often. Maybe that would change. It wasn't that he didn't want to, but between Tammy, Aiden, and the challenge of getting product, Jackson hadn't had many reasons. He wished he could convince himself that he wasn't thinking that chilling with a Klown Killer and smiling may become synonymous. He felt like a cartoon where an anvil was dropped onto some fucker's head and all of a sudden he was loopy, seeing stars and hearts.

It wasn't that Jack thought any of this shit was a good idea. In fact, he knew it wasn't. It was more that he wasn't sure he gave a fuck, which was by far the most dangerous aspect of it all. As soon as the crew caught a guy slipping, they were on him. He couldn't afford to get sloppy, and fucking the enemy was messier than anything else he was able to imagine.

Still, he'd wasted too much time dealing with Tamara. He wanted to actually feel something for someone, at least lust, and maybe more. Wanting Evan set Jackson's body on fire and he didn't fear the burn even though he knew he should have.

The redhead had to be new to the crew. If he'd been with them for a while, Jackson would've noticed him. Evan stood out in all the best ways. Maybe the street wasn't ingrained in him like it was in Jackson. After all, he still wanted to see him after he found out which gang he banged with.

Jackson wished he'd punched Evan harder; maybe that would've deterred him. It would've been easier if he had been turned off, walked away. Anything.

Jackson knew he had two legs of his own and could have used them to walk the hell away from the whole situation. Instead, he found himself walking toward it, walking toward *him*.

"Hoped you'd come," Evan said with one of those coveted smiles stretching across his busted lip. Amid the darkness that was ensconcing the park, it glowed. It was challenging for Jackson to shift his perception. He'd made himself believe that Evan had lived a life of privilege and he still saw him that way, though it was easy to predict that he hadn't. Rich kids didn't end up in street gangs. Still, when Jack looked at him, he couldn't help but think he was too beautiful to be wrapped up in the lifestyle, too good. Jack doubted Evan could even fight. After all, he hadn't thrown a punch after Jackson had clocked him on the court. Having the body for it didn't make a guy a solid fighter. Evan was contradiction: a beast in the sheets and seemingly meek on the streets.

"Hoped you wouldn't," Jackson replied honestly. He stood a few feet away from where Evan was sitting on the bench, wearing a maroon t-shirt that Jack wanted to rip off for various reasons.

Evan nodded knowingly. "Guess you're disappointed then?" he asked, rising to his feet and starting to make his way toward Jack.

Jackson considered pulling his gun on the motherfucker, unsure what his intentions were. Though he didn't trust people to begin with, he certainly wasn't going to have any certitude in a fucking Klown Killer, regardless of how hot he was.

Goddamn, he was really hot, though. Instead of reaching for his Glock, Jack pushed a stray strand of hair off his forehead and licked his lips, able to smell the faint scent of weed as Evan drew closer. So close. Evan was going to kiss him. Jack wanted to be kissed. He didn't crave kisses, but he was hungry for this one. As soon as he parted his lips and closed his eyes, he felt a clenched fist connect with his mouth.

"The fuck was that for?" he snapped, holding his cheek and turning his head so he could spit blood over his shoulder.

Before Evan could answer, Jackson returned the blow, earning another swing and a sardonic laugh from the redhead, whose lip had split open again, causing blood to stream down his chin. The asshole *could* fight. Jackson regretted doubting it as he readjusted his jaw.

"Now we're even for earlier." Evan grinned, lifting his shirt to wipe his face. Jackson couldn't help but admire the toned abdominal muscles and the way they flexed as Evan panted for breath. "Like what you see?" he asked with a smirk, openly aware of Jackson's gaze drinking him in.

Jackson closed the space between them and tugged Evan's shirt over his head, unable to stand seeing him in that color, or a shirt at all for that matter.

"We doing this?" Evan asked as Jack traced his fingertips over the cuts of Evan's six-pack. He smelled like soap, cigarettes, and peppermint, a combination that was driving Jack crazy. A loaded question, though Jackson could choose to take it at the surface if he wanted to. "Jackson?"

Heaven to hear his name coming from those lips. "Don't know what 'this' is," he muttered in reply, his voice reflecting the tentativeness he was feeling. Whatever "this" was, he knew they shouldn't be doing it. He wanted to believe that he could take one more taste, but it seemed unlikely that he wouldn't be back for more, no matter how bad of an idea it was. He was taken by surprise when Evan dipped his head and slotted their mouths together, hard.

The kiss was as painful as it was passionate, with bruised lips moving together as their tongues swirled wildly through the metallic taste. Fingers tangled in hair as bodies pressed close, desperate from the days spent aching for each other. It was impossible to ignore how consumed they had been since their first meeting, and, it seemed, neither was quite sure exactly what it meant. All Jackson was positive about was that they needed to fuck, and they needed to do it as soon as humanly possible.

They kissed their way behind the rock, where they proceeded to strip the rest of their clothes off as expeditiously as they could. As soon as Jackson slid the lube packet into Evan's hand, he immediately pushed Jackson's bare chest against the boulder and began to prep him roughly, making Jackson nearly crawl out of his skin, evidenced by moans coming from his mouth. With lips fastened to the back of his neck, Evan probed and scissored until Jackson demanded, "Get the fuck in me."

Reaching down to grab a condom out of the pocket of his discarded pants, Jackson turned to see Evan tear the gold foil with his teeth and roll the magnum over his dick. The volume of their collective sigh increased with each inch Evan pushed in. As soon as he was filling Jackson to the hilt, he started to roll his hips, slow at first, then to a backbreaking pace that had both men groaning at the sensation. Jackson reached around so he could dig his fingernails into the flesh of Evan's clenched ass cheek, prompting him to give him more.

"Couldn't stop thinking about this ass, this perfect fucking ass," Evan crooned as he slammed into Jackson, hunching over his back and driving into his prostate.

"Yeah?" Jackson asked, his voice broken by a moan.

"Yeah," Evan confirmed, grabbing on to the bones of Jackson's hips tighter and angling up. The shift had Jack shaking and groaning. He felt Evan trying to fuck him into submission; that he was intent on giving Jack the banging of his life to ensure he extracted a promise that they'd see each other again. "So fucking hot, Jackson."

The sound of his name rolling from Evan's lips was overwhelming. He'd never told a guy he'd hooked up with his name. It felt as intimate as getting bent over a rock in the middle of a fucking park could. Though all his thoughts were being fucked out of his mind, he knew that he wanted to hear it again. "Say it again."

"So hot, Jackson," Evan croaked. When Jackson's hand dropped to his cock and he began to tug, Evan knocked it away. "Going to fuck it out of you."

"Never," Jackson panted, trying to grasp onto the surface of the rock to steady himself, without much success. He gasped when he felt Evan's arms wrap protectively around his chest, giving him the support he needed. "Ain't going to work."

"I'll get you there," Evan assured, fastening his lips to Jackson's earlobe and sucking hard. "Want it?"

"Yeah." His voice was wavering from the force with which he was being fucked, body jarring forward only to be pulled back with each jolt.

"Tell me you want it," Evan grunted.

"I want it," Jackson moaned, squeezing his eyes shut as his knees grew weak. "Give it to me."

With that, Evan drilled into Jackson, his dick absolutely assaulting the sensitive spot inside him with each thrust. Undulating cries broke out of Jackson's throat as he spilled his seed onto the boulder in front of him. Evan wasn't far behind, emptying into the condom with a whimper of Jackson's name. They struggled to catch their breath for a few moments, the fervency slipping away as they drew air into their lungs, leaving them paused with questions.

"Am I going to see you again?" Evan asked, bending over to hand Jackson his pants before shimmying into his own.

"We can meet here Tuesday," Jack replied, sniffing uncomfortably as he pulled on his black sleeveless top. He wished he could have told Evan to fuck off, but Jack didn't have it in him. Not after the asshole made him come untouched.

His thoughts were interrupted by Evan reaching behind him. For a moment Jack thought he'd misread the sitch. But the Klown had taken his phone out of his back pocket.

"What are you doing?"

"Want to see you before that," the redhead answered, typing his digits into Jackson's cell. "So I'm giving you my number," he pressed send to place a call to himself, "and taking yours."

Jackson narrowed his eyes, not sure what to make of the man standing before him. "Don't fucking call me."

"You got a wife or something?" Evan asked, raising his eyebrows.

"No I don't got a fucking wife. What the fuck are you looking for?" Jack questioned when he noticed Evan's eyes darting around the area.

"My shirt."

"Tossed that shit back there," Jackson answered with a grimace. "Look better without it. Red ain't your color."

"Clashes with my hair?" Evan grinned, and Jackson scowled.

"Not kidding about that shit," he said gruffly, giving Evan a once-over before walking away.

"I'm going to text you," Evan called after him. "You said not to call but nothing about texting."

Jackson shot up both middle fingers without looking back and then picked up Evan's discarded t-shirt and dumped it in the trashcan.

"Asshole, that's full of fucking used condoms," he shouted as Jackson laughed all the way home.

13

Evan (8:45pm): Hey
Jackson (8:49pm): What?
Evan (8:50pm): It's Evan
Jackson (8:55pm): I know that. U put ur name into my phone
Evan (8:55pm): Oh
Evan (8:57pm): What're u up to?
Evan (9:00pm): ?
Evan (9:05pm): u there?
Jackson (9:15pm): I don't text
Evan (9:16pm): You're texting right now, so you sorta do
Evan (9:25pm): Hello?
Jackson (9:35pm): 432 St. Lawrence Apt. 9. Come over @ 10:30 if you want to bang.
Evan (9:37pm): C ur good @ texting. C u then.

Jackson couldn't help but smile as he tossed the phone onto his nightstand and made his way into the kitchen where Amy was making macaroni and cheese.

"What're you doing tonight?" he asked, attempting to sound casual.

"Was going to chill here. Isaiah's handling some business, so..." she shrugged, "I figured I'd take it easy."

Jackson nodded, unsure of how to approach the subject without coming off shady. He decided to with the direct angle. "I got someone coming over so if you could fuck off for like two hours, that'd be good."

Amy's eyes lit up and she punched out a laugh. "Somebody met someone," she teased in a melodic voice, smiling at her brother.

"Stop," he warned, trying not to grin. "Just fucking. Nothing serious."

"Must be kinda serious if you're letting her come over here. Tell me about her. Is she hot? Less annoying than Tamara?"

"Less annoying than you," Jackson replied, earning an eye roll from his sister.

"I'll scarf this down and go over to Gigi's," she said with a wink. "I'm more than happy to get out of here anytime you want to get laid. I'm sure it will help with your wicked mood recently."

Jackson let out a sarcastic laugh and began cleaning some of the shit off the floor.

"And cleaning, too," Amy noted. "You have a crush."

"Fuck off," he huffed, but he wondered if maybe he did.

By the time he heard a knock on his apartment door, he'd scrubbed nearly every flat surface and vacuumed the carpet. He'd felt safe enough to have Evan come over since Jack's place was out of the thick of it, plus everyone knew Amy lived here and with her and Isaiah being close, no one wanted to fuck with that.

With ten extra minutes left before Evan arrived, Jackson had decided to prep his ass, in hopes that he could get the Daywalker in, and *in*, and then get him the fuck out quickly.

Jackson found that nervous energy was surprisingly productive.

"Hey," Evan grunted, waiting for Jackson to wave him in. Before walking past, he leaned over and pressed a peck against Jackson's lips. In that moment, he seriously considered telling Evan to leave, but stopped himself. Jackson didn't do little kisses "hello." He didn't do little kisses at all. "This is really fucking nice."

Jackson tried to see the place through Evan's eyes. The apartment was small but clean with white walls and gray furniture. Evan seemed impressed; the couch wasn't ripped, there were no holes in the drywall, and the kitchen tiles weren't cracked.

"Do you have a roommate?" Evan asked, turning back from peeking at the two bedroom doors ajar across the living room from each other.

"None of your fucking business," Jackson bristled, not liking how comfortable the redhead seemed. Jackson walked into his bedroom, sort of annoyed when Evan followed. Jackson wanted him there, but he also wanted him to stop prying in his life.

"That's what I called you in my head before you told me your name," Evan tossed out as he unzipped his backpack and let it rest on the crook of his elbow. "'Cause that's what you told me when I asked."

"You ask too many questions," Jackson admonished, sitting down on the edge of his bed and watching as Evan pulled out a baggie of cocaine.

"Want to bump a few lines?" He smiled when he realized that he had just asked another. Jackson lifted his eyebrows and shook his head as an adult would at a child's antics.

"Let me see what you got." Jackson took the baggie from Evan then stuck his pinky into the powder.

"It's good stuff," Evan defended, studying Jackson as he rubbed his finger against his gum line.

"Nah it's not," Jackson replied with a grimace. "Ain't sour enough, man. This shit was cut like three times. Not horrible, but not good. Think they used vitamin C and B twelve, maybe some talcum powder." He handed the bag back to Evan, stood up, and walked over to his closet to pull out an eight-ball from a shoebox on the ground. "Don't fuck around with it too much, but I do keep some for myself."

"So you deal?" Evan asked as Jackson used a razor blade to cut lines on the dresser.

Jackson couldn't believe this damn Klown couldn't take a clue. "You ask too many fucking questions," he repeated angrily.

Evan threw his hands up in surrender and waited for Jackson to finish the cut.

"Go ahead." Jackson handed Evan a rolled-up twenty.

The redhead leaned over and inhaled a long line, tilting his head back when he was done, then sighed as the drug hit him. "Fuck."

"Yeah, don't take much," Jackson agreed, bending over to snort his own and grinning a bit when he felt Evan's hands rubbing his ass.

"Perfect ass," he whispered as he hunched over Jackson's back and began to kiss his neck. As soon as Jack finished his line, he turned around to catch Evan's mouth. Sucking on his tongue, gnawing on his lip, they ripped off their clothes fast. Damn, he couldn't get enough of this hot-ass man.

"Fuck me," Jackson urged, climbing onto the bed and getting on his hands and knees.

"Going to eat your ass first," Evan muttered, about to dive in when Jackson reached back and swatted him away.

"I don't do that nasty shit," he said, "and I'm already prepped so get the fuck in me."

"Really? That's it? No foreplay?" Evan asked, clearly unimpressed. "We have a fucking bed. We should make the most of it."

"Are you going to keep complaining or are you going to get on me?" Jackson groused. He was unsure enough about having this Klown at his place; he wasn't trying to make it a goddamn marathon fuck session.

"How about you get on me. Ride it," Evan prompted, lying down on his back and looking at Jackson eagerly. "Want to watch you fuck me."

Jackson didn't want to admit he'd never done that since it wasn't a practical position in the park. He'd sat on a few of his dildos when he'd fantasized about having a dude underneath him, but he'd never actually gotten on a real cock.

Evan was looking insanely hot as he stroked his huge cock slowly, his eyes blown out from the coke and his lips puffy and pink from punches and kisses.

Jackson clicked his tongue in surrender and reached for the condom Evan had thrown on the bed earlier. The redhead grinned and rested his hands behind his head on the pillow as Jackson rolled the rubber over that glorious thick cock.

He hovered over the redhead, pulling his ass cheeks apart with one hand so he could line Evan's cock up to his entry with the other. Jackson moved down on the shaft, slowly, wanting to get his bearings and give Evan show. With the drugs pulsing through his body Jackson felt freer, more open. He was willing to say things that he would have otherwise held back. "Going to be so good for you," he murmured. He hardly recognized himself, his tone so meek and submissive.

"Yeah?" Evan sighed. "You like that? Being good for me? Pleasing me?"

Jackson bit his lip and nodded, moving down on his lover's cock slowly until his ass cheeks were resting on Evan's pelvic bone. "Yeah. I like that."

"Bet you want me to throw you around a little bit too. Spank that ass?" Evan patted Jackson's butt playfully as he began to move up and down Evan's shaft.

"Mmm, yeah, I want it like that."

"I'll give it to you however you want it."

"Yeah?" Jackson questioned, throwing his head back as he rolled his hips on Evan's dick, lost in the freedom of it all. He was fucking a guy, in the bed he used to share with Tammy, in a room that had never felt like his own until that moment.

"Plan to keep that ass nice and full of my cock. Show you how proud I get when you do what I like. You want that?"

"Want you to be fucking proud. Want to make you feel that way." Jackson arched his back and reached behind him to grasp onto his ankles while still rocking on Evan's cock. The redhead couldn't take his eyes off Jackson's hard dick sticking straight up toward the ceiling as he rolled his body.

"Are you real? Am I really here?" Evan asked, eyes moony. He reached down to intertwine his fingers with Jackson's, taken aback when he batted his hand away.

"Don't get fucking weird," he chided, giving Evan an unimpressed look. "Not used to the good shit. Just keep your mouth shut, all right?"

Evan laid his head back on the pillow while Jackson leaned forward, resting his hands flat against the redhead's chest for leverage as he popped his ass on his cock. "Get it," Evan crooned, eyes growing wide when Jackson moved a hand up to his mouth and covered it.

"Shut the fuck up," he demanded, his voice breathy from his efforts. "I'm close." He sat up straighter and used his free hand to pump his cock in sync with the rhythm of his hips. It only took a few more thrusts until he was shooting streams of jizz onto his lover's chest. He panted as he felt Evan's cock twitch and release deep inside of him.

Without pause, Jackson eased himself off Evan and lay on his back a few feet away from him, hands resting on his sternum, eyes staring at the ceiling. He was crashing from the rush of the cocaine and sex, and was feeling more awkward than sated.

"I don't cuddle," Evan announced as he tied off the condom and tossed it onto the floor.

"I didn't fucking ask you to," Jackson scoffed, refusing to look at the man who was lying a few feet away from him. The silence was deafening; he didn't know what to say. After a few minutes that felt like several hours, Jackson muttered, "You can go."

The words were hardly out of his mouth and Evan was already scrambling to throw his clothes back on, apparently unfazed by the come that had dried onto his skin.

"Want to fuck tomorrow night?" Evan asked as he tied his shoes.

"I don't know, maybe," Jackson replied, twisting to get his cigarettes off his nightstand. Before he could bring one to his lips, Evan laid a quick kiss on them and left the room.

Jackson listened carefully to make sure the front door closed, and once it did, he jumped out of bed to lock it. He didn't trust that the redhead wouldn't come back and gank his shit while he slept.

Jack feared Evan had already stolen enough.

14

Evan (11:35pm): U around?
Jackson (12:27am): Am now. What?
Evan (12:28am): Finishing up some shit. Fucking horny
Jackson (12:30am): Got 2 hands don't u? Use 1 of them
Evan (12:32): Wanna C U

Jackson sighed as he stared down at the screen of his phone, trying to will himself to pull back. Whatever it was between them couldn't become a nightly thing. He didn't want to become wrapped up with a fucking Klown Killer or, really, any man at all. Men were supposed to be for fucking, not for anything else, but Jack could feel himself wanting more. He'd been dealing with massive amounts of bullshit all day, and he found all he had been able to focus on was the fact that he should have kissed his lover back when he pecked him good-bye the night before. He should have let him hold his goddamn hand. He should have allowed himself to get lost in the moment and let his desires lead his way.

It was too much, too soon. Evan had made Jackson realize that he could have feelings for a man in a way that didn't just center around sex, which was disturbing, to say the least. He didn't want to be like this, be gay or whatever. Enjoying getting fucked was one thing, but it was entirely different to want something more than that from a dude.

No matter how hard he tried to control his thoughts and emotions, it seemed his mind was intent on going on a journey to learn what it all meant.

He thought about what could happen if he denied Evan and played some sort of disingenuous game of hard to get, limiting himself when he would much rather indulge in the sexy Daywalker.

Maybe Evan would hit up Humboldt to get off, fuck some other dude, and move on. A strange pang of jealousy made Jackson cringe. He didn't want Evan with anyone else.

Jack wanted Evan to all to himself.

Amy was at Isaiah's, so there was no reason, except fear, to tell Evan not to come over, and Jack was no quivering pussy.

Jackson (12:45am): All right. How soon til ur here?
Evan (12:45am): 10 mins. Don't prep urself.

Jackson rolled his eyes and tossed his phone onto the bed next to him. He didn't know what it was about Evan that made Jack feel the way he did, but simultaneously he loved and hated it. He thought of tons of reasons why wanting Evan like this was a bad idea, but not one seemed compelling enough to turn Jack away.

He steeled himself when he heard the knock on his door and made his way over to it, resolute in what he was going to do.

"Hey," Evan greeted, walking into the apartment and regarding Jackson skeptically as he hung by the door. "What?" It looked as though the redhead's hackles were rising, like he was becoming aware that he had walked into a potentially dangerous situation. He tensed as Jackson approached.

"Come here," he urged, slipping his hand behind Evan's ear to cradle the nape of his neck. Then Jack pulled him in for a kiss. From the moment their lips touched, lights exploded behind Jackson's eyes. Evan sucked Jack's tongue like he sucked dick. Hard and with purpose. And Jackson gave as good as he got, grabbing Evan around the waist and slamming him against Jack's raging dick. Evan exhaled into him and Jackson swallowed the breath down, letting it swell in his lungs and consume him.

"What was that for?" Evan gasped once they pulled apart.

"Told you, you ask too many questions," Jackson chided, rubbing his thumb against his bottom lip as he admired Evan's.

"Wasn't fucking complaining." He regarded Jackson with a squint and a wry smile. "You're hard to read, you know that?"

"Like you're easy?" Jackson shot back with raised eyebrows.

Evan shrugged. "Never said I was." He stared through him as if he wasn't fazed in the least by the assertion. Like he'd heard shit like that his whole life, but had never found himself with someone who made him guess. "You're defensive."

"And you're not?"

"Not really, no." Evan shook his head.

"Got to be if you want to survive," Jackson preached. "You should know that."

"Guess I don't care."

"About surviving?" Jack couldn't understand that shit. He regarded Evan and realized the redhead seemed different than he had the other times Jack been around him, more flat and apathetic.

"Yeah." Evan nodded. "I do, so I don't really think about it."

Jackson wondered who had fucked Evan up so bad, and examined why Jack felt compelled to look out for him. "Can tell you're new to the street." Jackson gestured for Evan to follow him the few feet over to the kitchen.

"Wrong. Grew up on the street," he stated with a tsk. "I've been on my own since I was seventeen and before that…" He trailed off, as if his life story wasn't worth telling.

Jackson studied Evan for a moment to see if he was going to add anything else, and when he didn't, Jack clarified, "New to the gang then." He opened the refrigerator. "They catch you slipping once and there won't be a twice. Want a beer?"

"Thanks." Evan stretched out his arm to take the beer. Before he could pull back, Jackson grabbed his wrist and Evan narrowed his eyes. "What?"

"Guess I know what you were up to tonight," Jackson stated, noticing the maroon paint on Evan's fingers. He pulled his arm back then made his way over to the couch. "They got you tagging?"

"Among other things," Evan replied, as Jackson sat down on the couch next to him. "Who's asking a lot of questions now?"

Jackson gave him the middle finger. "Can't stand the color." He really couldn't. For as long as he could remember, maroon and blue were synonymous with fucking bottom feeders. There were many gangs on the South Side and most of them didn't really get under Jack's skin, but the KKz did. They were always trailing behind Dem Demonz trying to take things that they'd established and make them their own. The Klowns didn't put in the work, and Jackson couldn't fucking stand leeches. It was hard to think of Evan like that, mostly because Jack didn't fucking want to.

"Don't think it looks good on me?" Evan asked with a fake pout. "I'm hurt, man."

"Fuck off," Jackson laughed. "Shit fucking bothers me."

"Not usually this sloppy." Evan took a swig of his beer and wiggled his fingers. "I was distracted all night."

"Oh yeah?" Jackson licked his lips and smirked when he caught the look in Evan's eyes, and was able to see the smile behind them. "Why?"

"You know why," Evan gruffed, scooting closer so their thighs touched. "Want me to say it?"

"Don't give a shit." Jackson shrugged while nudging the side of his nose with the pad of his finger. He turned away, but smiled when he saw Evan's face moving closer in his peripheral vision.

"Was thinking about you," Evan muttered as he reached down to place his beer on the floor then began to pepper Jack's neck with kisses. "Can't get you off my mind."

"That right?" Jack asked in between letting out a soft moan when Evan straddled his legs and began licking and sucking the sensitive skin below his ear more ardently. "You're going to mark me up," he accused between his purrs.

"That a problem?" Evan questioned, his voice muffled as he continued to distribute hickey bites.

Jackson thought about it for a moment as best he could with a hot man Hoovering the life out of his neck. It'd probably be good if the boys saw he was hooking up with someone. It'd be normal to get out and fuck around after being tied down to one woman for so long.

He wasn't sure if it was a rationalization or not, but he figured he would go with it regardless. "Not at all," he hummed, leaning his head back to give Evan better access. Jackson slid his hands under the waistband of Evan's jeans and grabbed a firm hold on his ass as the redhead rolled his hips. "I think about you, too," Jack admitted quietly, gratified he could feel Evan's smile against his skin. Jack tilted his chin down to urge Evan up and they began to make out eagerly.

As their tongues intertwined, Jackson removed his hands from Evan's ass and made sure their fingers laced together. Evan squeezed Jack's hand gently and licked his lips before sucking on his tongue like a boss.

"I want you to," Evan whispered against Jackson's mouth, his warm breath fanning over Jack's face.

"Want me to what?" he questioned, nibbling on the redhead's bottom lip, remembering it was only a few days ago when he'd busted it on the basketball court. So much had changed in such a short period of time, and it made his head spin.

Two weeks ago, he never would have imagined that he'd be making out with some dude on the couch in the living room that he once shared with Tamara. He'd lived a dangerous life for most of his twenty-three years, but had never felt so alive as when he was in Evan's arms.

"Think of me," Evan whispered, pulling back far enough so Jack could look in his eyes. "I want you to." Evan searched Jackson's face, clearly looking for a positive response. It was crazy how different Evan looked when he was this close; the freckles brushed across his skin, making him appear innocent and pliant, when Jackson knew he was anything but.

"Good," was the only reply he could muster, wanting to say a million more things but not allowing himself to go there, realizing that as treacherous as an aloof Evan was, an earnest Evan was far more perilous. The more the redhead softened, the quicker Jack felt himself falling, and he knew the end result could be catastrophic.

Still, the way that Evan was holding Jackson's hands, as if he would float away, proved that he wasn't the only one with his head stuck firmly in the clouds. Evan was a dream that could easily become a nightmare, and as vigilant as he wanted to remain, Jackson wasn't afraid to close his eyes.

15

Evan had grown to hate the Drexel. It wasn't that he ever liked it much to begin with, but the amount of time he'd spent there recently had solidified his opinion. The owner of his stolen credit card had finally cancelled it, which was problematic to say the least. He needed a new stream of income and he needed it fast. After he shared the news, Luis had suggested that Evan hit up the club to collect as many card numbers as possible so they could spread out the spending. Luis and Micah had spent the last few nights doing just that.

Working the credit card gig meant it had been a few days since he'd seen Jackson, which, after three straight nights together, felt like an eternity. He'd been busy at the club and every time he'd texted Jackson to see if he wanted to fuck, he seemed distracted and blew him off. He thought that maybe it was too much too soon, so Evan decided he'd chill and wait it out, which was hard as fuck on all fronts.

He'd never wanted anybody like he wanted Jackson, who was so fucking sexy that Evan wanted to rip his clothes off the minute he was around him, and he had. Evan had made Jackson ride him every time they'd banged in Jackson's bed. Evan couldn't get enough of watching the tough-as-shit street thug bounce on his dick and whimper from the pleasure. He loved how Jackson's powerful thighs flexed as he moved up and down on Evan's shaft and the way Jack's cock bobbed with each movement.

That cock. It was perfect, just like the rest of him. Evan wanted it in his mouth constantly. He'd never paid such close attention to any other dude's dick. He liked them well enough, but ass was much more appealing. Sure, he gave head and enjoyed it, but he'd never become that intimate with anyone else's cock mostly because they'd always been much more into his. Every guy he'd been with had gone crazy to slobber all over his dick, and while Jackson hadn't been an exception, the way he worked him made Jackson stand apart. Even the idea of Jackson being into his cock had Evan hard as a rock.

The fact that Jackson liked to be controlled in bed was the icing on the cake.

It was easy to get wrapped up in the sex when they'd been having so much of it. After the awkward first time in the apartment together, they'd spent the next two nights endurance fucking. Just slamming the hell out of each other, while their bodies pulled apart into orgasms: mind-blowing, body-shaking, muscle-spasming releases.

It was such a turn-on that a guy with a reputation of being ice cold on the streets was so warm and giving in bed. Jackson seemed intent on bringing Evan as much pleasure as possible, and in return he was compelled to give the Demon exactly what he needed.

Evan had never been in a relationship that had required him to be faithful, and if he had been, he was fairly positive he wouldn't be. He'd always been promiscuous, never satisfied by one person, always needing more. Yet, if the opportunity ever presented itself, he was pretty sure he could commit to Jackson. He sort of wanted to. It was crazy how Jack was able to fulfill Evan in ways he'd never imagined. He couldn't fathom anyone else being able to do the same.

"Hey." Micah nudged Evan with his elbow to get his attention. "Over there." Micah gestured to the bar where three women were throwing down shots and laughing wildly. Each one was more beautiful than the next with their dark raven tresses and attractive figures. "Wanna try them?"

Evan nodded, worried that the group dynamic might work against them, but not giving a shit enough to protest. He knew he had to get his head in the game, but it seemed his mind was intent on being elsewhere. Still, he followed Micah as he approached the girls.

"Ladies, ladies, ladies," Micah greeted smoothly with a huge smile that showed off his perfectly straight white teeth. "Doing shots tonight, huh? Can we buy you another round?"

It was obvious they were already well on their way to wasted, which was precisely why Evan and Micah waited until after midnight to hit up the club. The drunker the girls were, the better the chance the KKz could get what they needed the easiest way possible—by just taking it. When they worked in pairs, they couldn't use the "forgot my wallet" scam; it was too unbelievable. Instead, they got the chicks buzzed enough to not notice when they pulled their credit cards out of their purses, that the guys took a picture and put it back. They never took the card, because it would be obvious it was missing and they'd cancel it when they woke up in the morning.

"Uh, yeah, sure," the brown-eyed girl replied, looking at her friends with a giggle. "That'd be good. Washington Apples."

While Micah called the bartender over to order the shots, Evan shoved his hands into his pockets and nodded his hello. "I'm Evan."

"Nice to meet you," the bustiest of the women said, not so subtly checking him out. "I'm Tamara, this is Amy and Kylie." She gestured to the other girls as she introduced them, but her eyes stayed fixed on him. "You're adorable."

He'd been called a lot of things in his life, but adorable wasn't one of them. He'd been a cute kid, but he and Paul had always been too naughty to be considered adorable by most adults. "Adorable, huh?" he stated, clearing his throat. "That's a new one."

"You don't like it?" she asked, pushing out her bottom lip into an exaggerated pout. "I could call you something else if you want. How do you feel about 'daddy'?"

Her friend, Amy, smacked her arm and rolled her eyes. "You look desperate," she chided softly, thinking that Evan couldn't hear her, but he could.

"Well maybe I am?" she retorted, turning to Evan. "You see my ex, Amy's brother, literally never fucked me."

"Tams," Kylie exclaimed, punching out a laugh while Amy looked like she was going to actually punch Tamara.

"What?" She blinked innocently, swaying slightly on her heels and grabbing hold of the mahogany bar to steady herself. "It's true. Jackson wasn't into fucking I guess, or maybe he wasn't into fucking me. I don't know." She sniffed and turned back to Evan. "You're a guy…"

"I am," he confirmed, alarm bells going off in his head. What were the chances? Jackson wasn't a common name. Evan couldn't believe he was standing at a bar with Jackson's ex-girlfriend, and, evidently, his sister as well.

Evan glanced at Amy, who seemed to be seconds away from crawling under the bar and dying of mortification. She had the same blue eyes as Jackson, just as beautiful and just as sad; as if they'd lived a thousand lives and all of them were a struggle.

"Here we go," Micah interrupted, passing the shots around.

"What are we toasting?" Kylie asked, holding up her shot glass.

"Evan," Micah prompted. "Want to do the honors?"

"Uh." He glared at Micah, always annoyed when he was forced to be more involved than he wanted to be. "To brown hair and blue eyes."

Tamara's face immediately lit up, thinking the toast was for her, and threw back her shot. She didn't waste any time getting back to business. "So Evan, why wouldn't a guy want to fuck his girlfriend?" she questioned.

Amy took a deep breath and put her clutch on the table, gesturing for Kylie to do the same. "We're going to dance." She grabbed her friend's hand, obviously wanting to get away from the oncoming train wreck. "Watch our shit, Tammy."

"I'm coming," Micah said with a grin, giving Evan a wink at how damn easy their task had become. Little did he know that it had gotten much more complicated than he could imagine.

Evan considered not taking Amy's credit card for a moment and going for the other girls', but he knew Micah would wonder why he hadn't snapped a picture of all of them. Evan didn't know shit about Amy and he certainly didn't have any loyalty to her just because he was banging her brother.

"Fine, but don't touch me. I have a boyfriend who will literally murder you if you do," Amy warned Micah, clearly unimpressed by the fact that he had invited himself to her dance party.

"And a brother that would do the same," Tamara added as she watched them walk toward the dance floor. She pulled their purses toward her and looked up at Evan. "So tell me about yourself," she prompted, batting her eyelashes. "What are you into?"

"Yayo and fucking," he answered truthfully.

She smirked. "Ah, is that right?" She opened her purse and dug through it until she produced a small bag of cocaine. Glancing over her shoulders to make sure there were no eyes on them she started pouring a few lines onto the table. While she did, Evan readied his phone to take the pictures and made his move. Tamara giggled as he leaned into her, placing a tender kiss on her bare shoulder so he could slide Amy's and Kylie's bags toward him undetected. "So this is half of what you want," she flirted once Evan straightened up. "Guess we'll get to the other half afterward."

He nodded, aware of how fucking weird it was that Jackson's ex-girlfriend was trying to bang him, and that Jackson had an ex-girlfriend at all. "You first."

"A gentleman," she cooed. "Haven't been around one of them in a while."

Evan cringed at the dig on Jackson and at the allusion that Evan was a gentleman when he was anything but. As Tamara leaned over to snort the first line, he quickly opened up Kylie's purse and took a picture of her card. Girls made it so damn easy to steal from them with their tiny little bags that didn't hold a wallet. They let their identification and credit card hang around loose, easy to grab without being caught. When she went for her second line, Evan got Amy's number. Just as he snapped the picture, he saw a text come through.

Jackson (1:34am): U around?

Evan grinned, happy to hear from the Demon after days of radio silence.

"Here you go," Tamara chirped, handing Evan the rolled-up ten spot. "It's not the best shit, but it's good enough."

Evan nodded and leaned over to bump the remaining lines, tilting his neck and squinting his eyes once he inhaled, never tiring of the rush the drugs gave him when they hit his head. He sniffed and threw a slight smile Tamara's way before pulling his phone back out.

Evan (1:37am): Yeah
Jackson (1:38): Wanna fuck?
Evan (1:38): C U soon.

"Uh, some shit just came up, so I got to bounce," he told her with a grimace.

Her face fell. "Really?" she asked, arching her eyebrow. "Are you serious?"

He nodded. "Yeah, but I'll see you around, okay?" As he walked away from the table, leaving a forlorn Tamara behind, he called to Micah, "Yo."

Micah waved his good-bye as he grinded against Kylie's ass.

Evan was about to grind against some ass, too, and he couldn't fucking wait.

16

Though the L ride from the North to the South Side didn't take long, it felt like forever when Evan was heading over to Jackson's to fuck. The cocaine he'd bumped with Tamara was still charging through his system, making him feel both jittery and euphoric. As he scrolled through his camera roll, he couldn't help but laugh at how Jackson had protected his sister without even knowing he did. The pictures Evan had taken of Tamara's and Kylie's cards were clear as day, all of the numbers visible and perfectly in focus, while the picture he took of Amy's was obstructed by the text message Jackson had sent him. Evan didn't believe in a greater power, but he couldn't help but think that the universe was in some way trying to protect him from an epic fucking-shit-up with Jackson. Evan deleted the photo and brainstormed his excuse for the remainder of the ride.

When he reached his stop, he jumped out and made his way to the apartment building on St. Lawrence, really fucking ready to get on Jackson. Evan almost felt bad for his ass, because it was going to be taking one hell of a pounding.

"Hey," Jackson greeted as he opened the door. He was wearing a wife-beater and basketball shorts that hung low on his hips. Evan could see the outline of Jack's cock and how it hung heavy against the mesh fabric. Evan was tempted to drop to his knees right there and fuck Jackson with his mouth, but he held himself back so he could loop his arms around the other man's waist and lean down to slot their mouths together.

The kiss was as full of want as it was of tongue. "You look so fucking sexy," he muttered against Jackson's lips, knowing that though it was the drugs and alcohol compelling him to share his amorous thoughts, he really fucking meant them.

Jackson grunted as Evan pushed him against the wall and kicked the door shut behind them. "Fuck off," Jackson scoffed quietly, returning the kisses and sighing when Evan's hand cupped his dick over his shorts. Then, slowly, Evan began to pump his hand back and forth to work his lover to maximum hardness. Peeking down, he saw the fabric tenting as a result of his ministrations. He knocked his hard-on against Jackson's dick as they continued to make out, loving the physical manifestation of Jackson's attraction to him.

"So hard for me, aren't you?" Evan crooned, moving his lips down to Jackson's neck. The brunet hummed in response, which wasn't good enough. "Want to hear you say it. Tell me how hard I make you." Jackson remained quiet save the soft moans tumbling from his lips as Evan sucked marks into his skin and slowly stroked his clothed cock.

"Tell me," Evan prompted again, increasing the pace of his jerking to reflect urgency, "c'mon."

"Like a rock, get me hard as a rock," Jackson breathed, letting out a near silent gasp when Evan immediately dropped his knees and ghosted his mouth over Jackson's bulge.

"Turns me on when you tell me." Evan yanked down Jackson's shorts so his cock could spring free. "Mmm." Evan took him in and started to swirl his tongue sloppily around the thick shaft. "Taste so good," he mumbled as best as he could with a mouth full of cock.

Glancing up, he saw Jackson lean his head back against the wall and close his eyes as he tangled his fingers into Evan's hair and exhaled heavily as Evan continued to work him.

"You think of me?" Evan murmured, lapping up the come that was beading on his slit, letting long rivulets extend from the head of Jackson's cock to the tip of his tongue. "Over the last few days?"

"Yeah," Jackson admitted, looking down at Evan with hooded eyes. "A lot."

Evan caught the flush creeping across Jackson's cheeks and couldn't help but grin that the badass was blushing. "What'd you do when you thought of me?"

"You know what I did," Jackson sighed, rubbing his forehead, looking frustrated. "Don't need to fucking say it."

"Want you to," Evan coaxed. "Don't you want to be good for me?"

"Oh, shut the fuck up," Jackson snapped, his skin now a deep crimson. He kneed Evan in the chest then walked to the bedroom, Evan on his feet and laughing as he followed. He could hardly believe that shit had come out of his mouth when it had, and without the influence of cocaine, he wasn't going to fucking go there. Jackson took the lube out of his nightstand and pulled off his shirt, watching as Evan did the same.

"I liked it, you know," he mumbled, taking a condom out of the pocket of his jeans before letting them drop to the ground. "When you talked like that. It was fucking hot as hell."

"Yeah, well you're going to have to deal with me being less hot," Jackson stated, lifting his eyebrows in challenge as slicked up his fingers and dipped them into his asshole, "because that shit ain't me."

Evan tsked that the brunet was starting without him, but smirked at the visual, thinking it would be impossible for Jackson to be less hot. His body was thick with a broad chest, strong trunk, and muscular thighs, just the way Evan liked it. "It seemed like it was."

Jackson flipped him off with his free hand and bit his lip as he continued to work himself open.

"Was going to eat that ass," Evan pouted, crawling onto the bed and on top of Jackson. He grabbed the lube, wet his middle finger, and gave Jackson a naughty grin as he slid it into his ass beside his digits.

"Not happening." Jackson shook his head. "It's too fucking weird."

"You'll love it when you let me," Evan assured him.

"You're a fucking perv, man," Jackson accused, not able to hide the amusement in his eyes.

"All you gotta do is let me rim you once and you're going to be a slut for it," Evan teased, shoving another finger in to meet Jackson's.

"Fuck," he moaned, biting into his lower lip so hard Evan was sure Jackson was going to draw blood.

"Want you to be a slut for me. You going to be my slut tonight?" Evan pressed a kiss against Jackson's collarbone as they continued to work in tandem to prep him.

"Suck a dick," he spat, not enough venom in his tone to make him appear the least bit angry.

"Just did," Evan replied, looking up at him, then sticking his tongue out. "And I fucking loved it."

Jackson stared for a moment before growling, "How about you stop being a lazy piece of shit who makes me do all the work and actually fuck me, prick? How's that sound?"

With a smile, Evan pulled his fingers out, making room for Jackson to do the same and patted his lover on the thigh, indicating he should flip over. "Might make you cry again, though. That a'ight?"

"You're a fucking asshole, you know that?" Jackson groused, getting on his hands and knees.

"Am what I eat," he retorted, rolling the condom onto his cock.

"Nasty motherfucker," Jackson chided, unable to hold back his laughter. He grunted when Evan's teeth gnashed hard into the flesh of Jackson's butt, and then he gasped when Evan smacked his hand flat against the same area.

"You have no idea," he assured, rubbing the pink skin before spanking Jackson harder.

"Do it again and I'm going to fuck you up," Jackson warned at the end of the low groan that had leaked from his lungs.

"Wish you would, ho," Evan shot back, slapping his cock against Jackson's ass crack.

Jackson moved to turn over, but Evan grabbed him by the neck and choked him out as he shoved his cock fully into Jackson's body. Fingers dug into the sheets as Evan began to thrust his cock deeper and deeper inside of the tight hole.

Laying his chest flat against Jackson's back, Evan wrapped his arms around tattooed shoulders for leverage as he forcefully snapped his hips. "Like that?" Evan whispered into his lover's ear, teeth nibbling on his earlobe. "When I show you how I own that ass?"

"Fuck off," Jackson whimpered.

"Going to be a good boy for me? Take everything I give you?" Evan rasped hotly in Jackson's ear. He smirked when the brunet let out a whine then turned and buried his blushing face into the pillow. "Gets you shy, huh? Don't have to be. Fucking love hearing you."

The only sounds in the room were the muffled moans coming from Jackson and the sound of Evan's balls slapping rhythmically against his lover's full ass with every thrust. He straightened up so he could give the man below him some space, deciding he'd try another tactic to get him to open up. Slowing his pace exponentially, he inched his cock out of Jackson's hole so just the tip was left inside before easing it back in.

Jackson let out a frustrated grunt and looked over his shoulder.

"What?" Evan asked with faux innocence. He peered down at his cock moving in and out of Jackson. "Look at this ass," he crooned, using his thumb to pull a cheek back to give him a better view. "Stretching so nice for my cock. So puckered and pink."

Jackson bit his lip and screwed down his eyebrows.

"You should see what I see, Jack. Looks so fucking pretty taking my big dick. Swallows it up so good. You like it?" He couldn't help the feeling of deep satisfaction wash through him as he watched Jackson's cheeks turn bright red again.

"Yeah," he replied softly. "I like it."

"Want to be good for me?" Evan asked, reaching around to wrap his fist around Jackson's leaking cock and angled his hips up to hit Jackson's prostate.

"Fuck," Jack punched out, shaking his head. "I want to be."

"Be what, baby?" Evan urged.

Jackson cringed. "Good for you," he replied quietly.

"Then tell me how you want it. Be good for me and tell me how." Evan ran his thumb over the slit of Jackson's dick and traced the slick digit around the head.

"Pound it like you hate it and then come all over my ass," Jackson grunted out, then tucked his head between his shoulder blades.

"Mmm." Evan hummed, spanking Jackson's ass with his free hand, loving the groan that escaped his lips. Evan dropped his lover's cock and dug his fingers into his hips, holding him steady in preparation. "I can do that." Without another word, he began driving into Jackson with such force that he was afraid he was going to split him in two.

Jackson managed to grab a hold of his cock while Evan rammed him. When he demanded that Jackson "fucking come" his lover obliged and his knees wobbled while his body tensed.

Evan jerked his cock out of Jackson's body to shoot his come all over his ass. As he was panting through the aftershocks of his orgasm, Evan rubbed the come into Jackson's skin, loving how slick and wet it made his thick ass. "So good for me," he praised as Jackson collapsed face down on the bed.

Following their usual protocol, Evan climbed off the bed and began to pull on his clothes, and nearly tripped with surprise when he heard a tired voice tell him to stay.

"With you?"

"Stupid fucking question," Jackson groused. "Don't make me regret it."

Wordlessly, Evan climbed back into the bed and wondered if he had, in fact, fucked the bad boy into submission.

17

Evan didn't expect Jackson to be a koala bear when he slept, clinging on to Evan's body like he was a eucalyptus tree. It hadn't started that way. They remained on opposite ends sides of Jackson's king-size bed, spent from the rigorous fucking. "Stay" was the last word he had said before passing out. Evan wasn't sure why Jackson had asked him to stay if all he planned to do was sleep. The cocaine had dissipated from Evan's bloodstream but he still felt speedy, unable to relax his mind enough to drift off. Instead he watched the way Jackson's back rose with his slow and even breaths, his sticky ass draped with the sheets while the upper half of his body remained uncovered. His face was turned to the side on the pillow and his pout was puckered from the way his cheek was being pressed. He looked peaceful and innocent: everything he was not during waking hours. When Jackson turned onto his back, Evan felt his body tense. He was getting closer and as much as Evan wanted to be tender, he wasn't convinced he knew how to be.

He figured he must've fallen asleep sometime after Jackson's first roll toward him, because when he opened his eyes next, tattoo-sleeved arms were wrapped around his chest and muscular legs around his knees. Though he feared that he wouldn't know what to do in a moment that reflected real intimacy, instinctively he did. After pushing brown hair back from Jackson's forehead, Evan gently rested his lips against it, awestruck by the comfort his lover seemed to get from holding him. Jackson had said he didn't cuddle, but being tangled up with him was everything Evan never knew he wanted, but suddenly really fucking needed.

The second time he woke up, the early morning sun was streaming under the slats of the blinds and bathing the room in an amber hue. Jackson was still holding him tight and Evan decided that now was as good a time as any to indulge in some of the sweetness he secretly craved. Cautiously, he closed the space between their faces and as gently as possible he rubbed the tip of his nose against the end of Jackson's. Evan hadn't ever noticed the soft brush of freckles that spread across Jackson's nose and couldn't help but think that they were the cutest fucking thing Evan had seen in a long time. When he nudged him again, Jackson sniffed, dug his face into the pillow, and held him tighter.

Venturing to make his next move, Evan gently raked his fingers through Jackson's hair, startled when his head shot up and his blue eyes opened wide.

"Fuck, sorry," he grumbled, peeling himself off Evan, who grabbed Jack and pulled him back.

"Been like this all night," Evan informed Jackson, arms looped protectively around his waist. "I like it."

"No shit," Jackson looked abashed. "All night?"

"Did you miss the part where I said I liked it?" Evan teased. He wasn't going to admit that he'd considered pushing Jack off at first, that the connection had been overwhelming and it had taken hours for Evan to get used to it.

Jackson closed his eyes, as if he was hoping that Evan would disappear. Instead, still entangled with his body, gazing at him softly, Jack asked, "Guess you're used to this shit, huh?" Sharing your bed with a fucking dude?"

Evan laughed lightly. "Not really. I didn't have a bed for like four years until recently."

"What?" Jackson looked perplexed, as if he couldn't imagine what Evan was telling him.

"My sister kicked me out of the house when I was seventeen. Been on my own ever since," he explained. "Crashed in shelters, park benches, other people's couches, beds…you know."

"So you were homeless? Until when?"

"A month or so ago. When I got jumped in."

Jackson nodded.

"Living with my brother and a couple of the other boys." Evan paused as if he was unsure if he wanted to share the next tidbit of information, knowing the two men had a history of hating each other. He decided that he might as well go for it. "Kane. My brother is Kane."

"Fuck," Jackson sighed, shaking his head. "Can't fucking stand that fake-ass thug."

"Yeah well, he's not crazy about you either," Evan informed him.

Jackson shrugged, clearly not fazed by the revelation. Evan was surprised that he and Jackson were still holding each other as they talked, as if he didn't want to give up the touch. "Can't believe you didn't have a place to live."

"Don't make a big deal about it. It's whatever." Evan sloughed it off as if it was nothing.

"You got what you need now though?" Jackson asked softly.

Evan nodded. "Most things." He paused. "Remember when you said that I asked too many questions?"

Jackson nodded again.

"Well, you're asking too many questions," Evan stated.

"You got a gun? You never seem to be strapped."

Evan shook his head. "Nah. Had some access to money, but you can't order a piece online, so I haven't gotten one."

Jackson sighed. "So you roll with the KKz but you don't pack heat? Sounds like a great fucking way to get your ass killed."

Evan bristled, loosening his hold Jackson, who in turn pulled him closer.

"Stop," he ordered softly, nestling his face into the crook of Evan's neck. "It's not..." He shook his head, his nose tickling Evan's skin. "Ain't like I'm judging you, all right? I just know this shit."

"And why do you care what the fuck I do?" Evan felt defensive, but his voice was less insistent than he intended it to be.

"I don't," Jackson assured, immediately letting go of his body and turning away. Evan was left staring at the back of Jackson's head and considered allowing him to shut Evan out. He thought about climbing out of bed, but instead scooted closer so his chest was flank to Jackson's back and Evan's knees were tucked into the crook of Jackson's.

"You do," Evan corrected softly, "and I'm glad you do." He paused so he could lay a kiss on his lover's bare shoulder. "I'm not used to anyone giving a shit. It's been a while."

Jackson remained quiet and lay there. Evan took in the companionable silence, the tension of moments before dissipating as quickly as it appeared. "You always sleep with an AK on your nightstand?" Earlier this morning, he'd noticed the gun lying on the side table, and was surprised he hadn't seen it the night before.

"Mmmhmm," Jackson hummed, "and a Bible."

"You religious?" Evan raised his eyebrows. Jack didn't seem the type.

"Nah," he replied. "I should be, but I'm not. Every day I look at it and think I should read it, but I never do."

"It's overrated."

"The Bible?" Jackson laughed.

"Yeah," Evan confirmed with a grin. "It's basically full of shit that tells us everything we do is fucking wrong. Who wants to read something like that? Like the Ten Commandments. How many have you broken?"

Jackson shrugged. "A few I guess."

"See."

"You say 'see' like you proved something." Jackson turned his head a bit so he could look over his shoulder.

"That's the start of it," Evan said with a yawn.

"You know how to build anticipation," Jackson joked, then turned his head to look at the clock next to the Bible. "You should probably go."

"You got someone coming home soon?" Evan asked, rolling off him and climbing off the bed.

"Yeah, my sister," he stated with a sigh. "She lives here."

"And she doesn't know you're…" Evan caught his tongue, not wanting to label Jackson, knowing he wouldn't want anyone to say that shit about him, "… the way you are."

Jackson shook his head and watched as Evan buttoned up his shirt. "Kane know?"

Evan laughed sardonically. "Thinks he knows something, but I never told him shit."

"How'd he think it then? You don't, you know, seem like you are," Jackson stated carefully.

Evan shrugged. "Maybe because I'm not drooling over the skanky sluts they have hanging around? I don't know." Evan considered bringing up his run-in with Tamara, but when he was on his way out the door didn't seem like the right time. He buckled his belt and watched as Jackson grabbed his discarded boxers and threw them on.

"Got anything to drink?" Evan asked as Jackson trailed after him out of his bedroom.

"Want coffee?" he asked, prompting Evan to scoff and cringe.

"I don't fuck around with that shit," he shuddered. "It fucks with your system."

"You've literally been shoving powder up your nose every time I've been with you." Jackson laughed, shaking his head at the irony.

"Yeah, well, that's different," Evan stated, nodding his head when Jackson held up a carton of orange juice from the fridge.

"Yeah, one's a completely acceptable pick-me-up and the other's a fast track to death," Jackson contended, getting a glass out of the cabinet and pouring some juice for Evan.

"You're awful judgmental for a motherfucker who sells the shit," Evan quipped, taking a sip and raising his eyebrows at Jackson.

"Yeah well, it's up to other people if they want to kill themselves. Ain't my responsibility to keep anyone alive but myself," he retorted.

"Cheery breakfast conversation."

"Coming from a guy who seems to ration his smiles, that's pretty fucking rich," Jackson shot back, grinning. The expression quickly fell from his face when they heard the apartment door open.

"Jack?" a woman called curiously. Evan presumed it was Amy. She turned the corner to peek in the kitchen. Shitfuckshit. Amy. With her mouth hanging open, "Evan?"

Jackson's sister turned as pale as a ghost as she looked back and forth between the men and then wordlessly hurried into her room.

"You got to fucking go," Jackson snapped, yanking the glass from Evan's hand and instantly dropping it due to his incessant shaking.

"Want me to...?" Evan began, looking down at the shards of glass covering the tile floor.

"Fucking go? Yeah. I do." Jackson's voice was heavy with emotion and Evan didn't fucking blame him.

Evan nodded and made his way out of the apartment, wishing he would've kissed Jack, but knowing he shouldn't.

The moment had passed.

18

Jackson spent most of the day holed up in his room lying in bed, trying to think of possible explanations for why Evan was sipping juice in the kitchen at the ass crack of dawn. The only feasible reason, besides the obvious, was that he was selling him some coke, which was unrealistic because typically, Jackson didn't do deals in the apartment or in his underwear. He had no idea why Amy came home when she did or why he was the unluckiest motherfucker on the planet. All he knew was that his sister was now privy to his deepest, darkest secret and there was no taking that back.

Not ready to face her, he waited until sometime in the late afternoon after he heard the front door open and close, to emerge from his room. He was supposed to meet up with Luke in a few hours to target shoot at the warehouse, but that wasn't fucking happening. Instead he decided to get wasted on some Jack Daniel's and play video games.

The text messages from Evan started flooding in around dinnertime.

> *Evan (6:36pm): Hey u good?*
> *Evan (6:45pm): ???*
> *Evan (7:02pm): Feel like ur ignoring me*
> *Evan (7:05pm): R U?*
> *Jackson (7:07pm): Fuck off*
> *Evan (7:10pm): Yeah?*
> *Jackson (7:11pm): Yup*
> *Evan (7:12pm): So ur gonna push me away now?*
> *Jackson (7:12pm): Yup*
> *Evan (7:14pm): Not surprising. Exactly what a pussy would do.*

Jackson (7:15pm): Fuck u. Come over here and I'll show u what a pussy I am.
Evan (7:16pm): Already did last night bitch. Remember when u were my good boy?

Jackson threw his phone across the room and rubbed his forehead, wishing he could erase every memory and moment with that asshole that was stuck in his mind. He figured his only chance at doing so was to drink more. He cringed as he took another swig, tilting his head against the overstuffed pillows of the couch, and closed his eyes.

He should have never allowed himself to go there—to let Evan into his house, into his body. He hated how badly he wanted him, wanted whatever the fuck they had. Jackson chugged the liquor, so aggravated when he reached the bottom of the bottle that he thoughtlessly spiked it against the wall, watching as the glass shattered from the force. He'd broken too many things that day.

He attempted to climb to his feet but gave up as soon as he stumbled, dropping onto his hands and knees, and crawled across the floor to his phone. "Of course," he grumbled, looking down at the cracked screen and the messages beyond it.

Evan (7:31pm): So that's it? It's done?
Evan (7:32pm): Guess there wasn't much there anyway
Evan (8:27pm): Fuck u and fuck me for giving a shit
Jackson (9:14pm): I gve a shtt 2
Evan (9:20pm): Ur drunk
Jackson (9:20pm): so
Evan (9:21pm): Anything ur drunk ass says doesn't count
Jackson (9:22pm): Ohyeh?

He lay down on his stomach, letting his cheek rest against the carpet as he squinted, trying to focus on the blurring screen. Evan's statement felt like freedom, an opportunity he was going to take with all of his inhibitions lying among the shards of glass in the corner of the room.

Jackson (9:24pm): Fcking crazy abut u

Evan (9:25pm): Stop ur gonna regret this when u look back at ur messages tomorrow
Jackson (9:26pm): U said it dont cunt
Evan (9:27pm): Did u just call me a cunt?
Jackson (9:27pm): count
Evan (9:28pm): Yeah well it does now
Jackson (9:28pm): U cant do tht
Evan (9:29pm): Can do whatever I want
Jackson (9:29pm): 2 me
Evan (9:30pm): Not true. You won't let me eat ur ass out.
Jackson (9:31pm): Cum here nd do it then
Evan (9:32pm): Don't tempt me. You're too drunk and you told me to fuck off earlier. Not gonna be someone's regret.

Jackson grimaced, hating that he'd made Evan feel that way and hating even more that he did regret wanting him. Shit was easier when he didn't have to talk to the guys he fucked, when he didn't kiss them, wake up wrapped around them, or want them the way he craved Evan.

Jackson (9:34pm): want itwant u
Evan (9:35pm): Ur gonna sober up and wish I wasn't there. Did u talk to ur sister?

Sometime after the last drop of alcohol had been consumed, he'd forgotten all about the awkward run-in hours earlier. Now, just like that, all the shame came back, crashing over him like a wave and making him feel like he was drowning.

Jackson (9:38pm): Don't worry abut it
Evan (9:38pm): So it went ok?
Evan (10:01pm): Ur done talking to me now?

He wanted to say yes, desperate to lick his wounds and forget about the events of the day. He wanted to end the conversation that he knew was going to mortify him as much, if not more, than his run-in with Amy had earlier. He wanted to be done talking, but he knew he couldn't be.

Jackson (10:02pm): NO not sure wht tosay
Evan (10:04pm): Been thinking about u all day. Wanna C U.
Jackson (10:05pm): Cme here
Evan (10:05pm): What about ur sister?
Jackson (10:06pm): Dont worry abutit
Evan (10:06pm): Okay

Without giving it another thought, he sent a text to Amy. Somewhere deep in his skull, his sober mind was screaming for him not to do it, to attempt to save some sort of face, but his sober mind was flooded with Jack Daniels, not at all able to win the battle it was too drunk to fight.

Jackson (10:07pm): Don't cme hme 2nit
Amy (10:10pm): I was planning on staying at Isaiah's anyway. Are we going to talk about this or pretend it never happened?
Jackson (10:11pm): Dnt know wht ur talkin abut
Amy (10:18pm): Got it. It never happened. But if it had... I wouldn't care. I hope you know that. I love you and I always will. Don't give a shit who you love.
Jackson (10:20pm): not abut luv
Amy (10:25pm): Well then, I don't give a fuck who you fuck. Is that better?

He stared down at his phone at his sister's succinct reaction. For him, his preferences were world crushing and painful, the secret that had always torn him up from the inside. To Amy, it was "I don't give a fuck who you fuck" and "don't give a shit who you love." The only person he had ever loved didn't give a fuck or a shit. As reluctant as he was to look her in the eyes again, the fact that she was so accepting made the prospect less intimidating.

Thing was, he didn't want her to see him differently.

He rolled over onto his back and stared at the ceiling, attempting to muster the energy to sit up. Once he did, he groaned at how fucking disgusting the room was. He figured he could make himself look somewhat less disgusting if he at least cleaned up the broken bottle. His submerged reasoning skills allowed him to pick up the pieces of glass without care and he ended up giving himself a good-size gash in his palm.

While he was wiping blood onto his white wife-beater, he heard a knock at the door. He forced himself to his feet and stumbled to it, opening it slowly to see Evan standing there with his hands in his pockets. As soon as the redhead saw him, his eyes went wide. "What the fuck happened to you?" He grabbed him by the wrist and examined the cut on his hand.

"Broke a glass," Jack slurred, yanking his arm away. "Ain't a big deal."

"Looks pretty deep to me," Evan disagreed with a click of his tongue. He closed the door behind him and frowned. "Do you have anything to clean it up?"

"In the bathroom," Jackson sighed, realizing that Evan wasn't going to drop it. Jackson staggered toward the bathroom, not protesting when he felt steady hands on his waist, supporting him. He swung open the medicine cabinet and leaned against the wall as Evan looked through it.

"Here." He pulled out hydrogen peroxide, cotton balls, gauze, and tape. "Think you can probably do without stitches if I pack it enough."

"You a doctor, too? That the next bomb you're going to drop on me?"

"What other bomb did I drop on you?" Evan asked with a laugh, turning on the faucet and letting the water warm up a bit before he took Jackson's hand and held his underneath it for support. Jackson refused to flinch even though it hurt like a muthafucker.

Evan wadded up some toilet paper and dabbed the area dry before wetting a cotton ball with the chemical.

"That you're a KKz," Jackson stated. "Fucking hate it."

"But you're bleeding red," Evan teased, much to Jackson's dismay. "I'm just kidding, man."

"It ain't a joke though. This shit's a big deal. We're never going to be able to be together, you know that? I mean," he cleared his throat, "if that's what you were hoping for, it ain't ever going to happen."

Evan nodded as he cleaned the wound. "I'm here though, so it's kinda happening, right?"

"You know what I mean," Jack stated, watching as Evan laid a bunch of gauze on his hand and then wrapped it with tape.

"Why don't we worry about that shit another time?" he suggested, dipping down to press a soft kiss against Jackson's lips. "You taste like Jack Daniels."

"Am I supposed to say something really fucking gay like 'you taste like heaven'?" Jackson smiled when Evan broke out into raucous laughter.

"I mean, I hope not," he said as he caught his breath. He slowly peeled Jackson's tank top off him and tossed it onto the floor. "Where's the rest of the glass?"

"In the living room," Jackson replied, annoyed that he was still embarrassed even when the alcohol was supposed to assure him that he wouldn't be.

"Let's get you into bed and then I'll go and clean it up," Evan suggested, looping his arm around Jackson's waist and guiding him to his bedroom.

"I can walk," he groused, earning a chuckle from the redhead.

"No you fucking can't," he disagreed, pulling back the comforter so Jackson could climb into bed then draped it over him. Evan made his way into the living room to clean up the broken bottle.

Jackson heard cleaning-up noises and glass hitting the trash bin before Evan came back to the bedroom. Pulling off his t-shirt and then shorts, he climbed under the covers behind Jackson and Evan wrapped his arms tightly around Jack's chest.

"Think I'm crazy about you, too," he admitted quietly, his nose nudging the nape of Jackson's neck.

"You said that shit didn't count," Jackson replied sleepily. "Said it wouldn't count."

"Well, I changed the rules," Evan stated.

"Can't change the rules," Jackson argued, grinning when Evan held him tighter, knowing full well that that the bastard could and did.

19

Jackson woke up feeling like shit. His head was pounding, his stomach was churning and his hand was throbbing, but none of it seemed to matter much with Evan's body cocooning him. As he rested his hand on top of the redhead's and allowed their fingers to intertwine, he admonished himself for being so gay. He couldn't help it. Evan made him really fucking gay. Before Evan, Jackson thought his attraction to men was only physical. But with Evan, Jack realized it was emotional too. He'd never experienced anything like it and found himself wondering if Tamara had felt that way about him. He couldn't imagine how badly it would suck to have that level of desire go completely unrequited.

He grinned when Evan instinctively pulled him in closer, their bodies growing more accustomed to each other; their minds becoming more accepting of what was going on between them. The easy way out would have been to deny it, pretend like whatever it was didn't mean shit and go back to their separate lives. Neither of them had ever had it easy, exceedingly used to the discomfort of taking the more difficult path.

It hadn't always been worth it.

Bad decisions had led to relentless struggles and strife, but this was different. Regardless of how messy they were on paper and how intent their pride seemed to be to get in the way, in the flesh everything was simple. They'd spent two nights together, skin to skin, laying a foundation for a relationship that they both could feel comfortable in.

As good as it felt to get lost in the moment, Jackson was pragmatic enough to know that whatever happened within the confines of his apartment was a fantasy…a dream that would keep them blindly grasping for it as it predictably moved farther out of their reach with each graze of their fingertips.

It wasn't practical to think it could be anything more than what it was. Still, he couldn't help but feel close to Evan. There was so much they didn't know about each other, but what they didn't know paled in comparison to what they did. Sharing their deepest secret had tethered and liberated them. They were tied together by their most intimate feelings and set free by their release. With each other they were not a façade of themselves, as they had always been around family and friends. They understood what no one else ever could.

What they never let them.

"How's your hand?" the sleepy voice behind him asked as warm lips brushed against Jackson's shoulder.

"Better than my fucking head," he muttered back, grinning when he felt the kiss on his temple and then another on his jawline. "Drank too much."

"No shit. You polish off that whole bottle of Jack yourself?"

He scoffed, "I'd be dead." Clicking his tongue, he tried to remember how much he had drank. "Probably half."

Evan hummed and nestled his face into the crook of Jackson's neck. "So did you like it?"

"Like what? The Jack?"

"No," he replied. Jackson could hear the grin on his face and wondered why it was there. "When I ate your ass."

"Fuck you," he laughed, shaking his head. "That didn't fucking happen."

"You sure about that?" Evan questioned, turning his lover's shoulder so he was flat on his back and hovering over him with a mischievous glint in his chocolate eyes.

"Positive, motherfucker. Never black out, remember everything," Jackson replied, reaching up to push one unruly clump of hair off Evan's forehead and tsking when it fell back down again.

"Everything?" he questioned, ginger eyebrows raised.

"Mmmhmm," Jackson confirmed, rubbing Evan's thigh before letting his hand travel back to his ass. "Getting me fucking hard."

"So, you remember when you told me you were crazy about me then?" Evan pushed, ignoring Jackson's admission, his persistence causing Jack to let out an aggravated sigh.

"I do."

"And you meant it?"

"Yeah."

"Why?" Evan studied Jackson's face as if he was waiting for a change in energy, a laugh or a jeer.

"Fuck. I don't know. Why'd you say it back?"

"Because that's how I fucking feel."

"Right," Jackson stated, narrowing his eyes, trying to understand what was so difficult to comprehend. "Me too."

"So you're crazy about me?"

"Yes and right now you're driving me nuts, man. How about instead of asking stupid fucking questions, you put that pretty mouth to better use, hmm?" He grinned when Evan licked his lips and began to crawl down Jackson's body. "That's right," he praised as the redhead took Jack's hard cock into his wet and wanton mouth. "Suck it good."

X

Evan had left shortly before Amy got home. As much as Jackson hadn't wanted him to go, he knew that he definitely didn't want him running into his sister again. As supportive as Amy had been in their text messages, he knew that it was one thing to say it and another thing to show it. He was still coming to terms with his feelings for Evan; he didn't need to deal with wondering about anyone else's acceptance. He and his siblings were taught to despise fags, that it was unnatural and disgusting for men to be with other men. In turn, he'd spent a good amount of his life hating himself and was sure that if Amy and Luke ever found out what he really was, they'd hate him, too.

"How are you?" his sister asked, sitting down next to him on the couch where he was playing video games.

"Fine. Why wouldn't I be?" He was sure that he was coming off defensive, but he figured it was better than being a pussy. He wasn't about to become some pansy-ass around her just because she knew he fucked dudes.

"Just a normal question, Jack," Amy replied evenly, giving him a soft smile.

He nodded, eyes fixed on the television screen in front of him. "Yeah, well, I'm fine."

"Good."

They sat there in silence for a while. Jackson knew he should man up and broach the subject but was unsure how to do it.

"So I left Isaiah's yesterday morning because I got the worst period cramps ever. I'm talking ripping pain. I made an excuse to leave because I wasn't about to stay and blow up his toilet."

"Fucking nasty." Jackson laughed, shaking his head. "Why the fuck are you telling me that?"

"Because as surprised as I was to see, you know, him here, that wasn't why I ran away. It wasn't like that."

"All right."

"Like I told you last night, I don't care. I'm not like you, Luke, and Dad. I've never cared what other people did in their bedrooms."

Jackson rolled his lips in and pursed them tightly, thinking for a moment before he spoke. "I don't know if I'm...like that though." He paused. "I mean, I like what I like and that don't make me a bitch, but I never, you know, felt a certain way about a guy. Never thought I was a faggot or whatever."

"And now? Do you feel a certain way about Evan?"

Amid the mayhem of the last couple of days, Jackson had forgotten that Amy had called Evan by his name when she saw him in their kitchen. "How the fuck do you know his name anyway?"

"I met him and his friend, Micah, at The Drexel the night before last night. They bought us shots and kinda fucked around for a while. Tammy was hitting on him pretty hardcore, though. They did a few lines together and I guess she thought they were going to go get it on or something afterwards, but he peaced out."

"Wait, she thought she was going to bang Evan?" Jackson was skeptical.

"Mmmhmm." She nodded. "Guess he's bi or something?"

"I don't know what he is," he replied, taken aback by the information. He had no idea if Evan was into girls, and chided himself for assuming he wasn't. The thought of Evan fucking anyone else made Jackson feel nauseous, and it was even sicker to think of him fucking Tamara. "So Tammy liked him?"

"Seemed like it. Talked about him a lot after he left, and seemed pretty disappointed. He's cute, but she's not over you, so maybe she just smelled the money."

"What money?" he huffed, well aware from the confession of his prior homelessness and the quality of his cocaine that Evan wasn't rolling in cash.

"His money. Never thought you'd be interested in a North Sider. That surprises me more than you being into a guy, to be honest," she answered with a shrug.

He couldn't blame Amy for thinking that Evan was North Side. After all, Jack had too. There was something about the red hair and freckles that made him seem way softer than he actually was. "He's South Side."

Amy screwed up her face in disbelief. "Really? Are you sure? I don't know many South Side guys that would be caught at some hipster bullshit place like The Drexel. He and his friend seemed pretty fucking comfortable there."

"I'm sure they are. Fuck." He rubbed his forehead and let out a wry laugh. "They got him on the party crew. You got to check your credit card and make sure nobody's buying shit with your number."

"Wait…he's a Demon? How have I never seen him around? Is he new?"

"Um, no. He doesn't roll with us," Jackson stated, immediately regretting opening his mouth. He was actually more ashamed to admit that Evan was a Klown Killer than he was for Amy to know that he was into dudes to begin with.

"He's not…" She shook her head vehemently. "Jack." She let out a deep sigh and closed her eyes. "Are you fucking kidding me?" Her voice was growing shriller, as it always did when she was getting stressed out. "He's a KKz?

"I didn't fucking say that," he replied, trying to keep his temper even. He wanted to blow up and tell her to fuck off, but he knew that he'd seem shadier if he did.

"You didn't have to. They were both wearing red the other night. Holy shit. I don't know why I didn't put it together." She was on her feet now, pacing the room. "I can't fucking believe this, Jackson. What the fuck?"

"Stop, all right?" He sighed. "Just sit the fuck down, you're making me dizzy."

She threw her finger up at him. "Do you know how bad this is? Like, you have to know how bad it is, right? Do you even know if he's into you? He could be using you to get pictures and shit and put a mark on your fucking head."

"Ames," he warned, his voice dropping low. "Don't talk about shit you don't know about."

"Oh I know about it. I know that we can't trust Klown Killerz. I've known that my whole fucking life. We were taught that shit in the womb. How could you?" She let out a sputtering breath. "I can't believe this. I can't fucking believe it. Are you crazy? If anyone finds out you're not the only one who's going to get killed. I'm going to get killed and then they're going to make Luke eat our toes or some shit before they kill him."

"You seriously need to chill the fuck out," he ordered. "Sit your ass down and shut the fuck up."

She did as she was told, recognizing Jackson's tone and knowing that she should comply.

"I trust him, okay?" he said softly. "He's not going to do shit."

"You have feelings for him." She glared. "You said it wasn't like that, but it is."

"Told you not to talk about shit you don't know about, Amy," he stated again. "Go cancel your credit card and tell Tammy and Kylie to do the same, all right?"

"Jackson, if this gets out…"

"Go," he demanded, sighing when his sister left the room.

None of what Amy had said fazed him as much as the fact that Evan could be into girls and that he was on the party crew. Two things that really rubbed Jackson the wrong way.

They were going to have a talk.

Soon.

20

Evan didn't paint people. The curves of their bodies and angles of their faces never interested him as much as cityscapes. The circumstances of his life had compelled him to create new worlds that he could get lost in rather than reflect the features of the people he ran from. He constructed buildings from their foundations, making them taller and stronger than he felt. He adorned edifices with countless windows, always left open or cracked so hope could pour in and fears could seep out. Tree-lined streets reminded him how to breathe, pumping oxygen through the atmosphere, off the canvas, and into his lungs.

He didn't paint people until the day he no longer desired the anonymity of his cities. The streets didn't feel like his escape anymore, not like Jackson did. Cerulean skies gave way to pale blue eyes and bus routes to pink pouts.

Evan didn't paint people until he painted Jackson.

His features were perfect; from the gentleness in his eyes to the thickness of his thighs, the fullness of his lips, to the cuts of his hips. Evan had noticed how gorgeous Jackson was when they first hooked up, but it was different now. A man who had been so brash and hard was dropping his guard, and the moments of softness only made him more breathtaking. Jackson was the most beautiful contradiction, so Evan made his paintings the same. Fingers grasped the stems of vibrant flowers while crimson blood poured from an adoring gaze.

He didn't get overly excited. He'd learned from an early age how to keep his affect flat. It was easier that way. Becoming too invested led to hurt and while physical pain was manageable, emotional pain was not. The swell of feelings that were surging inside him, coupled with the rush of cocaine, had become overwhelming. Dropping his paint brush to the hardwood floor, he watched as red paint splattered against it. Without thought he pressed his palms against Jackson's claret tears, smearing them to the sides of the canvas; scarlet sunbursts. The stinging in his eyes prompted him to lift his paint-covered hands to his cheeks and wipe away his own sadness, or maybe it was happiness; he couldn't tell.

He sat on the floor for a while, staring up at the painting, idly wondering if he loved it or hated it and what it meant either way. He wasn't sure how long he'd been studying it when he heard his phone vibrate. Rubbing his hands against his bare torso to clean them off, he crawled to his bed to grab it.

Jackson (10:46pm): U around?
Evan (10:47pm): What's up?
Jackson (10:47pm): Gotta talk to U
Evan (10:48pm): Sounds like I'm in trouble
Jackson (10:48pm): U wish
Jackson (10:48pm) U R trouble though
Evan (10:49pm): Heard that b4
Jackson (10:50pm): I bet
Jackson (10:51pm): Come over
Evan (10:52pm): 3 nights in a row?
Jackson (10:52pm): U got a problem with that?
Evan (10:53pm): Not at all. Think ur getting attached tho
Jackson (10:54pm): I'm not
Evan (10:55pm): Ur not?
Jackson (10:58pm): Am I supposed 2 be?
Evan (10:59pm): I dunno
Jackson (11:05pm): Ur fucking weird
Jackson (11:06pm): Get ur stupid freckled ass over here
Evan (11:07pm): Wait I have freckles on my ass?
Jackson (11:07pm): Ur about to have me on ur ass. When R u gonna be here?
Evan (11:08pm): Hour. I have to shower. Was painting and got shit all over me.
Jackson (11:09pm): Tagging aint paintin
Evan (11:10pm): It literally is & diff kind of painting
Jackson (11:10pm): With a fucking paintbrush n shit?
Evan (11:11pm): Like that
Jackson (11:11pm): U Paint?

Evan (11:12pm): Yes with a fucking paintbrush & everything
Jackson (11:12pm): No shit what do u paint?
Evan (11:12pm): None of your fucking business. Remember that?
Jackson (11:13pm): Clever
Evan (11:14pm): Always. C U Soon
Jackson (11:15pm): Don't shower
Jackson (11:16pm): Wanna C what u look like w paint all over u
Evan (11:18pm): Fuck off
Jackson (11:19pm): Don't
Evan (11:20pm): Fine

He didn't shower, but he did wash his hands and his face, not wanting to look like a serial killer on his short walk to Jackson's apartment.

"Where are you off to?" Luis called to him from where he, Jamal, and Kane were hanging out in the living room smoking blunts and playing video games.

"Fuck off every night now. Never chill with the boys," Jamal said with a smirk. "You got a girlfriend?"

"Something like that," Evan replied, noticing the dubious look he was getting from his little brother.

"Well, tell her to hop off your dick 'cause we're having a boys' night tomorrow night," Luis informed him. "We're going to hit up Teasers."

Evan could think of at least twenty things he'd rather do than go to a strip club, but he knew that if he was going to keep up appearances, he had to fucking go. He hadn't spent much time with the other guys and the fact that they were already asking questions wasn't great. It wasn't an issue that they thought he had a girlfriend, but it would be when they started to wonder why he spent all his time at *her* place and why *she* never came around.

It was expected that the girls KKz dated would be down for the gang. They'd hang out and become a part of the scene, doing favors for the guys and bringing around other girls. From what Evan understood, sometimes guys would lend their girls to other members, passing her around like she was a piece of meat to gain respect from the other boys. The thought of it never affected him before, but now, he couldn't imagine how the fuck they did it. They must not have given a shit about their girlfriends. He and Jackson weren't like that, committed and shit, but there was no way he'd be offering him up to some other dude. It made him feel pretty fucking sick to think about it.

"Think she'll let you go?" Jamal teased as he took a hit off his blunt. "You at the 'got to ask permission' stage yet?"

Evan tsked and shook his head; the thought that he'd ever ask permission to do shit was laughable to him. He'd never be that guy. He wondered if Jackson would ever expect him to be. If he did, he was in for serious disappointment. It wasn't that he enjoyed letting people down; it was just that he always did. It was better for people to have low expectations when it came to him, and he knew it. The moment that someone starting demanding shit of him was when he ran. He wasn't sure if it was selfishness or fear that made him that way, but he didn't spend too much time considering it. Since it didn't change the outcome, there didn't seem to be much point.

"That stage doesn't exist for Evan," Kane stated with a slight laugh. "Asshole doesn't answer to anyone. Never has. Never will."

"You're a stubborn motherfucker then, huh, Goodwyn?" Luis questioned as he sipped his forty.

He shrugged. "Guess you could say that."

"It's got to be the red hair," Jamal stated knowingly. "I read this study once that said that redheads are actually more temperamental and stubborn than the rest of the population. They got this devil's rage inside of them. Real inhuman, no remorse."

"Bullshit." Evan laughed at the absurdity, rubbing his forehead as he did. Jamal was funny as fuck, but he said the wildest stuff and often had Evan's mind spinning from the stupidity. Still, he kept things interesting enough and that could be endearing.

"No joke. I really did," Jamal promised. "I don't know if it's 'cause they're born feeling like too gingery and shit, but they take that shit out on other people. Like you..." he paused and gestured toward Evan, eyes wide. "I ain't ever trying to fuck with you. You got real red hair, none of that auburn shit. You were born with that rage. I can see it. You feel too gingery, don't you, man?"

"Too gingery?" Kane howled. "You feel too gingery, Evan?"

"You know, there are times I think I do," Evan replied with a grin. "Sometimes I feel like I don't give a fuck about anything. It must be when I'm feeling too gingery. My pubes get real hot, like they're literally on fire, and I want to punch shit and rage out."

"That's what the fuck I'm talking about." Jamal nodded. "There ain't any reasoning with a redhead that's feeling too gingery. You just got to get the fuck out of the way. That's it." His face was dead serious as he shook his head in disbelief that his theory was all coming together.

"You're smoking some crazy-ass shit right now. Give me a hit," Evan said, approaching the bigger man, who cowered as he did.

"Really?" Luis laughed, putting Jamal into a headlock. "You're a fucking spaz, man."

Jamal huffed and pushed him away.

"What if a redheaded woman approached you? Real smoke bomb, a'ight? Huge titties, smoking body. Would you fuck her or would you be too nervous that she'd get 'too gingery' on you?" Kane questioned a laugh in his voice.

"I'd never fuck a ginger. No way," Jamal stated emphatically. "She could be a fucking rodeo queen and I wouldn't let her ride."

"We got to find him a hot-ass ginger and see if he resists," Kane said to Luis. "It'll be our own twist on the study."

"Don't sound like a bad idea," Luis agreed with a grin. "You ever get too gingery and just rage-fuck your girl, Evan? Pound the shit out of her?"

"Likes it when I'm too gingery. Begs for that shit."

"My man," Luis exclaimed, shaking Evan's hand with a big smile. "Go out there and break her pussy."

"Thanks for the pep talk." Evan laughed, taking one last hit off Jamal's blunt before handing it back to the theorist, who took it from him quickly but refused to look into his eyes. "I'll take care of it."

"Tomorrow night, man," Luis reminded him as he left the room. "You better fucking show."

"I will," Evan called back, stopping in his bedroom so he could slide his still-wet painting under his bed and slip a few magnums into his back pocket. Whatever the fuck he'd smoked had gone straight to his head and his mind was swirling with a mix of mostly incoherent thoughts. He giggled as he walked down the dark street toward Jackson's apartment, curious what his impressions were on the ginger theory. Evan also wanted to know Jackson's middle name and if he liked pancakes or waffles better.

Evan didn't think it would be a deal breaker unless Jack said he liked French toast, because fuck that shit. Evan kind of considered whether to ask Jack if he thought he was Evan's boyfriend, but then laughed until his lungs hurt thinking it would make him sound like a fourteen-year-old girl. Still, he wanted to know if he was.

Evan (11:50pm): Hi
Jackson (11:52pm): Where RU?
Evan (11:54pm): Almost there
Jackson (11:55pm): Why RU texting me then?
Evan (11:56pm): Wanted to say hi & ask if I'm ur boyfriend
Jackson (11:58pm): R U 12?
Evan (11:59pm): 14
Evan (12:00am): ??????? hello?
Jackson (12:02am): We can talk when u get here
Evan (12:02am): Do u like french toast?
Jackson (12:03am): no
Evan (12:03am): good

21

"What the fuck are you asking about French toast for?" Jackson sniped as he swung open the door to his apartment. He was surprised when eager lips pressed hungrily against his, the passion and want evident with every swirl of his lover's tongue. Grunting when his body hit the wall, Jackson smiled into the kiss as the redhead attempted to tongue his way through Jack, zealous hands traveling up the back of his wife-beater and then down the waistband of his basketball shorts. Large fingers kneaded his ass cheeks as Evan's mouth dropped to Jack's neck and began to suck marks into his skin. "Got to talk to you." He gulped in air.

"About what?" Evan asked breathlessly, lifting his head and looking at Jackson with blown-out brown eyes.

Jack sighed and pointed out the obvious. "You're high."

Evan rubbed his thumb against his nostril and shrugged. "Usually am."

"Why?" Jackson studied Evan's face, searching for the fluctuations of emotion he saw in the early morning hours, only able to find impassivity hidden by carnal desire. "You got a habit or something?"

"Did I come here for therapy or to fuck? 'Cause if it's going to be therapy I'll go get off somewhere else," he growled, the venom in his voice sending chills down Jackson's spine. The anger. The antagonism. He'd seen it many times before; he just hadn't wanted to see it in Evan.

"You're an addict." Jackson wasn't sure if he'd uttered the realization aloud but when Evan pulled away, yup, he had.

"You're an asshole," Evan replied, yanking his wrist back and jutting his chin out when Jackson wouldn't let him go.

"Where you going? Going to find some other guy to fuck?" he challenged, eyebrows raised high and teeth gnashing into his bottom lip. "That's what you want, huh? Well, you can go right ahead, but I want you to stay." He dropped Evan's arm and threw up his hands in surrender. "Up to you."

The redhead exhaled breath noisily and glared. "Don't say shit about it again. Sick of people telling me what I am."

"All right," Jackson agreed, knowing that it wasn't a promise he could keep long-term, but would honor for the night. They had other shit to talk about anyway. He looked at Evan, recognizing how closed off he was with his arms crossed tightly over his chest and his back slumped. "Hey," Jack said softly, resting his hands on Evan's hips and squeezing them gently. "I like pancakes."

"Yeah?" Evan's mouth broke into a grin.

Jackson nodded. "Don't know why you give a shit, but I do."

"Honestly," Evan began with a laugh, "I have no clue. It popped into my head, so I asked."

"Hmm," Jackson hummed, dropping his hands and making his way into the kitchen with Evan trailing behind him. "You want some?"

"What?"

"Pancakes." Jack grabbed a pan from the drawer and glanced over his shoulder for the go-ahead.

"I could eat," the redhead answered, narrowing his eyes as he watched Jackson take out some pancake mix and get to work. "You're making me pancakes right now?"

"Looks like it."

"You need help or something?" Evan pulled himself up onto the counter and let his legs hang, closely watching Jackson whisk the batter.

"Pancakes are pretty fucking easy, man," he said with a smile. "I got this." He desperately tried to remain nonchalant as he poured the mixture into the hot pan. "So you wanted to know some other shit, too, right?"

"Don't remember." Evan dropped his gaze to his knees.

"I bet," Jackson mused as he waited for the batter to bubble. "You into fucking girls?"

"What?" Evan's head shot up and he looked at Jackson as if he had two heads.

"My sister told me she met you at some club and you were going to fuck my ex. You into girls, too?" Jack asked with an uncomfortable sniff.

"Not really. I never liked it, but I did it when I had to."

"When you had to?"

"If I needed a place to stay or some shit. Only fucked them when I needed something," Evan explained with a shrug. "You were in a pretty serious relationship with her though, weren't you?"

"I don't know. I mean, it was serious, yeah, but I don't think I was ever in it."

"She said you two never fucked," Evan informed him, drawing an aggravated huff from Jackson.

"She's got a big fucking mouth, don't she?" He shook his head as he flipped the pancakes. "I tried to avoid it as much as possible."

"You try to fuck me as much as possible," Evan stated, looking down at his palms, which held a red hue from, Jackson guessed, paint.

"Yeah, 'cause I want to fuck you," he replied simply. "Didn't want to fuck her. Just," he sighed, "don't like girls like that."

"I don't either. Never have."

Jackson nodded. "What about credit cards, you like them?"

Evan punched out a laugh. "You're hitting all your talking points right now, aren't you?"

"Seems like," Jack said with a smirk. He put a few pancakes on a plate, took out a fork and knife, and handed it all to Evan. "Don't got any syrup though."

"You're not going to eat?" The redhead rested the plate on his thighs and took a big bite. "So good," he complimented with his mouth full.

"Not hungry," Jackson stated. "You going to answer my question?"

"I like them," he replied matter-of-factly.

"They cancelled their cards," Jackson informed him.

"Good."

"Good?"

"Mmmhmm," Evan nodded. "Got to do what I got to do, you know that. But it doesn't mean I'm interested in going out of my way to fuck over people you give a shit about."

"Only care about Amy," Jackson said, leaning his back against the refrigerator. "Don't fuck with her again."

"Didn't even get her numbers," Evan said. It was partially true after all. He didn't, but it wasn't as if he hadn't tried. There didn't seem to be any point of going there, especially when Jackson had made him pancakes and was looking sexy as hell.

"That right?"

"That's right," Evan confirmed, putting the plate on the counter.

"So, they got you on party?" It was more a statement than a question, even though Jack hadn't phrased it as such. He knew exactly how they were utilizing Evan. The redhead nodded. "They're fucking using you 'cause you're hot."

"You think I'm hot," Evan teased in a sing-songy tone, smiling when Jackson straightened up and moved closer so he could stand between Evan's legs and rub his thighs.

"Know I do," Jack assured him, licking Evan's lips, a clear indication that Jack wanted to be kissed. Evan eagerly obliged, hunching down to connect their mouths and draping his arms over Jackson's shoulders as their tongues tangled languidly.

"Don't like that they got you doing that," Jackson muttered, once they peeled their lips apart. "Don't like them treating you like a whore."

"Not fucking anyone."

"Don't got to."

"Whores fuck for money. If I'm not fucking, I'm not a whore," Evan explained with a yawn.

"Coming down?"

Evan nodded. "You pissed me the fuck off so I think it accelerated shit."

"Blaming it on me, huh?" Jackson didn't want to look at Evan differently after recognizing his addiction, but it was impossible not to. His toughness and stubbornness remained intact, but his edges were softened and his heart was fragile. Jackson felt an overwhelming desire to take care of him, but when it came down to it, he knew he couldn't, not when it came to the drugs.

Cocaine was a storm that couldn't be controlled, not in the way Evan needed it to be. Jackson's mom had been an addict. He knew the manipulation and mayhem that ensued when you were in a relationship with someone who was in a relationship with drugs. He wanted to believe that he would able to help him, but it was unlikely. It didn't mean shit to want something for an addict if they didn't want it for themselves. To be with Evan, Jack knew he'd need to accept the fact that, at least for now, he was going to be with a functional addict and there wasn't shit he could do about it.

He wasn't a fucking saint himself; he drank too much and smoked like a goddamn chimney. He enjoyed violence and got off on pain. It would be hypocritical to put himself above Evan and look at him like he needed to be fucking saved. Still, the irony of being a dealer and ending up fucking a guy with a constant cold wasn't lost on him.

"C'mon," Jack urged, signaling for Evan to jump down. "You look fucking beat."

"I hate talking. Fucking wipes me out," Evan informed with another exaggerated yawn. "You literally drained the horniness from my cock with all your blah-blah."

"Do you ever stop and reflect on the crazy-ass shit that comes out of your mouth? Because you come up with some fucking stupid shit," Jackson chided without malice as he led Evan into the bedroom and helped him out of his clothes. He traced his fingers over the streaks of red paint that spread across his lover's toned abs. "Goddamn," he muttered, taking in the view and thinking it was even better than he'd imagined it. He patted Evan's ass as the redhead crawled into the bed.

"We were going to fuck," Evan mumbled, snuggling under the covers, his hooded lids making it exceedingly clear that they weren't going to be. "Came over so we could fuck."

Jackson rolled his eyes and disrobed, climbing into the bed next to Evan. Whether or not they had sex, he'd gotten what he sought from the night; some answers he'd needed and others he wished he hadn't found out. He raked his fingers through soft red hair as the sleepy man molded himself around his body. "No you didn't."

"I didn't?"

"No."

"Why am I here then?" Evan asked, tucking his face into the crook of Jackson's neck and peppering the skin with soft kisses.

"You came over to be my boyfriend," Jack whispered, too uncomfortable to say the word loud, though the concept didn't feel unnatural, at least not with Evan.

"And?" he asked, shifting his head so he could gaze up, his eyes filled with as much fear as hope.

"And you are."

22

Mornings were Jackson's favorite times with Evan. Jack hadn't realized why that was until his *boyfriend's* addiction came to light and everything began to make more sense. Stolen moments of tenderness seemed more indulgent now that he knew they were snatched from Evan as well. Those serene early hours were the only chance for their time to be truly the two of them without Evan's albatross ghosting over everything they said or did. He was softer, with the ability to show a greater breadth of feeling than when he was high. Unlike the erratic swells and crashes in his inebriated state, the dawn brought emotions that undulated gently with slow rises and gradual dips.

Jackson had never imagined he'd want to be so close to somebody, not only emotionally but physically. When Tamara had lived with him, they'd slept on separate sides of the king-size bed, each claiming to need their own space. With Evan, Jack couldn't get near enough. They laid their heads on the same pillow, their bodies intertwined. Their limbs were like strings, tangled up and tied together. It felt right to be bound to him.

"What're you thinking about?" Evan asked, resting the palm of his hand on Jackson's cheek, a small smile pulling up his lips when he leaned in to Evan's touch.

"You," Jack replied quietly, licking Evan's lips as he gazed at Evan's freckled face. "Like you like this."

"Like what? Dirty?" he laughed softly, looking down at the paint cracking on his skin. "Wanted me to come over all nasty and didn't do shit about it."

"What was I supposed to do?"

"Lick it off?" Evan suggested, earning him an eye roll and a chuckle.

"Shit's probably toxic. Trying to kill me already, huh? Been together a few hours and your freckled ass is already looking for an out." He took hold of the hand on his cheek and pressed a kiss against the back of it.

"No way," Evan protested. "Not getting rid of me that easy." He grinned and slotted his fingers between Jackson's. "You ever watch *Seinfeld*?"

"Some of them."

"Ever see the one where George's fiancée dies from licking the envelopes for their wedding invitations? You think that could really happen?"

"No it can't fucking happen unless he laced them with arsenic or some shit. That'd do the job," Jackson replied, lifting the covers so he could peek at Evan's muscular torso and trace his fingers over the streaks of paint. "This goddamn body, man, I swear."

The redhead grinned, wrapped his fingers around Jackson's wrist, and guided his boyfriend's hand down so he'd grip his dick. "Don't forget about your favorite part," he flirted, turning onto his back to give Jackson better access. Evan rested his arms behind his head and focused on Jackson's face as he jerked him off slowly.

"Who said it's my favorite part, hmm?" he smirked, thumbing the slit and dragging some precome down the shaft.

"You fucking love it," Evan crooned, sighing as Jackson continued to work on him. "Tell me all the time."

"Do I?" he questioned, raising his eyebrows with interest. They'd had a lot of filthy sex: hard-core fucking aimed at rapid, explosive orgasms. Even when they'd woken up in the middle of the night, they'd banged hard. It was always hot as fuck and Jackson was sure that he'd gotten lost in the moment and spouted off some mortifying shit.

"Mmmhmm," Evan confirmed with a nod. "It's so sexy when you let go like that."

"Tell me what I say," Jack prompted, dropping his free hand to his own cock and beginning to yank off with the same rhythm he'd established on Evan.

"You're going to blush," the redhead teased, grinning. He licked his lips and waved Jackson over for a kiss. "Come here."

Incredibly turned on by the conversation, which was feeding his impending orgasm, Jackson devoured his lover hungrily. Evan kept his lips connected to Jackson's while he reached for the lube that was sitting on the nightstand. He popped the top and hovered over Jackson, who grunted his annoyance when his hand was knocked off his lover's dick in the process. His aggravation quickly gave way to titillation when he felt Evan's wet finger circle around his puckered hole.

"Tell me," Jack directed once they'd peeled their lips apart, closing his eyes to relish in the care Evan was taking to prep his ass. It wasn't that he minded urgent and rough, but there was something to be said for the sensuality of going slow. He wasn't used to it, but he couldn't help but feel that it was something he'd eagerly get into more often.

"Umm..." Evan drawled, "I'll tell you some of my favorites. There was 'keep pounding. Swear that rod is hitting my fucking rib cage.' 'Splitting me the fuck in half with that big dick.' And then the variations of, 'I fucking love that huge cock. Fuck me with that perfect dick. Bust it open, give me that good shit.' You got a nasty fucking mouth when you actually open it. I could keep going."

"All right, all right." Jackson shook his head, cheeks burning from the words and the way Evan was fingering him while he uttered them. "Going to start calling it 'mine.' That's what all this boyfriend shit means, right? That cock's mine now."

"Yeah." Evan nodded, hooking fingers a bit and dropping his mouth open to 'Ooo' with Jackson when he hit the right spot. "Love that, don't you?"

Jackson's teeth dug into his lower lip as his head tilted back on the pillow.

"And I'm yours. Every fucked-up part of me...yours. Do you know what you're getting yourself into?" Evan asked.

Jackson nodded, though he wasn't entirely sure he did. However, he was convinced that he'd dealt with far worse shit than Evan could toss at him. Jack wanted him, and whatever came along with having him was shit he'd deal with. "Want every inch of you," he admitted, clicking his tongue and smirking at the offended look on Evan's face. "Talking everything—head to your toes, man. Want it all."

Evan slid his fingers out of Jackson, and moments later he felt the bump of the head of that huge cock against his hole. "Going to give it all to you," Evan promised, increasing the pressure on Jackson's opening. "Want to see your face when I shoot my load inside you." He raised his eyebrows expectantly, hoping for the go-ahead. "Let me fill you up."

Jackson knew he should've told Evan to put a condom on. He was admittedly promiscuous and, based on the fact that he'd wanted to fuck him without a rubber during their first hookup, probably not safe about it. But the tip of that big leaking dick pressing against his entry had him fiending and nodding his head. He gasped at the sensation of Evan's skin touching his as the redhead's thick, warm cock pushed slowly into his ass. Jack felt his body tighten around Evan, squeezing him with every millimeter he shoved in. Having Evan's dick inside him had always felt fucking amazing, but there was nothing that could compare to the deliciousness of experiencing every pulse and throb of Evan's cock against Jack's walls.

"Goddamn, you feel so fucking good," Evan rasped, resting his forehead on Jackson's chest. Evan whimpered softly when he bottomed out, his hipbones resting on Jack's as his body shook slightly from the fullness. Pulling up a bit, Evan leaned his elbows on Jackson's shoulders and put his palms on Jackson's cheeks as Evan began to slowly roll his hips.

Blown away by the intensity of the moment, Jackson let his eyelids drop, and focused on the feeling of Evan moving like molasses in and out of him, brushing against every bump and ridge inside as he did.

"Open your eyes," the redhead whispered, nuzzling his nose against Jackson's before pressing a soft kiss on his lips. He forced himself to do as he was told, admiring how much like topaz his boyfriend's eyes were when he could actually see the irises. If he didn't know better, he would have thought the man above him was making love to him, with his slow pace and the adoring gazes that were broken only by passionate kisses.

Evan repositioned himself when Jackson began letting out soft, breathy moans with every one of those slow gyrations. Evan placed one hand on the pillow beside Jackson's ear and wrapped the other around his waist. In turn, Jackson looped his legs around Evan's thighs, allowing him to get even deeper.

Jackson's cock rubbed against paint-splattered ab muscles with every one of Evan's pushes and pulses at his prostate. Between the friction and the ardor, Jack knew he wouldn't last much longer. "Gonna come, Evan," he moaned, biting hard on his bottom lip as his boyfriend picked up his pace slightly. "Gonna fucking come." He groaned as jizz shot up Evan's chest and under his chin, and then panted as he watched Evan lean down and painstakingly lick up every drop. "So fucking hot," Jack sighed as he felt the familiar tightening in his balls. Closing his eyes, he trembled through another orgasm, giving his man more to clean.

"Give it to me," Jackson urged, once he was sure he'd been hit with his last aftershock, "want your come inside me, man." Evan's chin glistened from the spit that had trickled down it when he lapped Jackson up and he swiped his thumb across it to wipe away some of the saliva. "Come here," he directed, calling Evan down for a kiss.

Their tongues flicked and swirled as Jackson angled up his hips, allowing Evan to move farther inside. The redhead bit Jack's bottom lip, letting out a sputtering sigh as he painted Jackson's internal walls with his release. Collapsing on top of him, he pressed sloppy kisses against his broad chest and hummed as fingers raked soothingly through his hair.

"You're going to call my dick yours?" Evan whispered, drawing a soft chuckle from Jackson.

"Mmmhmm."

"Well, I'm going to call you 'mine.'"

"I like that."

"You do?" Evan questioned, looking up at him with soft eyes.

Jackson nodded and kissed the tip of his boyfriend's freckled nose. "I'm going to call you 'mine,' too. All of you."

"Even the shitty parts?" Evan asked with a frown.

"Especially those," Jackson confirmed. "They probably need it the most, huh?"

"They'd never admit it."

"But they do."

"Probably," Evan agreed, yawning then closing his eyes.

23

Evan had to be really fucking high to get through a boys' night at Teasers, so he got himself really fucking high. By the time he was leaning back in a chair with a stripper grinding on his lap, he could hardly see straight. The spinning lights that cast colors over the room were blurred, making him feel like he was floating in a sea of melted Skittles. Sugary sweet notes of the girl's perfume had his head lighter than the cocaine did, and he couldn't help but think how vanilla she was. He'd never understand why anybody would want tits smacking them in the face when a cock could do it so much better. Holy fuck he wanted Jackson to slap him across the face with his dick. He had a perfect dick. He almost wanted to get fucked by it...almost.

"Want to fuck you," the busty brunette cooed in Evan's ear, letting her tongue take a little lick of his lobe. "You want to go into a private room?"

"Nah," he said, tapping her thigh as a weak expression of pity. He wondered in the past if he would've gone for it to see what he could've gotten out of her. Maybe he would've plowed her and while she was still reeling from his dick, stolen her shit. Now, that type of scam and the couple bucks he'd get out of it didn't seem worth it. He didn't want to fuck things up with Jackson, who had made it clear that he expected fidelity.

Evan had never been in a position where he wanted to be faithful to someone before, but it was easy to only want to fuck one person when the person he was fucking was Jackson. He figured that banging anyone else would be a serious downgrade anyway, and was pretty sure when his boyfriend finally dumped him, he'd be fucked up over his ass indefinitely. He knew it would only be a matter of time until Jackson got sick of Evan's shit like everyone else did. So he figured that he should enjoy the hell out their relationship while he could before the inevitable happened.

"I won't charge you," she offered, licking her heavily lined lips. "If you're down."

The bass that was vibrating the room and the stripper gyrating on his flaccid dick had his stomach flipping. All he wanted was for her to fuck off so he could sit there in peace thinking about Jackson and all the things he planned to do to him when he got that ass in his hands.

"I don't fuck for free," he told her simply, drawing a scoff from the girl, who immediately climbed off him, shot him a dirty look, and moved onto the next lap.

"What did you do?" Jamal asked, laughing as he repeatedly elbowed Evan in the ribs. "You get 'too gingery' on her? Scare her off?"

Evan rubbed his forehead and smirked, wondering when "too gingery" was going to die the death it deserved to. "Asked her if she wanted to blow me in the bathroom," he told him with a shrug, glad that he was getting better at spouting off dumb shit that would make the guys think he was like them. "Guess she wasn't into it."

"You got to ask her if she wants to do something that bitches actually enjoy doing, like have her pussy eaten or get bent over the toilet." Jamal tsked, swigging his beer. "They don't like to give head."

It was obvious Jamal had never sucked a cock. Evan had to stop himself from waxing poetic about how awesome it was to have a big, dripping dick rubbing against your tongue and fucking into your mouth, knowing that his love of dick wouldn't go over well. He wanted Jackson so badly. His boyfriend tasted as good as he looked and he looked really fucking good.

Evan wondered how much longer he'd have to stay not to look shady.

"Thought you had a girlfriend, man. Why you trying to get some strange?" Luis teased. "You already getting bored of that pussy?"

"I'm here right now and she isn't," Evan replied, thinking that it was a pretty gross statement when he really thought about it, but they liked when guys treated their girls like shit.

Kane smiled and nodded at his brother. "He's always been this way. Fucks one after another. The hoes always lined up for it and Evan was like 'now serving number sixty-nine.'"

They all broke into laughter, with the redhead thinking that it would be accurate if Kane had swapped out "dudes" for "hoes." The other guys went back to their ogling and he excused himself to the bathroom, ready to bump a few lines and take care of his waning buzz.

Even though cocaine was his first love, they had a rather tumultuous relationship. She always left him needing more thanks to how quickly she burned through his body, and he'd never stop coming back for it. The closer he got to Jackson, the more he realized that his feelings toward him weren't so different; any time with him wasn't enough and he wasn't going to stop angling for more.

He chopped a few lines on the counter by the sink, throwing his finger up at a guy who gave him the side eye from the urinal. "Worry about pissing, a'ight?" he snapped, rolling up his paper as he glared at him. The man turned away and Evan shook his head at the audacity the motherfucker had to pass judgment. Leaning over, he brought the tube to his nose and inhaled the three lines in rapid succession, letting out a pleasured moan and throwing his head back as the drugs hit hard.

He rubbed his thumb under his nose to clean up the excess powder and looked at himself in the mirror, a small smile pulling up his lips. He looked really fucking good. He was typically confident, but when he was high he felt like he was the hottest fucker to walk the Earth. He wanted to show his man how hot he was.

Without much thought, he unzipped his jeans halfway and slid them, along with his boxers, down a bit until they were resting just low enough to show a flash of his pubic hair. Lifting his shirt to show off his ab muscles, he speedily snapped a picture.

Evan (11:46pm): Want U 2 C sumthing
Jackson (11:47pm): What do U want me 2 C?
Evan (11:47pm): Make sure no 1 else can C
Jackson (11:48pm): Not a fucking idiot. Send it.

He sent the picture and eagerly waited for the response. As he did, he idly wondered how long he'd been in the bathroom and then shrugged off the thought, assuming that the guys would think the stripper changed her mind or he found another one to bang.

Jackson (11:50pm): Mmm look good man but U left something outta the pic
Evan (11:50pm): ???
Jackson (11:51pm): Don't fuck around show me that cock
Evan (11:51pm): Where R U?
Jackson (11:52pm): Out w my bro and friend. Send it.
Evan (11:52pm): Only if UR gonna ride it 2nite
Jackson (11:53pm): Said U were busy bitch
Evan (11:53pm): I am now but I could cum by later
Jackson (11:54pm): Depends how drunk & tired I am
Evan (11:54pm): R U drunk now? Stop drinking.
Jackson (11:54pm): Fuck off. Send me a pic of ur dick.
Evan (11:55pm): Promise if I do ur gonna ride
Jackson (11:55pm): Send it

He huffed at the vague answers he was receiving and pulled his zipper down the rest of the way so he could whip his cock out. He pumped it a few times to get it even harder than it already was from his thoughts of Jackson riding him. He was sure when a person looked at Jackson Jablonic they didn't think, "Damn, I bet that guy can ride a cock." but holy shit could he.

Evan knew it was selfish to always beg for it when he was aware that Jackson preferred to be rammed from behind or fucked face-to-face, but watching Jack bounce on his cock was the single hottest thing Evan had ever seen in his life and he couldn't get enough of it.

He grinned at how stiff his dick was, took the picture, and sent it off before swiftly shoving himself into his pants. He hoped it would turn Jackson on enough to let Evan go over there. He needed to be inside of him, and wondered if a person had ever died of wanting, because if they had Evan felt like he was close to gone.

Evan (11:57pm): It's waiting 4 u to hop on it
Jackson (11:57pm): Fuck UR so hot
Evan (11:58pm): Like that?

He slid his phone into his pocket and headed back to the area where the boys were sitting.

"Where the fuck were you at?" Luis questioned, narrowing his eyes at Evan.

"Where do you think I was?" he asked, raising his eyebrows. He had found that turning questions around on them always gave him better answers than he could come up with himself. He was glad that he was getting better at playing the game, because shit was simpler when people weren't constantly on his shit.

"Met up with that honey," Luis said with a smirk, shaking his head at the revelation. "You're a dirty dog, Red. Bad as fuck just like your brother said you were." He slapped Evan's hand and rambled on about him being the fucking man and a bad motherfucker, while Evan just nodded along.

He'd been called worse after all. He grinned at his brother, who was enjoying the work of the woman on top of him, and flipped Evan the bird before grabbing on to the stripper's fat ass. Evan pulled out his phone to talk to the fine behind that was going to be working him soon. As discreetly as possible he opened his messages and couldn't help but smile when he saw a slew from Jackson.

Jackson (12:00am): Know I luv it
Jackson (12:01am): Gonna show U how much soon
Jackson (12:05am): Got me like a rock right now
Jackson (12:07am): Where the fuck did U go?
Evan (12:14am): Sorry ppl around
Jackson (12:15am): What kinda ppl?
Evan (12:15am): Kane & roommates
Jackson (12:16am): Killed my boner
Evan (12:17am): Fuck U no it didn't
Jackson (12:17am): Promise U fucking did
Jackson (12:18am): Don't bring them up when ur talking to me
Evan (12:18am): U asked
Jackson (12:19am): Now I'm fucking telling U not 2
Jackson (12:19am): Hate that U roll w them. Should be w me.
Evan (12:20am): I am w U

Jackson (12:20am): U know what I mean
Evan (12:22am): Can I cum over 2nite? Wanna kiss U
Jackson (12:24am): Kiss me Goodwyn? Now Ur tryin to be fucking cute
Evan (12:25am): Is it working?
Jackson (12:25am): Ur pretty cute
Evan (12:26am): So…
Jackson (12:27am): Text me when ur leaving & I'll meet U at my place
Evan (12:27am): 4 kissing?
Jackson (12:28am): 4 some nasty ass sex
Evan (12:29am): I love ass sex
Jackson (12:29am): I didn't… mean it like that
Evan (12:30am): U said it tho
Evan (12:31am): We gonna do sum kissing 2?
Jackson (12:32am): Maybe if ur good
Evan (12:33am): U like me better bad. I like U good
Jackson (12:33am): Done texting
Evan (12:34am): Ur getting good at it tho
Jackson (12:33am): Fuck off

He couldn't wait to do just that.

24

It was routine now that as soon as Jackson heard a late-night knock on his door, he'd open it and have his high-as-hell boyfriend all over him—wild kisses and groping hands overtaking his body.

"Missed you," Evan confessed breathlessly as he tried to swallow Jack's tongue whole.

"Saw you last night, fag," Jackson replied, still uncomfortable with endearments he desperately wanted to share.

"Not enough. Don't see you enough." Evan took Jackson's hand and led him into the bedroom. "Mine or yours?" he asked as he stripped off his clothes and lay down on the bed.

"Mine. Yours is shit," Jackson sighed before heading over to his closet and tossing Evan a small baggie of cocaine. Jackson yanked off his shirt and pulled down his pants, tentative about what was about to happen.

He knew he shouldn't do it, but watching his hot-ass boyfriend chop lines in the cuts of his abs was probably the sexiest thing he'd ever seen. He was aware that doing coke with an addict was fucked up, but his dick was hard, his heart was racing, and the redhead was so goddamn tempting Jackson felt powerless against the pull. After all, he wasn't trying to be Evan's father, mother, or fucking counselor; if his man wanted to get fucked up and fuck him all night, Jack was definitely down.

Evan lifted his head off the pillow and leaned back on his elbows, licking his lips as he looked at Jackson through heavily hooded eyes. "You want it?" he asked with a smirk.

Bastard. He knew damn well what Jackson wanted. He admired the way Evan's stomach and arm muscles rippled in the position and how proudly his hard-on was standing in the air.

"Take it." Evan smiled when Jackson climbed onto the bed and made his way between Evan's legs so Jackson could suck on the head of that gorgeous cock as if he needed to taste him to breathe. He let his tongue drag along the ridge and looked up to see a mischievous glint in Evan's brown eyes. "My good boy," he crooned, tangling his fingers into Jackson's hair, pulling as he ordered, "Suck that dick."

Jackson placed his hands on the mattress for the leverage he needed to slide his mouth down the length of his boyfriend's impressive shaft, taking him in inch by inch. Grinning around his cock when he heard Evan let out a broken moan, Jackson made his way back up and then down again, his pace gradually building with each movement. "Mmm," he hummed, knowing that the vibrations and sounds would get Evan going even more than he already was.

"So good to me," he complimented, tilting his head to watch Jackson eagerly run his tongue up and down, chasing his dripping spittle. "Fucking slut for my cock. You love it, don't you?" Jackson increased the pace by way of answer, and continued to fuck Evan with his mouth. Evan dropped his neck back on the pillow and groaned, "C'mon, blow the lines or I'm going to blow my load."

Jackson obliged, releasing Evan's cock from his mouth with a pop before crawling up his body with his hard dick dragging along Evan's thigh and leaving a trail of precome as he did.

"Nothing is fucking hotter than the way you get turned on when you suck my cock," Evan mused as Jackson took the paper out of Evan's hands, hovered over his torso, and inhaled the lines without lifting up.

"Ahhh," Jackson moaned once he was done. He squeezed his eyes shut and held on to either side of his head as the drugs crashed into his brain. "Thought you liked it when I ride you," he teased, remembering his boyfriend's obsession during their text conversation earlier. He let his tongue do a few licks around the inside of his lips, looking for the taste that he'd just put up his nose.

"Everything you do is hotter than the last thing you did, which was hot to begin with. You got me on fucking fire," the redhead admitted, grabbing Jackson roughly by the nape of his neck and slamming their lips together. The kiss was all tongue and teeth, nips and bites followed by lustful licking. Climbing onto Jackson's lap, Evan wrapped his arms around Jack's shoulders and began to grind his ass on Jackson's hard dick as Evan's cock rubbed against Jackson's torso. "Turn me on so much."

"I can fucking tell." Jackson grinned, using his thumb to swipe the rivulet of precome that was leaking from Evan's cock then put it into his mouth. "Snow ain't supposed to make you hungry, but I'm fucking starving for it right now." Jackson bit into Evan's bottom lip. "Going to suck it some more."

"No you're fucking not, comeslut." Evan laughed, kissing Jackson down to the bed. "I got things to do to you."

"What're you going to do to me?" Jackson wrapped his legs tightly around his lover's waist and his arms around Evan's neck to pull him even closer.

"You're a little koala bear, you know that?" the redhead grinned, the smile falling from his face when Jackson lifted one of his legs and let it slam down onto Evan's lower back. "Ouch, motherfucker, that hurt."

"That's the gayest fucking thing I've ever heard," Jack groused. "Don't say that shit to me again."

"That you're a koala bear?" Evan smirked. "What're you going to do? Cuddle me to death?"

"You know, I'm a grown-ass thug, man. Feared and respected in the streets," Jackson shot back, thinking that whatever hissy fit he was having wasn't necessarily helping his cause, but he still went for it regardless.

"Well, in this bed, you're my comeslut koala bear," Evan replied matter-of-factly. "And I fucking love it. Turn over, baby."

"Don't call me that either. Why do you call me all this stupid shit? It don't turn me on," Jack complained while doing as he was told, laying his chest on the bed.

"Like hell it doesn't. You always bite those dick-sucking lips and start dripping whenever I call you 'baby.' You can act like you don't like it, but you really fucking do."

"Fuck off."

"C'mon," Evan hummed, kissing Jackson's shoulder blades. "Don't have to be ashamed of what you like when you're with me. You got to let go."

Jackson tilted his ass sunny side up, ready for his lover's thick cock. When Jack felt a warm mouth instead he tensed as Evan began to lick and suck the flesh on Jackson's ass. He'd had a good deal of spanks and some bites, but he'd never allowed Evan's tongue to get acquainted with his asshole. Evan poured the coke from Jackson's tailbone to his mid-back and then dragged his tongue up his ass crack before snorting the line in one long inhale.

Jackson was feeling pretty fucking gone and found himself craving the sensation he got from Evan's lengthy lick. He pushed up on his hands and knees and presented his ass to Evan, silently begging the redhead to bury his face in it and flick his tongue against his opening.

"This a'ight?"

"As long as you stop fucking talking about it after you do it," Jackson muttered, doing his best to come off as pissed off, even though his drug-induced lack of inhibitions had him into it.

"You're going to love it." He could hear the grin in Evan's voice.

Evan dove in, his tongue making never-ending rotations of some of the best-feeling shit ever. He was lapping at Jackson's hole, swirling around the rim and then narrowing to push past the tight ring of muscles. He felt himself get looser with every pass and by the time the redhead had the full length of his tongue inside of him and was making large circles, he knew that Evan was right; Jackson was going to become a slut for it. Whimpers and moans were leaking from his mouth, giving him away and taking away his ability to deny that he liked it even if he wanted to. When Evan reached around to start jerking Jack's cock, he huffed out, "Stop," the pleasure too overwhelming to cope with in his hyper-aroused state. He wanted to make sure he still had a fuck left in him to ride his boyfriend.

"On your back," Jackson ordered.

"I'm still going," Evan's muffled voice protested. "This is what happens when you hold out for so long. I got to get my time in."

"Get on your fucking back. Need to bounce on that dick," Jackson demanded. He'd fought Evan and fucked Evan, but Jack was sure as shit he'd never seen the man move as quickly as he did when he peeled his mouth off his ass and lay back on the bed, ready for Jackson to get on top of him.

"Been thinking about this, huh?"

"You know I have," Jackson replied, licking his lips as he positioned himself over his lover's cock, spreading his cheeks open with his hands so that he could sink down on him. Jackson gasped as he took more of Evan in, not as stretched as he typically was from Evan's fingers.

"So goddamn tight," he groaned, throwing his head back at the sensation, until he realized that it may be too tight. "Holy shit. You okay?"

"Yeah, fuck off," Jackson snapped. "Ain't some delicate flower, Goodwyn."

"Take it slow, baby," Evan urged. "Don't want you to tear."

"Shut the fuck up with that 'baby' shit," Jackson growled, not wanting to acknowledge that as soon as Evan said it Jack's dick twitched and he bottomed out then used his thigh muscles to bring his body up and down on his lover's dick.

"Just like that, mmm," Evan moaned, his fingers gripping into Jackson's ass. Evan laughed when Jackson knocked his hands off him so he could pick up the pace, intent to do every ounce of the fucking himself. "Get it, baby."

"I'm going to fucking kill you," Jackson grunted, unable to hold back the smile that was pulling on his lips. The little shit. He rolled his eyes at Evan's proud look and then flipped him both middle fingers to ensure that the asshole got the message.

"You might kill me if you keep those fingers up when you're riding me," Evan warned.

Jackson laughed and bit his lower lip, concentrating on what he was doing before his boyfriend had started to torment him. "How about this? You shut your goddamn mouth and I'll ride you until you think your dick's going to fall off."

"I mean, I'll take that deal," Evan said with a huge grin. "Shake on it?" He extended his hand with hopeful eyes.

Jackson shook his head at what a dumbass the redhead was but reached his hand out and chuckled when Evan pulled him down, grabbed the cradle of his head, and smashed their lips together.

Sealed with a kiss.

25

Jackson stared at Amy all snuggled up on the living room chair. She was fucking around on her phone, looking like she didn't have a care in the world, while he was doing his best to channel his energy into willing her to go away. Since she remained unmoved, he relented. Clearly he was doing a piss-poor job.

"You headed over to Isaiah's or what?" Jackson asked, sniffing uncomfortably and nudging the side of his nose with his knuckle. Though he was trying to remain as casual as possible in his attempt to get her to fuck off, he was failing miserably. His sister was typically long gone by 11:30 p.m. and he wanted to see Evan. A few weeks ago, he'd teased his boyfriend for saying he missed him after they'd seen each other the night before, but days without Evan were getting too long and just nights weren't enough.

They spent a good amount of the time they weren't together texting about mundane shit or what they were looking forward to when they reconnected that evening. It was weird, but he enjoyed hearing about what Evan was doing. Jack even found himself interested in the stupid stories Evan would tell about his roommates.

Jackson attempted to ignore they were KKz, the same way he tried to forget that Evan was, too. Originally, he'd told Evan not to talk about anything related to the gang, but Jackson had become so desperate to know more about Evan's life that the rule had been dropped. Jack had decided that Evan's affiliation to the KKz was like his cocaine addiction: two negative attributes that were incredibly problematic, but didn't change Jackson's feeling…feelings that had become surprisingly overwhelming.

Amy let out a soft laugh. "You know that you can have him over, right?"

"I know I can fucking have him over, it's my goddamn apartment," he shot back, taking a drag from his cigarette and blowing the smoke out through his nose. He noticed his leg was bouncing anxiously. He wondered if this was how Evan felt about his coke: jittery as hell when he couldn't have it. "So are you going or what?"

"Isaiah's in Mexico for a few days dealing with your distributors or whatever the fuck you guys call them. So I'll be sleeping here," Amy explained, sitting forward in her chair and tossing a baggie of weed to Jackson. "Pack the bowl again."

"You serious?" he questioned, raising his eyebrows to reflect his irritation.

"You don't want to smoke more? I'll make pizza bagels and we can play Doom," she offered. "It'll be fun."

"I mean about staying here for the next few nights," he clarified as he loaded the pipe. "Can't you go stay at Kylie's or something?"

"I live here, Jack," Amy reminded him as she sent an unimpressed glare. "Just because I'm gone a lot doesn't mean that I don't." She sighed and shook her head. "What're you so worried about? That I'll hear you guys or something?"

"Shut the fuck up," Jackson warned. Of course Amy knew they were banging, but he hated how casually she brought it up, as if it was normal that he was screwing a dude.

"Afraid I'm going to come at him for being with the KKz?" she pressed. "I'm not happy about it, but it's been a little while, right? How long have you two been together? If he was going to try shit on you, I think he would've probably done it already."

"Told you he ain't like that," Jackson replied, choosing to ignore Amy's question about their relationship. He hadn't really thought about it. Though it seemed like forever and no time at all, in reality it had been about three months since they first hooked up. He wondered if other people had the type of feelings he had for Evan that quickly or if he was just a schmuck.

"What's he like then?" she asked with a grin, taking the lit bowl from Jackson's hands and inhaling deeply. She held the smoke in her lungs until she started to sputter and then gave it back to him.

"Don't worry about it," he said coolly, taking a hit before pulling his vibrating phone out of his pocket.

Evan (11:42pm): On my way back from the club. Got what I needed FAST 2nite.
Evan (11:42pm): Ninja shit.
Evan (11:43pm): Went Ninja on their asses.
Evan (11:43pm): Ur not impressed?
Jackson (11:44pm): Only if ur a ninja on my ass
Evan (11:44pm): Love ur ass. Can I cum over and C it?
Jackson (11:45pm): What about me?

Jackson's eyes went wide when he realized what his question implied and frantically typed another text.

Jackson (11:45pm): Wanna C me 2?
Evan (11:47pm): Course I do. On my way
Jackson (11:48pm): My sister's here
Evan (11:48pm): Oh
Evan (11:49pm): Wanna meet @ park?
Jackson (11:49pm): Fuck no
Evan (11:50pm): Need U

He sighed and rubbed his forehead, trying to think of what he should do. The idea of having Evan around Amy was unappealing, but not having him come over at all for the next few nights was significantly worse.

Jackson (11:53pm): Come over
Evan (11:54pm): U sure?
Jackson (11:55pm): Yeah just don't tongue fuck my mouth as soon as u get in here
Evan (11:56pm): U love it tho :-/
Jackson (11:57pm): I'll survive
Evan (11:57pm): So if I can't kiss u can I at least get on my knees & suk dat cuk
Jackson (11:57pm): WTF. Don't be fucking weird ok? Can u handle that?
Evan (11:58pm): Can always handle it ;)
Jackson (11:58pm): I meant not being weird. U drunk?
Evan (11:59pm): C U SOON

Fuck. He couldn't help but feel that having Evan come over was an epic mistake. His boyfriend was erratic as hell when he was high, but easier to manage than he was when he drank, too.

"Was that Evan?" Amy questioned as Jackson slid his phone back into his pocket and gnawed on his bottom lip.

"Mmmhmm. He's gonna come by," he replied with a sigh. He brought the pipe to his lips and took a steady inhale, hoping that the weed would work to calm his racing mind.

"Does he sleep over every night?"

"None of your fucking business."

"What should I call him? I mean, when he gets here. Is he your boyfriend or…?" She pushed, grinning at the death glare she received in return. "C'mon, Jack, you gotta lighten up."

"I don't gotta do shit," he huffed, unamused. "Just call him Evan." He took a deep breath, feeling that he needed to give his sister some semblance of warning regarding which version of his boyfriend may show up in the next several minutes. He'd experienced Evan being wild and funny, soft and sad, and cold and nasty all within the same hour. "Y'know…" he began, "he was out tonight, so he's pretty fucked up."

Amy nodded. "We've all been there, right?"

"Yeah, I guess," Jackson answered halfheartedly. He'd gotten fucked up beyond belief, but he'd never been as gone as Evan was sometimes. "He was at a club so…"

"Stealing peoples' shit?" she questioned, with a click of the tongue. "That's what he does there, right?"

"Amy, if you're gonna…" He shook his head and took a deep breath. "I should tell him not to come."

A knock on the door sounded. Too late for second thoughts, and amid Amy's promises she'd be good, Jackson made his way over to answer it, deciding that they'd stay in the living room for a few minutes and then he'd drag Evan into the bedroom. It would be quick, and hopefully painless.

"Hey," the redhead greeted, holding up his hand for a high five. He laughed at the small grin that was pulling up Jackson's lips and walked past him, dropping his backpack in the entry. Taking a seat on the couch, he glanced over at Amy, who was looking at him with raised eyebrows. "You look nice," he said matter-of-factly, drawing a loud laugh out of her.

"First of all, I have zit cream on my face and my hair's in a bun so I don't. Second, that shit doesn't work on me, I still think you're a dick."

"Really?" Jackson exclaimed, flabbergasted that it had been literal seconds since Evan had entered the apartment and Amy was already starting with him.

"What? I think you're a dick, too," she informed her brother innocently.

Evan laughed at her response and threw his hands up in surrender. "It's fair, Jack. I kind of am a dick, right?"

Jackson felt his face heat at the familiarity when he realized that his smirking sister had picked up on it.

"C'mon, sit down, Jack," Amy directed, putting more emphasis on his name than she typically did. "You smoke?" she asked Evan, holding out the bowl to him.

"Nah, not really into drugs," he replied with a chuckle. "But I guess I could give it a try."

Jackson sat down on the couch next to the redhead, relieved that silly and flirty Evan had shown up. Pity Jackson couldn't take full advantage of Evan's good mood sans Amy.

Jack took the pipe from his boyfriend's extended hand and brought it to his lips, feeling a strong gaze locked on him as he hit it. He could feel heat creep across his cheeks and he admonished himself for fucking blushing. Evan looked at him with so much passion that it often left him feeling physically overwhelmed. It took all of Jackson's self-control not to climb onto his boyfriend's lap and get lost in him. Jackson forced himself to look away but found that Amy's indulgent back-and-forth between them wasn't much better.

"You two are fucking tripping me out," he groused, passing the pipe back to Evan. "Both of you got to stop looking at me."

"Weed's got you paranoid," Amy stated, but she turned to Evan nonetheless. "Tamara still thinks you're going to call her."

"Yeah?" he nodded, amused. "Don't have her number."

"Like you'd call her if you did," Jackson scoffed.

"Maybe I would," the redhead stated with a shrug. "Why not, right?"

Amy's eyes widened as she watched her brother's face go dark.

"What the fuck would you have to say to her? Hmm?" he questioned, rolling his tongue under his bottom lip.

"Get all the dirt," Evan said with a wide smile. "Find out all the bad shit about you so we can be even."

His sister looked at him, puzzled, as he rested his hand on Evan's knee. "Don't," Jackson ordered quietly. Over the last week Evan had been randomly going into a state of self-reflection that not only seemed out of the ordinary for a man who rejected the need for any sort of help, but also nerve-wracking for Jackson, who didn't know how to handle it.

"Did you steal my credit card number?" Amy asked as Evan passed the pipe to her. Jackson closed his eyes, wishing that he'd never invited Evan over, lived with Amy, or been born.

"Did you leave your bag out?" Evan questioned rhetorically, apparently nonplussed by the accusatory inquiry.

"So you did then?"

"Was anything charged?" he asked.

She shook her head. "Jackson told me to cancel it before you could buy anything."

"Ran that scam when I was like seventeen, man," Jackson told his boyfriend, eyes focused on his lips, prompting Evan to lick them salaciously.

"Smart."

"So, do I have to worry about you stealing shit here?" Amy asked, raising one eyebrow and looking at Evan expectantly. "Hmm?"

He placed his hand on Jackson's chest and smiled softly at her. "Only one thing."

"Fuck, enough," Jackson groaned, feeling his face catch on fire again. "No more." He got up and headed for his bedroom with Evan trailing behind.

"I'd be running to the bedroom if a guy said that to me, too," Amy called after her brother, who shot her the middle finger without looking back.

Stole it.

26

Due to an insane amount of bullshit they had to deal with in their respective gangs, it was rare for Evan and Jackson to get together any time before 10:00 p.m. There were some nights when Evan wouldn't go over until all the bars had closed and the rest of the city was long since asleep. Still, he always made his way to Jackson, not missing one night's opportunity to share a bed with him. It was strange. He'd spent years dreaming about his own space and a comfortable place to lay his head, but it had been easy to forgo it all if it meant more time with Jackson.

It was difficult not to wonder what could have been if he hadn't joined the KKz. While it seemed like a good idea at the time, and he did benefit greatly from what the gang provided him, he often considered how different things would have been if he would've delayed it a few weeks. He would have met Jackson, started fucking him, and eventually ended up in his bed every night.

Things were solid between them, more stable than any other relationship, familial or otherwise, that he'd ever had. He knew that his boyfriend wanted him to be around more often, and he could've been, if it weren't for his affiliation. As great as the gang had been for his circumstances short-term, it was fucking up his vision of the long term pretty epically. It was also ruining the first dinner they'd ever had together.

"Fuck," Evan grunted, pulling his phone out of his pocket to see that Cedric was calling him again. "I got to…" He sighed as Jackson waved him away. Climbing off the couch where they'd been sitting eating Chinese takeout, he made his way into the kitchen so he could answer the call. "Yeah?"

"You haven't answered your phone," Cedric barked. "C'mon, Red, we talked about this. What the fuck are you doing?"

"I'm on a date," Evan replied, dropping his voice low in hopes that Jackson wouldn't hear him. He realized he had no such luck when his boyfriend glanced over his shoulder at him with raised eyebrows.

"Ain't that cute," Cedric stated sarcastically. "I need to you hit up every corner on Grant from Greenway to Woodbridge. There's some shit going down and we got to get them marked tonight."

"That's like eight blocks," he huffed, knowing that it was going to take him hours to get the task done.

"Yeah, well at least it's September and not February, right, man? Not going to freeze your balls off. That's the silver lining right there."

Evan was too aggravated to shoot back a witty response, opting instead to confirm he'd take care of it and end the call.

"What?" Jackson questioned through a mouth full of chow mein.

Evan plopped down on the couch. "They need me to do some shit tonight. Going to have to leave when we're done eating or I'll never have enough time to get it done." He shook his head. "Thought I had the night off."

"Yeah well, that ain't going to fucking happen for a while. You're new. They'll keep running you until they find some other guy to do it," Jackson explained. "This actual business or the errand bullshit they tried to pull last week?"

"Actual business," Evan replied, remembering how livid Jackson had been when an O-G had called him late at night to get him some forties and Doritos.

"You better not be lying to me," Jackson warned. "If they keep sending you for dumb shit and fuck up our nights, I'm going to hunt them down."

"It's not errands." Evan took a bite of his food before admitting, "I'm over this shit. Not used to answering to people. I never did it before and I fucking hate doing it now."

"Blood in, blood out. They got you for life," Jackson stated with a click of his tongue. "Only way out is a cell or a casket, you know that. You ever been inside?"

"Yeah, a few months here and there for vandalism. Real dumb shit, but got popped enough that if I get caught again I'm going to have to do a year or two."

"Pigs don't let you fuck up people's property in peace anymore, huh?" Jackson teased, laughing when Evan punched him in the arm.

"What were you in for, hmm?" Evan asked with a smirk.

"Don't know why you're assuming I've ever done time," Jackson stated with mock indignation.

"You've been doing this shit for too long to have never been in prison."

"Did a bunch of stints in juvie, but only got one weapons charge that put me in MCC for a few months," Jackson replied, grinning.

"What?"

"Never would've guessed you were really a good boy," Evan flirted, placing his food on the floor so he could move closer to Jackson and press his lips against the skin under Jack's ear. Evan rubbed Jackson's upper thigh as he sucked a mark into his skin.

"Don't think 'good boys' go to prison, Daywalker." Jack laughed. "Just good at not getting caught," he said as Evan pushed Jack's chest down gently so he was lying flat on the couch.

Evan rested his body weight on Jackson and slid his fingers into his hair as they slotted their mouths together. "I caught you," he whispered as Jack bit his lower lip a little too hard, just the way Evan liked it. "Mmm."

"Fucking let you," Jack hummed, replacing his teeth with his tongue. He smiled into the kiss as Evan rutted the bulge in his pants against Jackson's crotch. He moaned when Evan's lips made their way back to Jack's neck. "Wouldn't have got me if I didn't want you to."

"That right?" Evan asked, his voice muffled against Jackson's skin. "Think I would've worn you down eventually."

X

Jackson knew it was true. Evan had him before he should have. Who would have thought a failed park fuck would lead to what they had? Jackson had never felt lucky in life. As far as he was concerned, being into guys when his father was a homophobic prick was the antithesis of luck. Realistically, falling for a cokehead who was in a rival gang wasn't necessarily stumbling across a four-leaf clover, but he felt like he had. Like luck, happiness had always seemed out of reach, until his arms were wrapped firmly around it, around Evan.

They kissed their breath away, only coming up for air when Jackson's head got light and fuzzy. Evan licked his lips and pulled down Jackson's sweatpants, stroking his hard cock slowly while he got control of his breathing. "Love your cock," Evan complimented, eyes focused on the glistening beads of pre-come that collected in his slit. "Think we ever fucked in MCC? That's where I was locked up, too."

Jackson laughed, putting his hands behind his head and gazing down at Evan as he was getting jerked off. "I'd remember that. Would've actually been turned on if I'd fucked you."

"If I'd fucked you," Evan corrected, swiping his thumb along the tip of Jackson's dick and dragging the stickiness around the head.

"Nah. Not there." He sighed at the sensation. "Always did the fucking."

"Then we definitely never fucked." Evan laughed.

"Never took a cock, Goodwyn?" Jack asked, surprised when Evan shook his head. "Not once?"

"Nope. No drugs could get me high enough to bend over and take it up the ass," he said with a click of the tongue. "Slept on park benches in the middle of January instead of bottoming."

"You don't know what you're missing out on," Jackson informed, closing his eyes and letting his head fall back as Evan wrapped his lips around Jack's cock. Evan licked up and down before coming up to the head to purposely lap up the pre-come he'd smeared a few moments earlier.

"I'll leave all that pleasure for you," Evan said as he jerked him off again. "My bossy bottom."

"You're always saying 'my,'" Jackson pointed out. "My bossy bottom, my koala comeslut, my baby, my man. Pretty fucking possessive, aren't you?"

"Over you? Yeah I am," Evan said with no shame.

"Why?" Jackson licked his lips and raised his eyebrows. "Told me you never grab on to anyone, why do you grab on to me?"

"You really want to know?" Evan asked, his tone reflecting a contradiction of challenge and vulnerability.

"I asked, didn't I?" Jackson studied his boyfriend's face, wondering if he'd go for it, if he'd open up. Secretly, he hoped he would, because there was no way Jackson would allow himself to go there first. He needed Evan to.

The redhead pressed a kiss against the tip of Jackson's dick and then onto his full lips before standing up and stretching his arms over his head. "I'll tell you someday."

"What the fuck? Get your dumbass back down here and finish me off," Jackson ordered.

"Can't. Got to go," he said, looking slightly apologetic, but more amused as Jackson pulled up his pants and gave him the finger.

"I'm gonna come in your leftovers."

"Mmm. Maybe you'll make that shit taste better."

"Didn't like it?"

Evan shrugged. "Like McDonald's better."

"So you're into the best coke and the worst food?"

Evan considered the question and shrugged. "Pretty much. Good coke makes even the shittiest food taste better."

"So you're not high right now?" Jack asked, surprised, thinking that he was usually better at identifying moments when his boyfriend wasn't inebriated.

"Nope. Burned off," Evan replied as he put his backpack over his shoulders. "You want me to come back?"

"Of course I do." Jackson sat up and looked at his boyfriend with a thousand thoughts jumbled in his mind, the most important making its way to the top of the heap. "Tell me now then. If you're not high. Tell me why you grab on to me."

Evan frowned, his body language revealing how vulnerable he felt. "You know why."

They'd been dancing around it for weeks and Jackson knew it was time. "Pretend I don't."

Evan looked like he was taking a moment to muster up his courage. "Because I love you," he admitted.

Then he turned on his heels and beat feet out of the apartment.

27

Evan exited the apartment building in disbelief that the words had come out of his mouth so easily, and was more shocked at how profoundly he meant them. He wasn't sure when it had happened, but somehow he'd fallen deeply and completely in love with Jackson Jablonic. At least that's what he thought the feelings were. Evan ached for his lover when they were apart and slowly healed when they were together. He hoped he mended Jackson, too—sutured the cuts and gashes that his hard life had left on him. His boyfriend made Evan want to be better, made him want to be everything.

Before Jackson, Evan had existed often wishing he didn't, his heart pumping blood that ran tepid in his veins. With Jackson, Evan was flooded with fire that sparked every cell of his body to life. He couldn't deny that much of their heat lit up the sheets, but it wasn't about the fucking. As incredible as their sex was, and it was by far the best Evan had ever had, it was the quiet moments spent talking, kissing, or holding each other that made him feel the most alive. He hadn't thought that love would be in the cards for him, believing that he was owed some sort of karma for showing so little to people who probably deserved much more. He wasn't sure what he'd done right in life, but it had to be something, otherwise he had a hard time understanding his luck.

Over the past several years he'd lost everything—his family, his home, his sobriety, himself—but none of that fazed him like it should have. He knew that some of his numbness could be attributed to the drugs, but it wasn't only that. He'd never cared about the things that were important to other people. If something didn't give him a thrill, he didn't understand the point to it, so he'd stuck to painting, cocaine, and men—anything or anyone that brought him that rush. After being with Jackson, he realized that no high could beat the feeling of being in love.

Evan always thought the concept of love was overrated, but that was because he hadn't felt it.

Until now.

Panic quickly set in when he considered that perhaps Jackson hadn't been alluding to love when he'd asked him why he grabbed on. Maybe he'd meant something different, more psychological. Had Evan really told a man that he loved him without actually knowing if it was something Jackson felt in return? It wouldn't matter either way. It wasn't as though Evan would be able to stop loving Jack if he didn't love him back. Evan was too far gone for that and expected that at some point he'd be left with his love while Jackson moved on to somebody less complicated.

Pain wasn't new to Evan. He'd dealt with it before and he'd deal with it again if he had to. Still, the agony of not having Jackson would be crueler than all the trials of Evan's past.

Reaching into his backpack, he put on his blue beanie, covering his head from the chill of the late September night. Though it was too early for it, the crisp air smelled like snow, making him want to pack some into his nose. He ducked into the alley so he could pour the white powder onto the back of his hand and snorted it up quickly before continuing on his way.

The night was going to be long. He couldn't go down the line from corner to corner. In order to have less of a chance of being caught, he needed to skip around and then come back and hit the ones he'd passed. Lighting up a cigarette, he started toward the farthest point, deciding to work his way back the best he could. The territory had been Dem Demonz's before it was taken over by the Block Boys, who had been struggling over the last couple of months to evade the cops, causing their numbers to dwindle greatly. Evidently, the KKz were making a move to take it over before the DDz could take it back.

Truly, Evan didn't give a shit. For the most part, he did what he was told and stayed out of the politics. The gangs wanted to get pissed about everything and he didn't have it in him to get worked up over corners as long as he was getting what he needed.

It seemed Kane thought Evan would be more invested in the Klown Killerz than he'd actually become. His brother had been making comments recently about Evan's marked absence at night and low affect in regard to gang-related business. Instead of worrying about letting him down, Evan wondered why his brother would've thought that Evan would get wrapped up in the scene.

He'd never understand why his family would expect him to be different when he never demonstrated a willingness to change. They always wanted him to be somebody else, but he knew only how to be himself. He never tried to tell them how to live their lives, but they didn't grant him the same consideration.

When he thought back to his childhood, he was unable to reflect on a time where they'd been truly supportive. To them, badgering him to get clean was showing their love, but that wasn't the type of love he needed. He'd spent his whole life screaming into silence and still nobody heard—until Jackson.

With Evan's siblings, it was always about how he could lessen their loads. The only time they'd looked for him was when they needed something. Growing up without parents was challenging for all of them, but they'd never treated him the way they treated each other. When Emma or Paul got themselves into trouble, the family rallied around them. It was always as if their poor decisions were a blip on an otherwise perfect record, while Evan's were who he was.

When he was fifteen, he met a guy named Jorge, who was visiting from Texas. They'd fucked around while he was in town and after he headed back home, they'd kept in touch texting each other. It wasn't that he gave much of a shit about Jorge, but he was gay, easy, and lived far away from Chicago. All qualities that made him significantly more attractive than he was. When he first suggested that Evan come down for a visit, he'd told him to "fuck off." He became more interested when Jorge sweetened the deal, sending pictures of the mansion he lived in with a huge pool in the backyard and telling him that his dad was going to Mexico running for his gang that weekend. Evan was enticed by the idea of freedom and spending time in a nice house, with an actual in-ground pool. He felt like he was entitled to an adventure. He'd never left Illinois. His life was flat and boring. He didn't tell anybody he was going before he did. It took him three days to hitchhike to Texas and once he got down there he stayed for four, fucking, smoking, and blowing copious amounts of Jorge's dad's cocaine.

He arrived back on the South Side eleven days later with gonorrhea and a coke habit. The first thing Emma did when he opened the door was ask him to take his little brother Sammy to the park. He argued with her, saying that Paul should take him, but she'd informed him that he was studying at Rachel's, as he had been all week. Apparently, he had SATs coming up and doing well on them was of paramount importance to the family. Evan never asked her if she'd noticed that he was gone, because either she had and didn't care, or hadn't and that was probably worse. So he took Sammy to the park, and when he came back home nobody brought up his absence, leading him to wonder if he'd dreamed it up and never actually left. His burning piss and craving for coke assured him that he had.

He shook his head at the memory, stomping his cigarette on the ground once he'd reached the first corner. There was nothing to their tag, just a stupid sad face in maroon. He sprayed it quickly, hoping that if he kept a good pace he'd be able to get back to Jackson when he was still at least half awake. By the time he'd hit all of the corners, his legs were sore and his fingers were cramped.

Evan (3:15am): Hey
Evan (3:23am): U awake?

A bit of anxiety began to build in his chest, worried that he'd said too much and Jackson was freaked the fuck out. He always left his ringer on so his texts would wake him if he fell asleep, but still there was no reply.

Evan (3:30am): Ignoring me asshole?
Evan (3:35am): U fucking asked
Evan (3:38am): Don't kno what u wanted
Evan (3:40am): 4 me to lie?

He sighed and walked briskly toward DDz territory. It wasn't nearby and he probably should've been able to talk himself out of it on his trek, but his stubborn mind was leading the way. He wasn't sure what he thought he'd accomplish by doing it, but he felt compelled to anyway. Getting out his blue paint can, he began to spray right over the DD's logo, immediately feeling calmer than he had moments earlier. Once he'd completed his piece, he stood back to admire it. Both he and Jackson could look at it as a "Fuck you," an "I love you," or maybe a "Fuck you, I love you." Regardless of how his boyfriend took it, Evan liked the work and felt pretty proud of it, and that felt like enough at the time.

*Evan (3:52am): **Going back 2 my place***
*Evan (3:53am): **When U wake up go 2 corner of Grant & St. Lawrence***
*Evan (3:53am): **I'm not there but something else is***
*Evan (3:55am): **If it makes u mad fuck u***
*Evan (3:56am): **If u like it fuck u anyway***

He lit up one last cigarette as he made his way back to his place, thinking how odd it was that he hadn't spent a night in his bed in months. He was in his room a lot during the day, but it felt strange to be alone at this hour. Once he closed the door behind him, he turned off his phone and rested his tired body down.

Before falling asleep he chided himself for being so forthcoming with his emotions.

He guessed it was just nice to feel them.

28

Jackson opened his eyes to see his bedroom bathed in sunlight. Letting out a quiet yawn, he turned over to cuddle with Evan, and was surprised he wasn't there. Panicked, he scrambled for his phone and sighed when he saw he had several missed texts and calls from his boyfriend.

"Fuck," he muttered, rubbing his forehead as he read them and realized Evan thought he'd been avoiding him due to what he'd admitted the night before. He was unsure how the redhead could jump to the conclusion that his confession had freaked out Jackson considering he'd practically pulled the words from Evan's mouth.

Still, it wasn't lost on him that it was a big deal. He knew Evan. Jackson understood that Evan didn't say that shit to people. They were similar that way, both reluctant to let themselves go for fear that if they did they'd never be able to drag themselves back. Jack had spent six years with Tamara and he hadn't been able to utter the phrase, even if just to appease her.

Jackson (8:45am): Fuck 4got to turn ringer on
Jackson (8:45am): Fell asleep
Jackson (8:46am): wasn't avoiding u
Jackson (8:47am): wanted to hear that

He looked back through all the messages, able to focus on the last few once his brain settled from the realization that he slept through his boyfriend's attempts to reach him. When Jack reread them, dread immediately pushed down on his chest at the thought of what the impulsive, most likely fucked-up-off-his-ass Klown had done to a Demonz corner.

Jackson (8:49am): what the fuck did u do?

Not stalling another moment, he rolled out of bed, put on his jeans and a long-sleeve shirt, pissed, brushed his teeth, and threw a Sox hat over his bedhead. Growing up, he'd liked the Cubbies, but DDz didn't root for any motherfuckers that wore blue. Jackson made sure to fasten his thin gold chain around his neck, knowing that if he saw his boyfriend it would drive him crazy, because for some inexplicable reason, it always did.

Shit, he wanted to see Evan. Jackson never thought he'd turn into such a goddamn needy bitch for someone, but Evan had changed everything. Jack chided himself for worrying more about missing out on a morning with his boyfriend than he was about whatever the hell Evan had done.

Regardless, he made his way out of his apartment building and headed toward the corner Evan had specified. He wasn't sure what he was expecting to see, but from the texts, he was thinking that it would most likely be something that would piss him the fuck off.

Every time Tammy had done annoying shit, he'd become increasingly checked out, until only the slightest sliver of obligation tied him to her. With Evan, it was different. The redhead was tough to handle, but even on his worst days, Jackson felt more compelled to pull him in closer rather than push him away, thinking that those were the times he had to care for him more.

Loving Evan was both the easiest and hardest thing Jackson had ever done.

Lighting up a cigarette, he pulled the nicotine into his lungs and exhaled into the damp morning air. Thick clouds rested one on top of the other, a stratified gradient of grays. It seemed that the sky was going to open up at any moment to dump a deluge of rain on the tired town, and he wished he was in bed with Evan when it did. Instead, he was standing on the corner of Grant and St. Lawrence, face-to-face with a blue koala bear that was hugging a can of spray paint.

He should have been livid that a Klown Killerz had the audacity to spray over the DDz' logo on one of their most lucrative corners. He should have been concerned by how impulsive his boyfriend was. He should have been aggravated that Evan had pulled him out of bed to look at a stupid koala bear, but Jack wasn't any of those things. He was mostly worried about what could have happened if any of his boys had been out last night and saw his artist at work.

He shook his head and let out a light laugh, feeling his cheeks warm when he realized that the image reflected how Evan saw him: attached and loving. The neediness of the hold was palpable. He wondered how the redhead so easily saw through him, felt his love even when he wasn't sure how to properly show it. He was glad he did.

> *Jackson (9:23am): ur fucking nuts*
> *Evan (9:25am): u want my nuts*
> *Jackson (9:25am): that 2*
> *Evan (9:26am): could've had them on ur face last night*
> *Evan (9:26am): would've fucked that hot mouth but u didn't answer*
> *Jackson (9:27am): Fell asleep man 4got 2 turn ringer on*
> *Evan (9:28am): that right?*
> *Jackson (9:28am): wasn't ignoring u*
> *Jackson (9:30am): missed ya*
> *Jackson (9:30am): don't like waking up without u*
> *Evan (9:31am): Thought it was cause of what I said*
> *Jackson (9:32am): no needed to hear that*
> *Evan (9:33am): yeah?*
> *Jackson (9:33am): yeah come over in an hour. Got something 4 u.*
> *Evan (9:34am): it's daytime*
> *Jackson (9:34am): I'm outside looking at a fucking koala know it's daytime. Come over.*
> *Evan (9:35am): u sure?*
> *Jackson (9:35am): said it didn't I?*
> *Evan (9:36am): alright c u soon*

Jackson snapped a quick picture of Evan's painting and send it off to Lyle.

> *Jackson (9:38am): on Grant & St. Lawrence tell them 2 cover it 2night*
> *Lyle (9:39am): KKz? A fucking blue koala?*
> *Jackson (9:40am): probably just some kid*

Jackson (9:40am): KKz are pussies but I don't think they rep koalas
Lyle (9:41): prob right lol

He slid his phone back into his pocket, making sure not to delete the picture. By tomorrow the tag would be gone, sprayed over with a black coffin. As stupid as it was, he wanted to keep it because it mattered to Evan, and that mattered to him. Honestly? Jack thought the whole thing was pretty sweet, and that convinced him that he was losing his fucking mind.

It was easier not to think about all the dangerous shit they did, as if keeping it out of his mind would make it so it didn't exist, but he knew he couldn't wish away the truth. If he could he would've erased their whole situation and all the surrounding bullshit, just leaving them; no colors. If a DD would've seen Evan on their corner with a can of blue spray paint and a matching beanie, they would've painted the sidewalk red with his blood.

Jackson had lost plenty of people and had taken even more, but the thought of living his life without Evan was too much to bear.

Unsure when he lost himself, when a random park fuck had taken over his life and changed everything, Jack knew his priorities were different now. He didn't worry as much about the gang, or his loyalty to them. He used to be ride or die Demonz. Every decision he made was based on the greater good of the gang. Now, he only wanted to ride with Evan.

Fuck, he was dying to ride him. He felt himself grow hard at the thought, wondering when he'd stop having such an immediate physical reaction to thoughts of his boyfriend.

He adjusted himself and started on his way to meet his dealer on Halstead, knowing that he could get Evan what he needed. The transaction didn't take long, but by the time he was done the downpour had begun. He kept his head down and pulled his hat down low as he walked the few blocks home. He got back to his apartment building just as Evan was opening the door to the lobby.

They didn't look at each other, eyes facing forward and boots squeaking from the puddles as they made their way over the slick tiled floor to the elevator. Standing several feet apart, they waited for the door to slide open, thin rivulets of water still trickling down onto the floor. Jackson tapped his fingers nervously against the thigh of his wet jeans, silently praying that nobody showed up to ride the elevator with them. As soon as the door slid open then closed behind them, they were on each other, mouths and hands locked together, damp bodies pressed close. Evan tasted like weed and gumdrops, a combination so intoxicating that Jackson was sure he got drunk on his lips.

"I love you," Jack told Evan, pulling away long enough to stare with sincerity into blown-out brown eyes and smiling into the kiss again when Evan leaned in with more hunger, obviously appreciating hearing his sentiment returned.

"Because of the koala?" he whispered with a soft laugh, nuzzling his nose into Jackson's neck.

"In spite of the fucking koala," Jackson replied, with a huff that made Evan laugh harder.

"You loved it," he stated matter-of-factly as he sucked a mark into Jackson's wet skin.

"Love you," Jack repeated, letting himself get swept past the dam they'd broken, washed away with the current. "Fucking love you."

"I love you," Evan assured him, admitting it to both of them once again. "Never loved anyone like I love you."

Evan's earnestness was dizzying and Jackson found himself leaning his body heavy against his lover's, thinking if he didn't he'd lose his balance.

Regretfully, they peeled themselves apart when the elevator opened, the short walk down the hallway to Jackson's apartment feeling like miles; Jack's lips tingled with the desire to reconnect.

"Amy here?" Evan asked as Jackson put his key into the lock and turned it.

"No." He couldn't ignore the fact that his hand was trembling as he turned the knob, everything feeling like too much and not enough at the same time.

He considered giving Evan what Jack had picked up for him, but decided to save it for another time. He dropped his backpack on the ground as he stripped off their clothes, ready to give himself to Evan instead.

Everything.

29

They'd woken up in love for the past several months, but it was different knowing their love was reciprocated by the person for whom they felt so profoundly. The simplest touches were more honeyed, tenderness leaking from fingertips and saturating skin. Words that tumbled from their well-kissed lips were quieter, while their meaning was louder. The pupils of their sleepy eyes were dilated from adoration; their obsession with each other the only source of intoxication. Freckled noses nudged and nuzzled, innocent acts between two men who had spent their lives being anything but.

"I'm so in love with you," Evan admitted, rubbing his palm up the soft skin of Jackson's side, relishing in every dip and curve. Their faces were mere inches apart, heads sharing the pillow as they always did.

"Been telling me that a lot," Jackson replied with a smile. It seemed every other sentiment out of Evan's mouth had been a confession of love, and Jack couldn't get enough.

"Fucking in awe of it," Evan sighed. "Never thought I'd be able to feel this way about somebody. Thought I'd spend my whole life being numb, numbing myself. I don't know..." He paused so he could press his lips against Jackson's, as if his boyfriend's puffy pout dripped the elixir that gave him the strength to continue with his thoughts. "It's weird. Thought I was made wrong or something."

"You were made perfectly," Jackson assured, tracing his fingers up the cuts of Evan's ab muscles. "Every fucking inch of you, inside and out. Perfect."

"You got a fucked-up definition of perfection. Don't think that being into the shit that I'm into makes me perfect," Evan disagreed, clicking his tongue and closing his eyes for a weighty moment. He felt a warm hand cradle his cheek and tilted into the hold. "Wish I was. For you."

X

Jackson sighed, tentative to ask what he wanted to, knowing that it would fuck up the air of the room, bring noise to the stillness and pummel the sweetness. Still, it seemed like as good a time as any to go there since Evan had brought up the topic. He'd been doing that more frequently recently, his demeanor surrounding it vacillating between anger and sadness, sometimes a strange combination of both. "You ever get help?"

Evan's brown eyes held more pain than Jackson had ever seen. "No. I honestly never thought it was a problem. It's always been like running away with my feet planted in the same place, you know? I liked being lost like that."

"And now?"

"Not sure I want to be," Evan said softly. "Makes me feel far away from you." A breathy gasp escaped his mouth as Jackson grabbed his hip and pulled him closer. He wrapped his arms low around Evan's waist as the redhead tucked himself under Jackson's armpits, resting his hands on Jack's shoulders.

"I got some money," Jackson stated, trying to keep his tone even and careful. "If you want to…"

"Stop," Evan ordered firmly, shaking his head as he did. "Not taking your money for this shit. I'll kick it myself."

Jackson gnawed the inside of his cheek, unsure if he should press. Tamara had been his only experience in relationships, and if he'd offered to send her to rehab, she would have hurried to pick out a place in Malibu and had it booked within the hour. He found that this was the only circumstance in which he wished that Evan would've been more like Tammy. "Baby," he began gently, deciding to go for it. "How long have you been hooked? Four or five years?"

"Around six," Evan corrected, cringing at the admission.

"You're not going to be able to do it yourself. You got to get help."

"Don't tell me what I can't do. I'm stubborn as fuck. If I want to do it, I'll do it," Evan snapped, pulling away, and sighing when

Jackson dragged him back and peppered kisses across his collarbone. He could almost taste Evan's racing heartbeat.

"Never said you weren't stubborn," Jackson assured, looking up with a smirk. "Won't ever argue with you about that, man." He attempted to soothe his lover by raking his fingers through wildly red hair as he scooted up to slot their mouths together.

The kiss was purposefully slow as Jackson endeavored to quiet Evan and slow the pounding in his chest. It seemed to work as he fell into the motion, his tongue sliding against Jackson's as his hands traveled up Evan's spine.

Jackson would've forgotten what they'd been talking about, so wrapped up in the emotions of the moment, if it hadn't been for the unexpected warmth that trickled over his lips.

"Sorry," Evan said, his face flushing red as he backed away and climbed out of the bed to shove tissues into his nose. Jackson watched as he wiped the blood off his mouth with the t-shirt he'd discarded on the floor the night before. "Fuck," Evan chided, as he attempted to stop the bleeding. "Sorry."

"Ain't afraid of blood, Goodwyn," Jackson assured him with a shrug. It was rare for Evan to get embarrassed, but it seemed from the red hue remaining on his face and his trembling hands that he was. "Come back here."

"Got to stop this first," he grunted, walking fully into the bathroom and closing the door behind him.

"Tilt your head back," Jackson suggested. "Treat it the same way you do when you get your ass kicked."

"Never get my ass kicked." Evan laughed.

"I kicked your ass," Jack reminded him.

"Fucking let you, bitch," Evan called back. "You were so shook that I rolled with the KKz I gave that shit to you."

"Then you punched me in the fucking face a few hours later. Pussy punch. I didn't even know it was coming and 'bam,' clocked me," Jackson tsked, grinning at Evan when the door opened and he came back into the room.

"That shit was hot as hell and you know it." Evan chuckled. "It turned you on."

"Everything about you turns me on," Jack admitted while Evan got back into bed and crawled on top of him. "Hot motherfucker." He grabbed his boyfriend's ass and kneaded it hard as they kissed.

"You must have it really bad if you don't mind when I bleed on you," the redhead teased as he nipped at Jackson's lip.

"You know I got it really bad."

"I love you." Evan looked deep into Jackson's eyes.

"You're pretty into that shit, aren't you?" Jackson wrapped his hand around the nape of Evan's neck.

"Going to tell you for as long as I feel it."

"How long's that going to be?" Jack asked, thinking it was a strange way to reassure him. Realistically, though he wanted to deny it, he knew there wasn't an endgame for them. They couldn't live their lives sneaking around; eventually they'd get caught.

"Depends, I guess," Evan replied. "We could run away from here and it could be forever, or we can stay and it could be months, years?"

Jackson let out a wry laugh and shook his head. "We can't just pick up and leave. We're in the mix of it. I got eyes on me and I'm sure you got them on you, too. They ain't going to just let us go because we fucking want to. I'm the top producer. Until somebody steps up to fill my shoes, I'm the go-to, and if I fuck off, you better be sure they're going to follow, and it won't be good."

"So then you can produce less, right? Don't pull in so much money and they won't miss you," Evan suggested as if it was an easy concept. Jackson almost felt bad for the dirty look he shot him.

"You're living in some sort of fantasy world, Daywalker. Didn't your brother explain how this shit worked before you got your ass jumped in?"

Evan shrugged. "I'm telling you, I don't think about this kind of stuff. I figure the worst thing that could happen is that I get my ass killed, and what difference does worrying about that make if I'm already fucking dead?"

Jackson sighed and tousled his boyfriend's hair. "Speaking of getting killed, I got something for you to try to stop that shit from happening. Sit up."

Evan did as he was told, draping his legs off the edge of the bed and keeping his eyes fixed on Jackson's ass as he walked toward his dresser. He opened the top drawer and tossed a Glock to Evan.

"Got it from my dealer yesterday after you spent the night fucking around on corners that you don't belong on," Jackson informed, noticing how Evan's eyes went wide as he examined the gun. "You got to be strapped, Evan. I'm not fucking around about this. You know how to shoot it?"

"Of course I know how to fucking shoot it," he replied. He bit his lip and looked up at Jackson, who was still standing over him. "This is a nice gun, Jack. Like really nice and pretty goddamn expensive."

"It's the same one I got."

"How much do I owe you?"

"Shut the fuck up," Jackson grunted, shaking his head.

"I can take care of myself, been doing it my whole life," Evan stated with enough edge in his voice to piss Jackson off. "Don't need a fucking sugar daddy."

"Better that you have a bunch of bitches' credit card numbers?" Jackson raised his eyebrows high. "Like that more than letting your boyfriend take care of you?"

Evan shot his middle finger up and glanced back down at the gun.

"Let me take care of you," Jackson urged, dropping to his knees in front of Evan. Jack slowly took the gun out of Evan's hands and placed it on the bed. The redhead tangled his fingers in Jack's hair and watched as he licked his lips. "I need you to let me take care of you, all right? All I fucking need."

"Why?" Evan sighed when Jackson grasped his semi-hard cock and licked the head to bring it fully to life. "Why do you need that?"

"You're my man. Always want to be down for you," Jack replied as he circled his tongue around Evan's shaft.

"And that includes going down on me, too, then?" the redhead asked with a grin, letting out a soft moan as Jackson began to bob his head.

"Mmmhmm," he hummed, mouth full of cock as he stared up at Evan.

"Going to let you."

Jackson pulled off Evan's cock for long enough to ask, "Let me what?"

"Take care of me. Going to let you take care of me if that's what you need."

Without another word, Jackson made clear he was going to do just that.

30

When the opportunity presented itself for Jackson to see some of Evan's paintings, he took it. For months, he'd told Evan to bring his shit over, but his boyfriend had shrugged off the request, stating that he wasn't about to lug canvases around the South Side. It wasn't that Jackson really cared about art, he didn't, but he cared about Evan. When he'd mentioned a few months ago that he seriously wanted to see his work, Evan had gotten shy, his pale face turning a vibrant pink, which Jackson found endearing.

They seized the moment when Evan's roommates left for a two-day drug run through Indiana and Ohio, knowing that there wasn't likely to be another chance for a while. It was strange to think he'd never seen Evan's place. He had a picture in his mind of what he thought it looked like, but as he stood in his boyfriend's bedroom, he realized he couldn't have been further off.

A single bed was pushed into the corner next to a window with kinked blinds that didn't do anything to stop the daylight from pouring in. The walls were a dingy white and there were splatters of multicolored paint all over the rotting hardwood floors. It smelled vaguely like mold, weed, stale beer, and acrylic, a combination strange enough to make Jackson's stomach turn. Empty baggies were piled on the nightstand and strewn over the bed; a junkie's touch.

Compared to the squalor he grew up in, it wasn't too bad, but he'd chosen to keep his space cleaner, feeling it would stop him from allowing himself to be like his father, as if a mess could make a man a monster.

"It's not much," Evan said, sounding apologetic, "but it's mine."

"It's nice," Jackson lied, grinning back at the smile on his boyfriend's face.

"You're full of shit." The redhead laughed, crouching down so he could slide a few canvases out from under the bed. "Here are some of them," he said as he leaned five paintings against the wall. He pointed to the piece in the middle. "That's my favorite."

Jackson nodded and bit his lip as he looked over the artwork, all featuring him in some degenerated way, each one more disturbing than the next.

Somehow every painting screamed in torture but settled into solace, leaving Jack wondering whose pain was reflected, his or Evan's. It was the first time Jackson had ever truly admired a piece of art, and he felt it in his bones. It was as if Evan had scooped out the marrow and spread it across each canvas. The paintings were as unnerving as they were beautiful—how Evan saw Jack, how Evan saw himself

"You hate them," Evan stated, his tone indicating that he knew he would.

"They're all me," Jack said in a hush.

Evan shook his head in disagreement. "No, they're all me." He sniffed uncomfortably. "My fears I think."

"Afraid of me?" Jackson questioned. "Don't act like it."

"Afraid of what I could do to you," Evan admitted, sitting down on the edge of the bed and pulling a baggie out of his nightstand. Jackson turned away as Evan snorted the cocaine, unable to watch him give in again. Jack's heart cracked with every line his boyfriend cut. He'd never seen a strong man be so weak; a slave to a substance.

"More worried about what you do to yourself than what you do to me," Jackson muttered, studying the paintings again.

"It impacts you though, right? What I do to myself?" Evan asked after he let out the familiar sigh of the last line bumped.

"Rather be destroyed by you than never fucking know you," Jack confessed, feeling the weight of the statement. Maybe Evan had ruined him after all. "You're really talented, Evan."

"At fucking up?" Evan teased wryly, getting up so he could come behind Jackson and drape his arms over his shoulders. Evan pressed a kiss on the back of Jack's head and breathed into his hair.

"At this shit," Jack replied, waving toward the paintings. "Love them."

"I'm more talented at other things," Evan flirted, reaching down and grabbing Jackson by the wrist to flip him around. Evan pushed Jack hard against the wall, cupping the crotch of his pants roughly.

"That right?" Jackson smirked as his boyfriend unzipped Jack's jeans. He kicked off his shoes and shimmied out of his pants while Evan yanked off Jack's shirt, leaving him naked while Evan remained fully clothed.

"This body," Evan crooned, rubbing his hands over every inch of Jackson's torso as he kept his eyes trained on his hard cock. "Want to get dirty? Be my muse?"

"What I gotta do?" Jackson grinned, knowing that whatever it was, he was putty in his lover's hands. Jack wondered how another person could hold that type of power over him, making him happily and dutifully kneel to his will.

"Just gotta take it like I know you can," the redhead stated as he dug his fingers into the fleshy bits of Jackson's ass. "Ready to do that for me?"

"Do I look fucking ready?" he retorted, knocking his dick against the thigh of his boyfriend's sweatpants and lifting his eyebrows. "Bet I feel ready, too. That big dick stretched my ass out good this morning."

Jackson never thought he'd be a morning person, but waking up next to Evan had a hell of an effect on his body. It was barely 9 a.m. and while they'd already banged hard once, he was more than ready to do it again. Everything about Evan was sexy, from the way he looked to his attitude. He had a perfect face and a body to match it. Just being next to him in bed drove Jackson crazy.

"Bend over and show me that hole," Evan directed. "Spread your cheeks, baby, c'mon," he prompted. He leaned down and spit into the gap, and Jackson's muscles contracted at the sensation. "Looks so good. Now, go lean your elbows on the bed, stick that ass in the air, and wait for me."

Jackson obliged, glancing over his shoulder to watch as Evan stripped off his clothes and grabbed two tubes, one paint and the other lube. "Don't get those two tubes confused," Jack warned, smiling at the grin on Evan's face.

"That rhymed," he stated, tossing the lube onto the bed and covering his palm with red paint. He smoothed it up each of his fingers carefully as Jackson narrowed his eyes.

"What are you doing?"

"Don't worry about it," Evan replied with an indulgent hum. "Finger yourself," he ordered, watching as Jackson popped the top of the lube, squeezed some out, and began to dip a digit in and out of his hole. He let out a breathy moan as he did, causing Evan to shake his head. "So fucking sexy, Jack."

Hands that were completely washed in crimson reached around and pressed onto Jackson's hipbones. Hunched over Jackson's back, Evan put his right hand over Jack's heart.

"Line me up," Evan directed, letting out a sigh when Jackson did as he was told. Evan pressed the thick head of his huge cock against Jackson's hole. He pushed back as Evan wiggled his hips, groaning when he bottomed out. He mounted Jackson and settled those paint-wet hands around his neck, squeezing gently so the paint left hand marks on his skin.

"Harder," Jackson rasped, overwhelmed by the desire to be fucked brutally and choked out. "Just don't let my body go limp."

Evan did as he was told. They were alike in a lot of ways: both having addictions to things that fucked them up. Jackson gritted his teeth as Evan drove into him hard, and he was desperate to feel the release he craved; a recharge and reset.

Jackson's body wanted to inch forward with each thrust of Evan's powerful cock, but the strong hands clenched tightly around Jack's neck held him back. The blood drained from his head as his body arched under the weight of Evan's, pleasure pumping through his veins as his mind floated away. He saw flashes of red hair in his peripheral vision; black dots dancing in front of his eyes before everything went dark. Evan's animalistic grunting sounded miles away as Jackson found a space in the quiet, his body trembling as he left it.

Gone.

He came to when he heard gunshots. Three distinct pops, in close succession to one another. His head was pounding as he tried to open his eyes, wondering if he'd dreamt them. If it wasn't for the bed being wet underneath him, he wouldn't have thought they were real.

Sticky puddles of come and sweat adhered the sheets to his thighs, and his body felt empty in a satisfying and alarming way.

"Evan," he croaked, voice as broken as his body felt. He willed himself to stand as the room spun around him, forcing him to the ground. He blinked several times, trying to get his bearings, looking past the open door at the streaks of red spread across the wall of the hallway.

"Evan," he called louder, closing his eyes again, willing his fuzzy brain to focus. When his eyelids lifted, he saw himself in the mirror that hung on the door of Evan's closet, covered in blood.

Maybe he was dead.

"Evan!"

31

Blood. Jackson needed blood to make its way back to his brain and carry with it the oxygen that would make him more coherent. Evan had choked him too hard. He wondered how long he'd been out. Closing his eyes tight, he hoped that when he opened them he would be lying on Evan's bed with his boyfriend on top of him, that there wouldn't be blood splattered across the wall, and that he'd know what the fuck was going on. No such luck. Finding himself in the same position he'd been in prior but now he had more panic pressing against his chest. He rose to his feet and steadied his wobbly legs, letting the worry guide him out of the room.

He passed the dead body in the hallway, sidestepping the busted skull and cursing when he got blood on his foot. He smeared it down the hallway, purposely pushing down his toe to rub it off against the floor, and into the kitchen where his boyfriend was pacing, Glock in his shaky hand, naked body splashed with blood. "The fuck's with you strangling me like that, bitch? You were supposed to stop before I passed out."

"You came like a motherfucker. What the hell are you complaining about?" Evan snapped, shooting Jack an aggravated look. "You see the dead guy in the hallway?"

"Mmmhmm." He nodded nonchalantly as he glanced over his shoulder at the carnage. "Who is it?"

"Jamal," Evan replied solemnly, tilting his head so he could see past Jackson.

"The one with the 'ginger anger' theory?"

"Yeah."

Jackson shrugged. "Kind of ironic, huh?" he smirked as the redhead stared at him completely unamused. "Thought he was on a run. What the fuck happened?" He took the gun from Evan's hands and placed it on the kitchen table before sitting on one of the chairs and pulling his trembling boyfriend onto his lap. "First time?"

"Yeah," he replied, finding that he was short on words and long on worry.

"Pretty decent shot."

Evan glared again but relaxed when Jack gently scratched circles into Evan's back, attempting to soothe his stress. "This doesn't fucking faze you at all?"

"It ain't you," Jackson answered. "And it could've been. So nah, this shit don't faze me." Evan nodded as Jackson tickled up his spine. "You did what you fucking had to." He paused and licked his lips, studying his lover's freckled face. "Going to tell me what went down?"

"Yeah, uh," Evan sighed heavily and rubbed his palm over his forehead, shaking his head as if he was in disbelief of what had occurred. "I squeezed too hard, got too into it I think. You blacked out. Thought you might've had a seizure but you were just coming. It was kinda weird. You were convulsing but like, eerily quiet. I'm used to you whining or whimpering."

"All right, all right." Jackson cringed. "You want to get to the part where you killed the dude or keep chitchatting about shit that don't matter." He knocked the side of his nostril with his knuckle and sniffed uncomfortably, quite done with discussing his partially conscious orgasm.

"I went into the bathroom to wet a few towels so I could clean you up or whatever, wipe off the paint. I was halfway down the hallway when I saw him standing by the doorway, looking at you. It freaked me the fuck out. I was kind of frozen."

"He saw me lying there like that?" Jackson questioned with a grimace. He could only imagine how he must've looked: bent over the bed, fucked out in a puddle of his own jizz with come leaking down the back of his legs. He was glad the fucker was dead. Nobody but Evan should be allowed to live after seeing that shit.

The redhead nodded. "So, he starts walking farther into the room. I think he was going to check if you were dead or something. He said your name. 'Jackson fucking Jablonic,' and let out this crazy laugh like he'd found something out, you know."

"How'd he know my fucking name? Don't know that fucker from shit."

"All the KKz know who you are," Evan replied, waving away Jackson's grin. "He's still talking but I don't know if he's on the phone or, you know, just talking to himself, but he keeps repeating 'They're fucking faggots' and shit like that."

Jackson rolled his tongue up tight between his bottom teeth and the interior of his lip. "And…?"

"Snuck into Kane's room, grabbed his AK, went back into the hallway, and called his name," Evan said, his eyes growing wider as he relived the moment. "As soon as he came out of the room I lit him up. Put three bullets right in his head. Sent him flying back. Done."

"Done," Jackson agreed, reaching up to rake his fingers through Evan's hair. It was hard to think of something to say to empathize with the emotions his boyfriend was experiencing, as he'd been far removed from his own for so long. "I killed my best friend. Sold my coke out from under me. Said it was stolen. Shot him in the head. Didn't think twice about it. Just fucking did it."

Evan's eyes widened, but if there was fear there, it didn't register. "Was it hard for you?"

Jackson shook his head and clicked his tongue. "Harder to distrust people around you than to take them out when they prove they ain't worth it." He paused and lowered his hand to the nape of Evan's neck. "Is it harder to shoot him or wait for him expose you, hmm? Sometimes you got to do the easier thing and not wait for the hard shit to fuck you in the ass."

"You like to get fucked in the ass," Evan reminded with a slight smile.

"You know what I fucking mean," Jackson chided with a grin and an eye roll. "Come here." He pulled Evan toward him, pressing his lips softly against his and kissing him sweetly. Once they peeled their mouths apart, Jack assured, "Everything's going to be all right."

Evan bit his lip and nodded. "What the fuck do I do now?"

"Get in the shower. I'll start taking care of shit out here. You guys got to have bleach," he said, patting Evan's bare ass so he'd stand up to check under the sink. Yup. They had bleach. He held up the jug with a grin. "Call me when you think you got all the blood off and I'll check you and get the tub."

He gestured with his head for Evan to get to it and watched as his boyfriend stepped over the body lying prostrate in the hallway to get to the bathroom. Without wasting another moment, Jackson wrapped a paper towel around his hand and began dumping drawers onto the ground. Once he felt the kitchen looked properly ransacked he made his way into the living room and did the same. After locating the laundry room, he stripped Evan's bed and tossed all his shit into the washer along with detergent and bleach. Moving from room to room, he fucked with everything and collected all the drugs he could find. He was tossing about a pound of weed into Evan's backpack when he heard his boyfriend call from the bathroom.

"Look good," Jack stated as he checked over Evan's body. "Got to rinse yourself with some of this," he said, holding up the bleach.

Evan did as he was told and moved aside so Jackson could join him. When they were done, Jackson scrubbed the basin while Evan looked on.

"It's a shithole out there, had to make it look like a robbery. Took all the drugs in the house. No good thief would leave any of them. Put the bags in your backpack. I'll carry it back to my place and you can have them back," Jackson explained, noticing the concern in Evan's eyes. "Hey, it's going to be fine," he promised. "You're not going to go down for this, all right?"

"Thanks," Evan said sincerely, leaning down to kiss Jackson. "What would I do without you?"

Jackson licked his lips and patted Evan's ass. "Wipe the gun and put it in a duffle, okay? Don't toss it too close by. Take it to a dumpster at least ten blocks away," Jack continued as he put some gel into his hair. "Buy some groceries on your way back so that when you call the cops you can tell them you were out shopping. Got it?"

Evan nodded and then followed Jackson into his now-trashed bedroom. "Got it. When should I call them?"

"Give it about an hour. They're going to search everything, so you may want to mess up your paintings," he suggested gently, knowing it was a fucked-up thing to have to do. He stopped pulling up his jeans so he could look Evan in the eye. "Glad I got to see them."

Evan gave him a half smile and lay back on the bed to finish watching him get dressed. "I love you."

"You got shit to do," Jackson reminded, giving him a kick on the ankle. "Get to work."

"I love you," Evan repeated. He grinned when Jackson climbed on top of him and slotted their mouths together.

"Love you too, Goodwyn," Jack whispered. "Now get the fuck to it and call me when they're gone. You'll stay with me for a while. Say you're sad or some shit."

"I kinda am," Evan admitted.

Jackson stood up and shrugged. "That's okay I guess. Always remember shit could be worse." Evan tapped his fingers on his bare chest as Jackson slung the backpack over his shoulder. "See you soon."

"Can't wait," Evan replied.

Jackson heard him muttering, "Shit could always be worse."

32

Jackson's head was aching as he made his way down the crowded South Side block. The adrenaline blast he'd gotten from the clean-up had waned, leaving him feeling like he'd been strangled by strong hands and pummeled by a nine-inch cock. It probably wasn't the brightest idea to ask Evan to choke him out when he was high as a kite, but goddamn, his man was sexy; bad decisions wrapped in a good time.

Everything about Evan made Jack want to do stupid shit, like make promises he couldn't keep and commit to things he shouldn't. He never realized he was so fucking gay. He knew he was into cock, but he was obsessed with a man, head over heels, heart busting in love.

His knees got weak when he kissed him. He swooned at the sound of Evan's voice. When Jack got lost gazing into Evan's eyes, he never wanted to be found. He lived for the laughter and relished the touches and tickles.

Jackson wanted Evan for life.

Jackson wanted to be tangled up in Evan every night and beside him every day.

Jackson wanted mundane moments and stupid arguments; he wanted it all, way more than he'd ever dreamed of.

He'd never felt so trapped, holed up in circumstances that were beyond his control. Being a Demon had always felt liberating and empowering. He owned the streets with his brash attitude and trigger-happy fingers. He loved the way his gang revered him and others feared him. But now, his affiliation seemed like a life sentence, creating distance from the person he wanted to be nearest to most of all.

He needed Evan closer, especially after what had gone down earlier that morning. As commonplace as it had been for Jack, he knew it would impact his boyfriend. He decided he was going to ask Evan to move in with him, at least for a while, and then never let Evan leave.

They could make it work. Evan was there every night anyway. Jack needed an excuse to get pissed off at Luke so he could tell him not to come over anymore. Jackson sighed, thinking how complicated it was going to be, but it would be worth it. He wanted Evan all the time and the only way for that to happen was to create a safe space.

Maybe he'd leave Amy with the apartment and get another one. He'd keep a bunch of his shit at the old place and move Evan in to the new one. It wouldn't need to be much, just a place where they could be free.

The idea of having their own place where they could walk around naked and fuck as loud as they wanted sent a tingle up his spine. That's what he'd do. He'd have to move some more product, but it would be financially feasible to have both places. Hopefully his boyfriend would be down to take the next step.

He lit up a cigarette as he turned onto Grant, shaking his head at the absurdity of it all. When he'd thrown Tamara out, he'd been so thrilled to have the bed to himself and not need to share his space anymore. It was crazy how Evan had changed everything. Jack had never been able to tell Tammy that he loved her, but with Evan, uttering those words was second nature.

Thinking of spending a lifetime with his ex had been awful, while considering a life without his lover was completely terrifying.

Fuck, he was gay.

He wondered what life would be like for them if they weren't into the shit they were into. Would they have still met? Fallen in love? Maybe they'd be guys who went out for beer and watched the Bears. They'd eat takeout on the couch in their little house in the suburbs while complaining about the percentages of their 401K and interest rates. He'd probably be in finance and Evan would be in sales and they'd be boring as fuck.

There were probably benefits to living a humdrum life, but it would never be theirs. They weren't built like that. They were issues and mayhem twisted up in a crazy fucking love and he wouldn't want it any other way. He'd take a hard life with Evan over easy shit any day.

Still, he knew his boyfriend needed help. Evan had told him a few weeks ago that he intended to kick his habit and, as Jack suspected, hadn't been able to without help. He knew better than to get too involved, push him too hard. He could've reminded him every time Evan blew a line that he'd said he wanted to stop, but it wasn't as if Evan didn't know. The beast had him heavy in its claws and the only way to pry it off was to get some real fucking help.

Jack had to take Evan to rehab, at the least outpatient. As independent as Evan seemed, Jack knew his boyfriend needed to be cared for, held down and loved, shown his ass was worth it. Evan had spent too many years around too many people who hadn't given enough of a shit about him. Jack was intent on loving him enough for all of them.

Selfishly, he knew that caring for Evan like that would heal Jack, too. It was powerful to love someone that intensely, to be connected to another person in such a visceral way. Getting lost in those feelings allowed him to think outside of himself, let someone else in. Just as he'd felt compelled to protect Amy when they were growing up, he'd do the same for Evan, steal him away from his situation and make him safe. Neither of them were saints—far from it—but maybe they'd save each other, sins and all.

As he turned onto St. Lawrence, the pound of weed in his backpack felt heavier at the sight of the three cops and a German Shepherd standing at the entry to the alley beside his apartment.

"Fuck," he muttered, gnawing on the inside of his cheek and dropping his cigarette to the ground so he could stomp it out. He glanced behind him, wondering if he had enough time to bolt in the other direction, but when he heard the deep bark of the police dog, he knew it was too late. He sighed and walked forward.

"Well, well, well, if it isn't our favorite Jablonic," Officer Marks said with a sarcastic grin. "How're you doing on this fine day, Jackson?"

"Was doing pretty good until I saw you fat fucks," he replied, raising his eyebrows as he approached them. "Know some people like the smell of bacon in the morning, but I ain't ever into pork."

"Talking a lot of shit for a guy who's got our Dottie here barking," Officer Green taunted.

Jackson glared at the dog who was snarling angrily at him. "Yeah, well I'm always pissing bitches off." He shrugged and attempted to walk past them, well aware that a pound of weed would get him a year and a half for intent to sell, and Evan's baggie of coke would round him out to a solid two. If he was black or didn't have the money for a lawyer it would be at three to five. America the beautiful.

He felt his heart begin to pound frantically in his chest. Prison never scared him, but doing time away from his addict boyfriend, who was knee deep in gang shit, sure as hell did. All of his daydreams of their own apartment, away from it all, began to drift from his mind as soon as he heard Marks say, "Not so fast, Jack. We're going to have to check that bag of yours."

"Thought you would," Jackson said as he tossed his backpack to the officer. Turning around, he placed his hands behind his back and awaited the cuffs, wondering if Evan would be down for him or if he'd move on to some other guy, stumble onto another life, just when Jack thought they'd be starting theirs.

The metal clasped tightly around his wrists by a disinterested policeman, who was going through the motions while Jackson stood frozen. He needed to get ahold of Evan, tell him what was happening, but he didn't know his number and wouldn't have access to his cell phone. He'd have to go through Amy and have her reach out to him.

For years he'd stepped up for his sister and now he'd expect her to do the same. He knew Evan would resist, but Jack would take care of him through his sister, the best he could.

He couldn't imagine how Evan would take this news while he was reeling from the events of the morning. The timing couldn't be worse, but that seemed to be their lot in life. Jack hoped Evan didn't spin more out of control than he already was—Jack's unpredictable, impetuous tornado of a boyfriend. He squeezed his eyes shut, willing them not to let his emotions leak out.

"You have the right to remain silent. Anything you say can and will be used against you in a court of law. You have the right to an attorney. If you cannot afford an attorney, one will be provided for you. Do you understand the rights I have just read to you? With these rights in mind, do you wish to speak to me?"

"Yeah," Jackson rasped with a wry laugh. "Go fuck yourself."

"Always been such a charmer, Jablonic," Green huffed as he shoved Jackson into the back of the patrol car. "Think I'll let that one slide. Eyes look a little misty and I hate to see a grown thug cry."

Jackson shot up his middle finger and then pressed the heels of his hands against his glassy eyes. For the first time in his life everything had felt so right; he wondered how over the course of two hours it could all go so wrong.

As the car pulled away from the curb and made its way to MCC, Jackson got himself in the prison state of mind, systematically rebuilding his walls and purging his body of its vulnerabilities. He couldn't let even an iota of his demeanor appear soft. He had to be made of stone, which he could be when the man holding the hammer that shattered him was on the outside, and he was going in.

He walked into the prison with his lips pursed tightly, chin tilted up and fists clenched into balls, ready to fuck up anybody who tried to mess with the good time he intended to do so he could get back into his boyfriend's arms.

He ran shit on the streets and he'd do the same in the joint. He needed to come in strong and then fade into the background.

He'd done it all before.

He knew the score.

It was time to get to work.

33

It was awful to see his roommate lying dead on the hallway floor, and it was even more disturbing knowing that he killed him. Sitting on the edge of the bed, Evan stared down at his hands, surprised they were capable of what they'd done. He'd never been soft, but he'd always felt more human and compassionate than he had in that moment. Even though he'd recognized the panic in Jamal's brown eyes, he hadn't hesitated. Maybe he could have worked it out with him, sworn him to secrecy, but he wasn't willing to live his life constantly worried about when the other man would open his mouth to spill his secret. When it came down to it, it was either him or Jamal, and Evan had made his choice.

Still, it was difficult to get his roommate's look of terror out his mind. And the blood…so much fucking blood. It wasn't that he was skeeved out, but really thinking about who it came from made it nauseating. The blood that was splattered all over the hallway had carried oxygen to Jamal's brain and flowed in and out of his heart. It had kept him alive, until Evan had killed him. He decided that the sight of blood was more worrisome when he was the one who had caused it to spill.

He forced himself to stand, knowing that he had a minuscule window of time to do everything that Jackson had told him to do. Before picking the gun up, he crouched over Jamal and pulled his cell phone out of his back pocket, intending to find out if he'd been on the phone with anybody when he was repeating "They're fucking faggots."

Man, Evan hated that word. Just thinking that someone would have the audacity to reference him and Jackson like that had Evan feeling significantly less remorse. His reprieve from guilt was short-lived when he saw that Jamal hadn't called anybody and a string of text messages that seemed to explain why he hadn't gone on the drug run with Kane and Luis.

> *Ma (9:16am): I feel bad you had to cut your trip short for me.*
> *Jamal (9:20am): Quit it. It's not a big deal. Going to grab the papers I printed out from your patient portal at the Clinic & bring them to the hospital. Don't want them redoing tests they already did & charge u more.*
> *Ma (9:23am): Can't afford this stay anyway, son. You know that.*
> *Jamal (9:24am): I got you, mama. Already told u that.*
> *Ma (9:25am): This cancer's too expensive for the both of us. Not worth fighting it. I'm going to bleed you dry and die anyway.*
> *Jamal (9:25am): Told u not to talk that way. I'm going to take care of u. We'll beat this 2gether. Going to grab the papers n come see u in a few.*
> *Ma (9:26am): Love you Jammy*
> *Jamal (9:27am): luv u more ma*

The acrid taste of bile rose up Evan's throat and permeated his mouth, causing him to jump to his feet and run to the bathroom. Hunching over the toilet, he vomited until he had nothing left in his system and then dry heaved some more. It seemed with one murder, he'd killed two people. As he cupped his hands and rinsed out his mouth, he thought back to conversations with Jamal, trying to remember if he'd brought up his mother. He might have once or twice, but Evan had made pretty good practice over the years of blocking out the words "mom" and "dad." They were empty titles to him, but clearly they weren't to Jamal. He was somebody's son. A woman who gave a shit about him would mourn his death, a death that Evan caused. He gave up just filling his mouth with water and splashed his whole face with it instead.

He wanted to curl up in the fetal position with Jackson wrapped around him, telling him that everything would be a'ight. When he told him shit like that, he actually believed it. Jackson had a way of settling him down like nobody else could. Evan needed that reassurance, but he knew he couldn't call him; Jack had too much to do.

Evan started with the worst thing first. Squeezing globs of black and blue paint onto a paper plate, he dunked his brush into them, letting it get saturated as he leaned all of his paintings up against the baseboards. After taking one last glance at his hard work, he smeared the paint over them, one by one, obscuring the subject in each. As much as he loved the smell of acrylic, he found himself repulsed by it when it was used to ruin pieces he felt so deeply about. At least he had the real thing to stare at until he could paint him again.

The scent of bleach wasn't much better than the acrylic. Painstakingly, he wiped down Jamal's phone and then the AK-47 before tucking it into a duffel bag. He zipped up his jacket, threw on a beanie, and headed out into the brisk September day.

The weather was perfect and he would've been able to enjoy it more if he wasn't walking to a dumpster to toss the gun he used to kill his roommate, who was still lying in a puddle of his own blood. It seemed that murder was a great way to ruin a nice day.

Evan dumped the gun in the dumpster a few blocks away from the grocery store Jackson told him to stop at. Evan decided to take a moment to smoke a cigarette outside the entrance. He wasn't in a rush to go in and buy a bunch of food he wouldn't be able to stomach. What he really had a craving for was coke. He wished Jackson hadn't taken all the drugs. If there was any time he wanted to get high as hell, it was now. It was probably better this way; no doubt part of the reason Jack took them to begin with. Evan knew that he couldn't talk to the cops fucked out of his mind, but damn he needed something. Drugs or sex. Sex and drugs. Drugs and Jackson. Jackson. He needed Jackson. He pulled his cell phone out of his pocket and opened his texts.

> *Evan (10:35am): Want u baby*
> *Evan (10:35am): need u riding my cock right now*
> *Evan (10:36am): fuck my stress away*
> *Evan (10:37am): want to kiss u 2 not just fucking*
> *Evan (10:37am): never just fucking with u*
> *Evan (10:39am): going to be over soon*
> *Evan (10:39am): even tho ur ignoring me*

Evan (10:40am): ily koala

He sighed at the lack of response and put his phone away. He decided to get a few of Jackson's favorite things in the store: two containers of Pringles, a few Twix bars, and some Gatorade. If his boyfriend was pissed for choking him too hard earlier, he'd surely soften once he saw Evan came bearing artificially flavored gifts.

Though he considered taking the long way home to avoid calling the cops, he knew that the sooner he got it over with, the quicker he'd be able to see his man. Before opening the front door, he threw a brick through one of the windows, figuring if they were making it look like a robbery they should probably go all the way. He waited until he'd been home for a few minutes to call 9-1-1, unsurprised when it took them a half hour to get there.

Shootings in the hood weren't top priority.

Once the cops got there, it wasn't difficult to channel some level of panic. When he really stopped to think about what had happened, stress wasn't a stretch. They asked him tons of questions, but he had answers for all of them. He'd spent his whole life lying to the police; doing it was second nature. He could tell by the way they were going through the motions that they weren't pressed by the case. Gangbangers ending up dead wasn't much of a loss to them. He'd be surprised if they even followed up. It wasn't lost on him that the best way to get away with murder in America was to be a white man standing over a black body.

The whole process was over before he'd felt like it had even begun. Questions gave way to nods, then hums and blank stares. He almost wished they would've grilled him more, at least pretended that Jamal's life mattered, which, Evan realized, was an ironic thought considering he took it.

With his head still spinning, he left the house to make his way to Jackson's apartment. All his anxiety began to wane as he rode the elevator up to his safe space; a haven he could wrap his arms around, a shelter that would tell him everything would be a'ight. He knew something was wrong as soon Amy answered the door. Her face was ashen and drained.

"Jackson was arrested," she informed Evan as she locked the door behind them.

"For murder?" he squawked, barely recognizing the tone of his voice.

"What?" She narrowed her eyes, shook her head, and let out a sputtering sigh. "You know what…I don't even want to know, do I?"

"Probably not," he relented, biting his lower lip. "What then?"

"Drugs. He thinks they have him on intent. Probably going to have to serve two," she said, wiping a tear off her cheek.

"Years?"

She nodded.

Drugs. His drugs. Once again, drugs had found a way to fuck up not only his life, but the lives of people around them. He wished he hated them as much as he should have. When tears began to stream from his eyes, he wondered if he was truly crying. He couldn't remember the last time he had. He'd probably had reasons to but none had ever felt as devastating as this.

Amy placed her hand on his shoulder and though he was quick to shrug it off, she put it right back where it had been. Without any further protest, he allowed her to pull in for a hug and hold him while he cried. It was as though twenty-one years of pain had found a way to flood out of him right there in his boyfriend's living room.

He had so much to cry about he was concerned that now he'd started, he'd never be able to stop.

Through all the tears, Amy held him tight, and though she didn't grasp on to him like a koala, she did a'ight.

34

Evan woke up in the same place, both physically and mentally, he'd woken up in for the last week. Being wrapped in Jackson's blankets while wearing his clothes kept Evan ensconced in Jack's scent and made Evan feel safe, at least until he realized that he was again lying in his boyfriend's king-size bed all by himself. He let out a labored sigh and closed his eyes, trying to remember what it felt like to be tangled up in Jackson. Their limbs were like strings intertwined through every crook and nook. Mouths rested against skin, always needing to be connected.

Evan ran his thumb over his lower lip and remembered how it vibrated slightly when he pressed it against his lover's pulse points, feeling the life move through him, becoming alive himself. Sighing, he sat up and rubbed his eyes, hoping, as always, that he'd somehow erase reality, and when he opened them again, Jackson would be by his side. Realizing he had no such luck, Evan reached for his bowl and packed it full of weed, glad that at least altering his mind helped him cope a bit more. He took a long hit off the pipe, letting the weed burn his lungs and then his brain, dulling the pain and the memories.

Glancing at his phone, he sighed when he saw that it was noon. He needed to get back to his place and show his face. He'd been avoiding Kane for too long, and if the slew of aggravated texts were anything to go by, his brother was beginning to get suspicious. Jamal had been more like a brother to Kane than Evan had ever been, and Kane was reeling from Jamal's murder. The thought of facing Kane's grief, knowing he was the one who caused it, was too much of a mindfuck to deal with when he was attempting to cope with his boyfriend's incarceration. So he did what he did best: avoided the situation by pretending he didn't exist. He wished he could do the same with Jackson, but he loved him too much.

The knock at the door startled him at first, but excited him when he considered what it meant.

"Come in," he called, giving Amy a half grin when she opened the door.

"Wake and bake, huh?" she questioned, raising her eyebrows skeptically, like Jackson did.

Evan shrugged.

"Brought you a donut for breakfast, lunch, or whatever you call it when you sleep so goddamn late," Amy teased lightly. "He's going to call in ten."

He scrambled to his feet, knowing the best part of his day was moments away.

"Still too small on you," Amy remarked with a shake of her head as she regarded too much of Evan's lanky legs showing in her brother's boxers.

He didn't respond, deciding instead to walk into the kitchen and shove the breakfast pastry into his mouth. When Amy's phone rang, he tried to grab it out of her hand, but a swift elbow to his ribs had him retreating and following her into the living room like a lost puppy dog.

"I'll accept," she stated, sitting down on the couch and glaring at Evan, who plopped himself down too close to her with hopes of hearing his boyfriend's voice sooner rather than later. "Hey, Jack." She paused. "Everything's all right. Just chilling on the sofa with my new roomie." She let out a sarcastic scoff. "Done with me already? Should I be insulted?" She handed the phone to Evan. "It's for you."

Evan took the phone from her hand and lay back against the armrest, immediately curling up into a protective ball. "Jack."

"Hey."

"I miss you," Evan admitted softy, as if Amy hadn't heard him utter the same sentiment at least twenty times by now.

"I miss you too, baby," he replied in a voice so low it was obvious he had other inmates on the pay phones beside him. "I'm glad you're still staying with Amy."

"Got to go back to my house at some point," Evan stated. "Just don't want to face them." He glanced at Amy and turned his head away to whisper, "And I like being in your bed. Smells like you."

"Fuck," Jackson mumbled with a sigh. "Wish I was there. Want to…" He paused and cleared his throat as if he was swallowing the words.

"Want to what?" Evan pressed, standing up and moving to the chair like the extra few feet would make it more difficult for Amy to hear. She was busying herself picking lint off her shirt, but stealthily listening to every word.

"Feel you," he confessed. "Fuck, I want to feel you." He clicked his tongue. "So empty without you."

Evan wiped the tears that were falling rapidly off his cheeks. He wondered if he'd cried this much when he was a baby; had anybody noticed then? Because Amy definitely noticed, tossing him a box of tissues.

"You cry too much," Jackson chided without malice. "Never thought you were a fucking crier."

"Yeah, well, I never gave a shit enough to cry about anything I guess. Seems like I give a shit about you."

"Seems like you do," Jackson agreed. Evan could hear the smile in his tone. "It's good 'cause I do, too."

"Did you talk to your lawyer? Any more news about your sentence?"

"Got my hearing tomorrow and Hank told me the sentencing will most likely be on Thursday."

"I want to be there," Evan stated, earning him a shake of the head from Amy and a soft "Know you can't come" from Jackson. "You're telling me it could be two fucking years, Jack, and you're not going to let me show up?" he cried. "Come the fuck on."

"Ain't safe, all right?" he snapped in a harsh whisper. "Don't stop being affiliated in prison. Got a set in here." His voice got impossibly lower. "Some of your boys, too."

"So that's it then? Not going to even get to lay my eyes on you?" The outburst earned him a warning from Amy and an annoyed "Don't make it more difficult for him."

"It's been a week, Goodwyn. Pull it the fuck together," Jackson groused. "Going to have, like, one hundred and three more. Can't do this every time I talk to you."

"I can't fucking take it."

"Ain't going to blame you if you don't wait for me, but I fucking hope you will," Jackson stated, tone even again. "I love you."

"I..." Evan let out of a sputtering sigh, "love you too. Just wish you'd let me visit. I don't even have my..." he squeezed his eyes shut, "paintings. Miss your fucking face."

"Fucking my face?" Jackson questioned with a laugh.

"That too," he admitted. "Got the prettiest fucking mouth. Miss those lips, such full lips."

"Holy shit," Amy exclaimed, jumping up from the couch and throwing her hands up. "That's my brother's 'pretty' mouth.'"

"Your sister doesn't like when I compliment you," Evan deadpanned, causing Amy to give him the finger.

"I do. Go in the other room," Jack said quietly. "Got another two minutes."

Evan hurried into his boyfriend's bedroom, slammed the door shut behind him, and lay down on the bed, palming his dick over Jackson's boxers. "Wake up rock-hard for you every morning."

"That right?"

"Mmmhmm," Evan confirmed. "Got me touching myself all the time. Thinking of you."

"Better fucking be."

"Only you," Evan promised. "Think of you sleeping face down on the bed, that thick ass uncovered by the sheets. You're still nice and stretched from all the fucking that knocked you out. I crawl on top of you and slide my big dick in. You're so warm. So perfect around me."

"Sounds good."

"Love burying my face in your neck, whispering shit in your ear."

"What kinda shit?" Jackson asked, sounding strained.

"How you're such a good boy for me, take my cock so nice. How I love you, never loved anybody the way I love you. Can't wait to fuck you for the rest of our lives."

"Our lives, huh?"

"Yeah." Evan felt his face flush at the admission. "You got a problem with that?"

"Not at all," Jackson replied earnestly. "Don't got a problem with that at all."

They sat in silence, just listening to the breathing between them; so far away, but still feeling the closeness.

"So you'll wait for me?" Jackson asked, breaking the silence. "Sounds like you're going to wait."

"Of course I will," Evan assured him. "You're the love of my life, man. The fuck can I do?" There had to be something he could do, he just wasn't sure what it was yet.

"Goddamn, I love you," Jackson muttered, the pain evident in his voice.

"So hearing tomorrow? Sentencing Thursday? Then we'll know how long you're in for."

"Yup."

"Thursday."

"That's what they tell me," Jack replied. "I got to go. Some fat fuck named Skank is pounding his fists." He paused so he could huff at the man waiting for the phone, "Yeah, hold the fuck on, you tubby tank of shit." He lowered his voice again. "I'll call around the same time tomorrow. Amy's phone, okay?"

"Yeah, okay," Evan said with a sniffle. "I love you."

"I love you too."

Evan hung up and walked the phone back to Amy, who took it between her fingers like it was contaminated. "You better not have spooged on it."

Evan rolled his eyes and laughed. "All clear."

"Good." She looked at him expectantly. "It's hard, right?"

"Not easy."

"I think you guys will make it work though. Two years isn't too bad."

"It's going to feel like thirty, but we'll be a'ight." He sighed and shook his head. "I got to go back to my house for a while. May stay over there tonight."

"You got a key now, so come over whenever," Amy offered. "Not going to bring anyone around."

"Thanks," he said before going back into Jackson's room and getting dressed. "Hey, Amy," he called as he zipped up his jacket. "Let me get your cell number."

She leaned against the doorway and caught the phone Evan tossed to her. "Here you go," she said once she'd typed it in. "Make sure you eat something other than the donut today, okay?"

He grinned at her and tousled up her hair as he passed by and headed out the door. As he walked back to his house, he looked at her number and repeated it aloud to himself, trying to commit it to memory.

He knew he'd be using it soon.

35

Almost dusk, which meant about go time. Evan tossed his supplies into his backpack and took one last look at his bedroom. Having his own space had seemed like a dream at first, but now it felt like a prison, a representation of a decision he made that would keep a distance between him and the man he loved. His canvases were still leaning against the wall, covered in moody colors that obstructed everything beautiful about them.

There was nothing left for him there.

Ever since he left home, he'd never stayed in one place too long and though it was not necessarily by choice, he'd grown accustomed to it. He wasn't as apprehensive of change as he was of standing still, but he guessed he was going to have to get used to that too.

He looked in the mirror and wondered if the shit that people had always said about him was true. Maybe he was crazy, impulsive, impetuous, and inconsiderate. He'd decided that he'd rather be every one of those things than nothing at all. He'd never be like *them*: so focused on clawing their way up ladder, trying to prove that they were worthy of things that were never really worthy of them to begin with.

Emma once told him that he saw things too small, never was able to look at the grand scheme of things, but she was wrong. He saw it better than any of them did. They were running in the rat race, while he was living, breathing, loving. He planned to do more of that. When it came down to it, his crazy, impulsive, impetuous, inconsiderate ass had found what people spent a lifetime looking for. As they were moving along on their humdrum path, ready to settle for a thrill-free existence, he had found his forever.

Kane had always been more like Evan than the rest of the family. Perhaps if he would've put more time into fostering a bond with his brother, things between them could have been different. The fact that he even reflected on it, and had wanted them to be, was a testament to how much he really did care for his brother. It was too late now to change things. If things went as he planned, he'd never see any of them again. He decided that rather than dwell on how uncomfortable that thought was, he'd be thankful for the time they'd spent together in the KKz.

"You got that look in your eyes," Kane commented when Evan walked into the kitchen.

"What look?" Evan questioned, glancing at his brother and Luis, who were eating their dinner at the table. It was strange to see them sitting there without Jamal. It had always been the three of them. Until it wasn't.

"You know what I'm talking about," Kane replied. "That crazy fucking look that tells me you're about to do something asinine."

"Asinine, huh?" Evan asked, raising his eyebrows and smirking. "I'd use the term inspired instead."

"Fuck." His brother groaned, shaking his head. He turned to Luis. "See, I told you he's been too quiet. Silence is the enemy of sanity."

"When did you become a philosopher?" Evan asked, pulling one of Luis's burritos out of the freezer and popping it in the microwave. He was going to miss those badass burritos.

"Think it started when our friend got murdered," Luis stated. "You remember him? Didn't make it to his funeral yesterday."

"Told you not to expect much from him," Kane reminded Luis with a click of his tongue. "Evan doesn't do obligations and he sure as shit doesn't do feelings."

Evan wanted to correct him, to tell him that feeling was all he'd been doing lately, that he was a gaping wound of bleeding, stinging feelings. As much as he should've hated the vulnerability and pain of it all, he didn't, because all those feeling were because of Jackson, were for Jackson. So instead of protesting his brother's incorrect assessment, he shrugged.

"But you got a girl, right?" Luis pressed. Evan could feel the discontent radiating off the otherwise affable man.

"Something like that," Evan confirmed, taking a bite of his burrito. He caught Kane shaking his head disapprovingly out of the corner of his eye. He knew that if it was up to Kane he would have a full-blown cover story; a fantasy heterosexual life to share. He didn't have the energy.

"There all the time so it's probably serious, yeah?"

"You could say that," Evan replied with a nod.

"You tell her you love her? Able to go there?"

"All the fucking time," Evan stated emphatically, taking both of the guys at the table by surprise.

"Really?" Kane asked skeptically. He looked at his brother like he'd been abducted by aliens and dropped back down to Earth as a pod person.

"Mmmhmm," he hummed, balling the wax paper in his fist and tossing it into the trash. "I got to go." Evan turned to Kane and licked his lips tentatively. "Don't know if I'll be back for a while."

Kane lifted his eyebrows in surprise but let them fall. Evan figured his brother realized that it had only been a matter of time until this happened. "You know the KKz aren't like Goodwyns, man. You disappear for too long and they're going to come looking for you."

Luis shifted uncomfortably in his chair. Gang loyalty ran deep with Luis.

"Know I've always been good at disappearing," Evan said with a weak smile. "I'll make them forget me the same way I make everyone else. Just got to stay gone for long enough to let it happen." He approached his brother and extended his hand, slightly taken aback when Kane stood up and hugged him hard.

"Never stayed away long enough for me," he whispered as Evan hugged him back.

"Will this time," Evan assured him, patting Kane's back before they parted.

Evan nodded at Luis, slung his backpack over his shoulder, and headed out into the chilly evening. He lit up a cigarette and let it hang between his lips as he walked toward his destination.

As soon as Amy told him that Jackson was sentenced to twenty-six months, Evan knew what he was going to do. Thanks to public records it was easy to get the name, badge, and vehicle number of the arresting officer via the computers at the library. He also familiarized himself with Class 4 felonies, and what kind of time was likely for those who committed them.

Even though he had more than he'd ever had before, he felt like it had been torn away when Jackson was arrested. He realized that though he'd always lived his life like he had nothing left to lose, there was something empowering about fighting to keep something he'd gained.

Before he approached the station, he pulled a baggie of cocaine out of his pocket. His last. He wanted to get clean and though being cut off cold turkey wasn't going to be pleasant, it would be effective. He'd been off the shit in the past when he hadn't gotten his hands on enough money or men to get it. It was what it was and he'd be a'ight. He'd have to be.

A little less than a gram was going to have him soaring and was no doubt enough to keep him fucked up through intake. Dropping his cigarette on the ground, he inhaled the powder in two fat scoops, savoring the way it rushed to his head and sent tingles up his spine.

He tossed the empty Ziploc in the trash and grabbed a can of black spray paint out of his bag. Making sure to shake it up as best he could with numb hands, he approached the police car. He couldn't help but laugh as he sprayed the "G-R-E-E-N" on the window. By the time he'd finished his message, he was practically howling and had, consequently, attracted the attention of a group of officers exiting the station.

"Somebody get Officer Green out here," one of the policemen barked as he ran toward Evan. "Fucked his wife, huh?"

A wild grin spread across Evan's face. "Stretched her out real good for him," he replied, grunting as the other man slammed him against his handiwork.

"Hey, Ben," the officer called to his partner as he came running toward the car. "This junkie motherfucker wanted you to know something." He yanked Evan back by the wrists so Officer Green could see the full message.

"Green I fucked your wife," he read aloud with a smirk. Officer Green regarded Evan, whose eyes were blurry, and he was fervently licking his lips. "Don't think Darlene's into cokeheads," Green scoffed with a wry laugh. "The squirting cock was a nice touch though, I have to say."

"Wanted to show you what a big dick looks like," Evan stated with as much of a shrug as he could muster while being restrained.

"When your bitch was riding mine, she couldn't get over how fucking huge it was."

"Okay, enough," the officer holding Evan said, attempting to silence him. "You going to take this one, Ben, or do you want me to?"

"This prick is worth the paperwork. It's going to be my pleasure," Officer Green stated, getting his cuffs out.

"Same shit Darlene said when she was devouring my dick," Evan taunted, laughing as Green threw his chest against the car hard and put the cuffs around his wrists too tightly. "You fucked with mine and I fucked with yours. Turnabout's fair game, motherfucker."

"Is that right?" the officer questioned, clearly becoming perturbed by Evan's continued assertion.

"That's right," Evan confirmed, groaning when Green pulled him back only to crash him into the car again.

"Ben, read him his rights," Green's friend prompted.

"You have the right to remain silent. Anything you say can and will be used against you in a court of law. You have the right to an attorney. If you cannot afford an attorney, one will be provided for you. Do you understand the rights I have just read to you? With these rights in mind, do you wish to speak to me?"

"Nah, man. Would rather talk to Darlene while she's riding my meat," Evan laughed. "All the shit she likes, 'That's right, baby.' 'Get it, Dar.' Enjoy the fuck out of that."

"You're going to enjoy the fuck out of prison," Green said through clenched teeth.

Evan knew he wouldn't enjoy it, but it would sure as hell be better than not seeing his boyfriend for two years.

He couldn't wait to see Jackson's face.

36

Wednesday

Jackson cringed as he received a scooped lump of some unidentifiable vegetables onto his tray, knowing that he was going to trash them along with the rest of the shit they gave him for lunch. He was intent on living off Ramen noodles for the entirety of his sentence. Twenty-six months. He was going to have to do twenty-six months. At least five times a day the reality of his circumstance hit him like a truck. Twenty-six months would feel like a fucking lifetime without Evan. If Jack were still with Tamara, he would've looked at the time as a vacation, but it certainly didn't feel that way with the redhead on the outside. The last two days had been especially brutal. Evan wasn't there when Jackson had called Amy. He tried to stop his mind from drifting to the dark place it felt so compelled to go to: thoughts of Evan moving on while Jack stood still. Forty-eight hours without hearing Evan's voice had been dismal. It was awful to imagine how painful it would be if he never heard Evan say he loved him again, that he missed him.

Jackson shook his head, trying to knock away the trespassing worry. His melancholy, uninvited thoughts were interrupted by the loudest guard in MCC, Big John, calling to the pimple-faced inmate in charge of the kitchen, from what seemed to be two inches behind him.

"Yo, Grady. Got a live one for you here. He's going to start tomorrow."

"He don't look alive," Grady said with a disgusted look on his face. "You sure he's healthy enough to work the line? Ain't going to give all the guys Hep C or something?"

"Nah. He's good. Dude was so high at intake that the guys said he was practically pissing cocaine," Big John boomed with a raucous laugh. "Just coming off a bender, isn't that right, Goodwyn?"

Jackson swung around so quickly that he almost snapped his neck. Wide-eyed, he watched as his boyfriend nodded. Evan was so out of it that it seemed to take his brain a moment to process that Jackson was standing right in front of him. When he did, his bloodshot eyes lit up and a small smile curled up the edges of his chapped lips. Evan looked paler with dark circles below his lash lines. In the worst shape Jackson had ever seen him

"Fuck," Jackson muttered, turning around to stare at the mystery meat in a chafing dish rather than the redhead. He tried to gain control over his spinning head, pounding heart, and the overwhelming desire he had to hold his boyfriend, kiss him, punch him, and fuck him. "What the fuck?" he mumbled.

"Huh?" the inmate behind the line questioned, startling Jackson, who was already on edge and hadn't realized he'd spoken aloud.

"I said what the fuck is that?" Jackson replied brashly, gesturing toward the meat and raising his eyebrows. "Bet you don't even fucking know."

"I just serve it, man," the inmate behind the counter said with a shrug, his tone vaguely apologetic.

"This is what you're going to have to deal with, Goodwyn," Grady informed Evan, who Jackson still refused to look at. "Pissy inmates who give us crap even though we don't got any more control over shit than they do."

"Can't wait."

Jackson could hear the playfulness in Evan's tone buried deep under exhaustion and irritability. Jackson did his best to walk on wobbly legs over to the table where the rest of the DDz were sitting.

From a safe distance, he allowed himself to glance at Evan, who was now sitting at the end of a table with his face in his hands. Though Jack could still see the outline of Evan's arm muscles through the thin orange fabric of the prison-issued jumpsuit, his body looked weak, as if his mental state had caused the physical to wane. Jack sighed at the sight of his lover.

Withdrawing from the amount of coke Evan had grown accustomed to would no doubt be brutal. Jackson wished he could help him through it: calm him during Evan's bouts of paranoia, hold him through the depression, soothe his anxiety, and make him food to abate the insatiable hunger. Instead Jackson had to watch Evan suffer, unable to do anything to make it more bearable. Being away from him was awful, but having him suffer right in front of Jackson felt like torture.

"You going to eat your meatloaf, Jack? Don't look like you're going to," Cecil commented, his fork already making its way over to Jackson's plate.

"That what this shit's supposed to be?" Jackson groused, tearing his attention away from Evan and pushing his whole tray in front of Cecil. "Ain't hungry."

"Awesome. Thanks, man."

Jackson nodded and feigned interest in the conversation the DDz were having while periodically looking at Evan, who had his arms crossed on the table and his forehead resting on them. Jack wondered what the fuck Evan had done, and more importantly why he'd done it. For a moment, Jackson permitted himself to question if his boyfriend had gotten himself purposely incarcerated, but there was no way anybody would choose to go to prison unless they were a lunatic or an idiot, and he was pretty sure Evan was neither.

As he and his boys were standing up to leave the cafeteria, he saw two prison queens approaching Evan. He couldn't hear what they said, but he knew the gist of it. He watched as Evan shook his head. One of the guys placed his hand on the crook of Evan's elbow, causing the redhead to rise to his feet defensively.

"Touch me again and I'll knock the fucking faggot out of you," Evan growled, prompting the guys to throw their hands up in surrender and retreat.

Jackson shook his head as he tried to hold back his grin. It was easy to forget that Evan was a hard-ass when he was so sweet and loving toward Jackson. He cleared his throat and followed the other guys out of the room while adjusting the hard bulge in his boxers.

Even though the food was horrible, he was suddenly looking forward to breakfast the next day.

X

Thursday

"What's with the fucking carrot top?" Jackson asked Cecil as they stood in the breakfast line. "Looks like he's got AIDS or some shit. Don't need that motherfucker infecting my oatmeal." He sniffed uncomfortably, trying to seem uninterested as he pressed his friend for information. "You hear anything about him over in D?"

"Yeah. We got him in D block. He rolls with the KKz. Guess he ain't in that deep with them. Supposedly none of the guys in here know who he is and they aren't crazy about having his back 'cause he's a coke fiend with a shitty attitude and a bad temper," Cecil explained.

"Ah, fucking KKz rat. Should've known," Jackson replied, watching as his boyfriend handed apples to the guys a few spots ahead of them. "They say…uh…what he's in for? Probably a drug charge or some shit if he's a junkie."

"Nah. Guess he got mad lit and tagged up an officer's car right in front of the station. Wrote some crazy shit like he fucked his wife or something. Like I said, dude's got a temper."

Jackson nodded. He knew all about that temper. He also knew that no matter how fucked up Evan got, he wouldn't be stupid enough to mess with a cop car unless he wanted to get caught. Jackson gritted his teeth at the realization that his boyfriend was in fact an idiotic lunatic who got his ass intentionally tossed into prison. Jackson's jaw was clenched tight when he reached Evan. The redhead stared straight in Jack's eyes as he handed him an apple. Jackson took it, unable to stop himself from shaking his head in irritation. "Dropping sheets off to every cot in C and D today starting at ten," he stated in Cecil's direction.

His friend gave him a confused look. "You do the same thing every Thursday, Jack."

"Just reminding you that I ain't going to be able to play ball today," Jackson informed, making sure he locked into Evan's gaze for a moment to ensure he got the message. From the small grin on his lips, yeah, he understood.

"Got it," Cecil confirmed. "We'll have to survive without your air balls."

Evan chuckled at the comment, causing both Jackson and Cecil to shoot him dirty looks.

"The fuck is you laughing at?" Jackson snapped, glaring at his boyfriend.

The redhead shrugged, clearly unaffected by the brashness of his tone. "You're kinda flat footed so it's not that surprising that you suck ass at basketball."

"You better watch your fucking mouth," Cecil warned as Jackson gnawed on the inside of his cheek, doing everything in his power to not slug that gorgeous freckled face. "KKz trash," Cecil snarled and gestured for Jackson to leave it and follow him to their table.

If Jackson hadn't been looking for it, he would've missed the wink he got from Evan. The simplest action caused a butterfly reaction in Jack's stomach. They fluttered and flitted inside him for hours as he did his job, going from cell to cell dropping off new linens for the inmates' cots and collecting the old ones. He felt particularly excited as he made his way to D block, knowing that one of the rooms would be Evan's. Though the redhead seemed out of it, Jackson hoped he'd comprehended that he should stay in his cell that morning.

The butterflies took flight as soon as he opened the door to D-48 and saw Evan lying on the bed. He looked tired and weak but that didn't stop him from jumping up as soon as he laid eyes on Jackson. He dropped the clean sheets in Evan's hands as Jack's body was slammed against the wall. The kiss was desperate and full of love; bodies connected from lips to hips as hands grabbed, grasped, needed.

"I love you." Evan exhaled the words into Jackson's mouth while taking his lower lip between crooked teeth and tugging gently. "So much."

Jack hummed in response, tangling his tongue with Evan's while pulling him impossibly closer. They melted into each other until reality ripped them apart. "We can't." Jackson panted, pushing Evan away. "You did this shit on purpose, didn't you? Got popped intentionally."

The redhead licked his lips and nodded.

"You're fucking crazy, you know that?" Jackson exclaimed with a wry laugh.

"About you. I'm crazy about you!"

"This ain't going to work here, Evan." Jack rubbed his forehead and sighed.

"It already did. Knew if I got a class four they'd throw me in here. Saw you three times so far. Going to get to look at you at least another two thousand one hundred and ninety. Three meals a day for two years. From zero to two thousand one hundred and ninety…I already did." He looked at Jack earnestly, Evan's face open and free of regret.

Jackson raked his fingers through Evan's hair and pulled him back down so he could slot their lips together. He may have been an idiotic lunatic, but he was Jackson's idiotic lunatic and he was insanely in love with him.

"Another one hundred and four for this shit. I do it once a week," Jackson said, staring into Evan's dilated pupils, knowing that they were blown out by love rather than drugs. Jack smiled back at the redhead's wide grin. "I love you."

"I love you," Evan stated sincerely. He stripped his bed and dumped the sheets into Jackson's bin so he could hand Evan his new ones.

"Proved that shit," Jack said with a smirk as he rolled his cart away and headed down the hallway. Two thousand two hundred ninety-four opportunities to see that beautiful man had Jack thinking he would've done the same fucking thing.

37

November

It had been three weeks since Evan had showed up at MCC and Jackson had to admit, time was moving more quickly. There was much to be said for having something to look forward to. He woke up every morning knowing that he would see his boyfriend in the cafeteria. Though they rarely spoke, they were still able to communicate via stares that lasted a few beats too long or stolen touches when Evan handed off food. Jackson never thought that the simple feeling of fingers brushing against one another would be able to make his whole body tingle with excitement. He always wanted more, but whenever he got aggravated by the distance between them, he reminded himself that every single one of their interactions was a moment that never would have occurred if Evan hadn't changed their circumstances.

There were benefits to talking on the phone, namely being able to actually speak, but there was nothing that could compare to being able to see each other day in and day out, living their lives together instead of ending a call and existing separately until the phone rang again.

Prior to their incarceration, they'd shared a bed nightly and Jackson found that he still missed his boyfriend throughout the day. He wondered if any amount of time with Evan would ever be enough or if he would always crave more minutes, months, years. His life was divided into two different schools of thought: the way he saw things before Evan and the way he saw things after.

Before Evan, Jackson had never allowed himself to think much of the future. It didn't make sense to plan for the days ahead when it took eight hundred sixty milliseconds for a bullet to leave the chamber and go through his head. After Evan, Jack was considering two years in the future and beyond—the span of his life and how he needed Evan in the full length of it.

Jackson placed his tray on the counter and moved it along the line, keeping his eyes trained on Evan. Every week he seemed to look healthier, with the color coming back to his cheeks and the strength returning to his body. There had been days when it was difficult for Jackson to look at Evan even though he was Jack's favorite sight. He couldn't handle the sick green hue of Evan's skin or the way his hands shook when he served the food. Just as the drugs had ravaged his mind when he was on them, they wreaked havoc on his body when he was off. Jackson hoped the pain and discomfort during withdrawal had solidified Evan's commitment to stay clean, but Jack knew that it was rarely the case for addicts. It would be a lifelong struggle for Evan, one that Jackson was prepared to support him through.

"Oatmeal?" Evan asked, holding out a bowl of lumpy oats to Jackson, who screwed up his face and grunted at the offering. "It's extra thick," the redhead stated, amusement dancing in his eyes.

"Fuck off," Jackson scoffed, holding back the smile that was threatening to pull up his lips. "Fucking weirdo."

He walked over to his table and glanced back at Evan, who was laughing as he ladled out hot cereal for the rest of the line.

He looked happy.

X

February

Evan wasn't sure why it had taken him so long to think of the most obvious way to communicate with his boyfriend. Maybe his brain had become so used to being flooded with drugs that he didn't function as well when he was off them. Perhaps the mere seconds he spent looking into his boyfriend's eyes hypnotized him and rendered him an imbecile when he looked away. Whatever it was, he'd wasted so many opportunities and didn't plan to miss out on anymore.

He grinned when he saw Jackson and his annoying friend enter the cafeteria. Lonely nights in prison were significantly less depressing when Evan knew he'd see Jackson's face in the morning.

Goddamn his man was perfect with his full lips and big blue eyes. Evan loved how dark and long Jack's eyelashes were and the soft dusting of freckles that brushed across his nose. Sometimes Evan wondered if anybody else noticed them and subsequently thought about bashing in their heads if they had. He didn't want other people that close to what was his.

Growing up, Evan had never been possessive of much, mostly because he never had that many possessions. What he did have was so ratty or unappealing that most people would overlook the items even if they were left lying out in front of them. There were certain things that he cared about, like his paint and art supplies, but the use of those materials caused them to naturally come and go. He never got too attached. With Jackson it was different. Though he wasn't a possession, Evan found that his need to have Jackson for himself made Evan possessive.

"Eggs?" he asked, offering Jack a plate of soggy yellow mush.

As he typically did, Jackson shot him a dirty look and shook his head.

"They're good today. You should try them," Evan suggested, causing his boyfriend to grimace and Cecil to do a double take.

"You're a creepy motherfucker," Cecil informed Evan with a shake of his head. "Real weird. No doubt that's why your own boys don't want to fuck with you."

"I'm not trying to fuck with guys anyway," Evan stated simply. "You can keep that gay shit. Open your ass wide all you want."

"Better watch your fucking mouth," Jackson jumped in, narrowing his eyes in warning as he crossed his arm over his friend's chest to hold him back. Jack huffed when the redhead held out the plate again, completely ignoring the irritation he'd caused in both men.

Jackson grabbed it and put it on his tray. "Probably poisoned this shit or something," he told Cecil. "Let's give them to Larry's celly and see if he fucking dies." Cecil nodded and glared at Evan one last time before heading to the table.

As discreetly as possible, Jackson slipped the small folded paper he'd felt under the plate into his pocket and kept it there until he could read it privately.

When he was alone in his cell later that day, he pulled out the note, smoothed it out, and smiled at the drawing of a koala holding a little flag that said "Hi."

He'd never turn down any of the disgusting prison slop again.

X

September

By far, Thursdays were Evan's favorite day of the week. On Thursdays he got to kiss his boyfriend. Without exception, he made sure to be in his cell at 10:00 a.m. every Thursday morning. Jackson usually didn't get to his room until around 10:45, but Evan was there at the top of the hour in case Jackson's rounds got messed up in any way. Evan would do his best to get his cellmate, Luther, to fuck off. Most of the time he was successful, but sometimes he wasn't. On those Thursdays, Jackson would show up and look like he'd been punched in the gut at the sight of Luther, perfectly illuminating Evan's feelings on the matter. Luckily, of the forty-eight Thursdays that had passed since Evan arrived at MCC, they'd made out for forty-five.

"Luther," Evan began as his cellmate perused his GED book, "can you go try to educate your dumb ass in the library for a while?"

"Fuck you, prick," Luther grunted without malice, completely used to Evan's delivery after living with him for eleven months.

"Seriously, I'm horny as a motherfucker. I got to jerk my cock. I mean, you can always stay in here if you want to watch. I'll give you a good show, but I'd really rather you fucked off."

The other man sighed and shook his head. "Why can't you just do it in the shower like the rest of us? I don't like being displaced."

"Ooo, using those new vocab words, man. I see you," Evan teased with a smirk. "C'mon. I don't ask for much."

"You ask for a lot actually," Luther informed him. "Always asking me for my Takis or gum."

"Speaking of gum, you got any?"

"Fuck, you're annoying as shit, Goodwyn," he groused. "If I don't give it to you, you're just going to take it when I leave."

Evan smiled as his cellmate tossed him a stick of Double Mint that was lying on his desk before taking his book and ambling out of the room.

As he always did, Evan chewed his gum and paced the small cell, waiting for Jackson to show up. Never had Evan anticipated anything as much as he did those two-minute meetings. His head spun for days afterward as he remembered the feel of puffy lips against his and fingers clawing at his body. The passion between them had never waned, but having each other in such small doses caused the intensity to be even greater than it had been.

As soon as he heard the door handle turn, he was on him, hunching over slightly to meet his lips and grasping onto the fleshy mounds of his ass as they kissed hungrily.

"I love you," Evan whispered between kisses as he kneaded his boyfriend's ass cheeks hard, hating the way the fabric prevented him from feeling his skin.

"Love you too," Jackson promised, dropping his hand down to stroke Evan's hard-on over his jumpsuit.

"Hang on," the redhead said, quickly unbuttoning his garment, so he could pull his already straining cock out. "C'mon. Let me see yours."

"Don't got time. Won't get done with my rounds by 11:30 and then Big John will put me on fucking washer duty instead," Jackson reminded him, licking his lips wantonly at the sight of Evan's dick standing so proudly between them. "Say 'good-bye' to Thursdays."

"I'm practically there already," Evan assured him as he licked and sucked on Jackson's neck, careful not to leave a mark. "You could put your fucking hand on it and I'll fucking blow." To prove his urgency, he wrapped his fingers around Jackson's wrist and brought his hand to his cock, letting out a deep groan as soon as Jackson touched him.

"All right, yeah, all right. Hold on," Jackson relented. He scrambled to undo his uniform and yanked his dick out, gasping when Evan immediately dropped to his knees and took him into his mouth. It took an estimated four bobs on his dick to have Jackson shooting his load down Evan's throat with a breathy groan.

"Mmm," Evan moaned, closing his eyes to savor his boyfriend's taste. "Fucking missed this." By the time he'd opened his eyes again,

Jackson had already tucked himself back in, his cheeks flushed red. "Bet I go quicker."

"That was two fucking seconds," Jackson laughed as he got down on his knees. "Goddamn. Dream of this motherfucker splitting me in half every night," he crooned as he swirled his tongue around the head of Evan's cock. Jack smirked when Evan let out a broken whimper. One fat lick up the underside of the shaft and a trip down his throat had Evan's legs shaking and his dick pouring out come.

Evan was still panting through his orgasm when Jack rose to his feet and slotted his messy mouth to his. The kiss was salty, sloppy, and perfect. Evan felt looser and more sated than he had in months.

"Can't wait 'til next week," Jackson flirted, lifting up his eyebrows as he pulled away.

"So fucking hot. You're so fucking hot," Evan groaned, grasping Jackson's ass again. "Drive me crazy every time I see you."

"You're the one that got your ass thrown in here for this torture," Jackson reminded him with a grin.

"Would go anywhere for this ass," Evan stated as he laid a playful spank on Jackson's behind. "Such a hot ass."

"All right, fuck off, Goodwyn." He grinned as he shoved Evan back. "I'm already behind. Going to have to bust my ass to get done in time."

"Fuck, I wish I could bust that ass."

Jack shook his head and handed Evan his clean cot sheets. "Give me your dirty ones."

Evan scrambled to strip his bed. "Came all over them for you."

"Romantic."

"You know me," Evan said with a smirk. He moved in close to Jackson again, this time resting his palm softly on his cheek and gazing into his eyes. "Love you."

"I love you." Jackson pecked Evan's lips, lingering a few seconds too long before pulling away.

Evan watched as his boyfriend left the room, thinking that Thursday forty-nine was a game changer. Fifty-five more to go.

38

November

Jackson had noticed that Evan had looked a little anxious that morning, but he wasn't sure why until he opened the note Evan had slipped him with his eggs.

> J,
>
> I wanted to talk to you about this in person, but we're too busy doing better things when we're face-to-face. I also know that I'm asking you to make a big fucking decision and thought maybe you'd want to read it over instead of listening to me vomit it all out and then have to leave.
>
> I want you to come away with me. When we've served our time I want to leave this city. I want **us** to leave this city. Fuck gang bullshit, fuck visibility, and fuck Chicago. I know you have more keeping you here than I do. If you feel the need to stay, I'll understand. I'll stay too and we can live our lives the way we did before we got thrown in. But I can't help think if we left, we could live them better.
>
> Until you, I never thought about the future. I existed from moment to moment. I want a future with you. I want all of that gay shit. I want to come home to you, go to bed with you, wake up with you. You. I want you for life. I want a life with you.
>
> I feel like this is our chance. There'll be a lag between when we're released and when the affiliated boys will be able to get word back that we're out. You got a month more than me, but you don't have to worry; I know how to live on the streets, always have. Four weeks out there and I'll come back

for you. We'll take a bus. Anywhere but here. Come away with me and I'll never stop loving you, or don't, and I'll love you then too. You got me for as long as you want me and I hope it's forever. I want you to know that it feels like forever to me.

Anyway, it's weird not doing drugs. I feel so much more than I have in years. I kinda hate it, to be honest, but it doesn't mean that I think it's worse. I hate a lot of things. It's just different I guess. Either way, I feel lucid and confident that getting the fuck out of here is a good idea. I hope you do too.

I love you.
    E

P.S.: I've fucked up a ton of shit in my life. I could blame it on the coke but that would be bullshit. I'm probably just a dick. Thought you should know I'm not going to fuck shit up with you, in case you're worried I will or whatever.

Though he knew that a proposition of this sort was imminent, it didn't surprise him any less. He wasn't worried about the inherent promise that went along with running away together; he wasn't even worried about the disloyalty to Dem Demonz, as his allegiance had long since shifted to Evan.

Jackson was worried about Amy.

He'd spent the majority of his life protecting her, so the thought of abandoning her didn't sit well with him. He'd made sacrifices for her before and he wouldn't hesitate to do it again.

Yet, staying in Chicago and going back to the way things had been scared him. It didn't seem like a stretch to think that it was only a matter of time until all the shit that had happened would happen again. Maybe Evan would revert back to old habits, cravings intensified by streets he only remembered through bleary eyes. They'd no doubt get caught again and this time perhaps they'd be on the other side of the bullet. Dark thoughts of death permeated Jack's brain; having to bury Evan and not being able to show at the funeral, having to say good-bye to the love of his life while not being able to speak.

Jackson knew what he wanted to do, what he had to do, but he needed to speak with his sister. He needed her to tell him that it was all right, that she'd be okay without him.

Two days later Jackson started his visit with Amy with, "I got to talk to you about something." He rubbed his fingertips over his eyebrows as he sat across the glass from his sister.

"Sounds serious." She frowned, shifting in the metal seat. "Everything okay?"

"Yeah, it's…uh, he wants to leave after we're released. Get out of Chicago."

"For a while or, like, for good?"

"For good. Wants to be done with all the shit, you know. Start over, I guess." Jackson cleared his throat uncomfortably.

"And what do you want?"

Jackson's eyes darted to the side to ensure that the guy next to him wasn't listening and dropped his voice low. "Him."

"For good?" she asked, a small grin gracing her painted lips.

He nodded and gnawed on the inside of his cheek.

"Where are you guys going to go? Better be far away. Like airplane far. They're never going to get on airplane to look for you," she whispered, "but they sure as shit will get in a car."

"I know. Just not sure if I'm going to do it."

"Do what? Move?" she questioned, her confusion apparent on her face. "You said it's what you want."

"Don't want to leave you here."

She sighed. "Haven't you suffered enough for me, Jack? Seriously. You got wrapped up in all this shit in the first place because of me."

Jackson scoffed and shook his head. "Ain't a fucking victim, Ames. Not going to act like I don't like banging."

"But you like him more," she stated with a smirk.

He hushed her, eyes darting around the room nervously.

"I want you to go. I'm fine here, Jackson. I have a life, a boyfriend, friends. I'm strong. Because of you I'm strong. You deserve to have a life, too. A life that you want," she urged, blue eyes the same color as his. "I want that for you."

Jackson nodded, not sure what to say in response.

"Do you know where you're going to go? Have you talked about it?" she asked, straightening out her bangs.

"We haven't discussed…I mean, I haven't even told him that'll I'll do it."

"He'll be really happy when you do." She smiled at Jackson, who grinned back.

"He will be," he confirmed. "We'll probably need your help with some of the logistics, moving my money or whatever."

"I got you. Whatever you need." She nodded. She stared at him for a moment, her face awash with an emotion that Jackson didn't immediately recognize. "I'm proud of you," she whispered. "Being with who you want to be with, going where you want to go. It's awesome."

"All right, enough of this pussy shit. Can't fucking it take any more," he groused, but the smile that was still on his lips had to give him away.

She tapped her fingers on the glass and gave him a smirk.

X

January

"Happy New Year," Evan crooned, pressing his lips against Jackson's and grunting when his boyfriend pushed him against the wall of his cell to go at him more fervently.

"Happy New Year, baby," Jack replied, fanning his fingers out as he grasped the cradle of Evan's head and slipped wild tongue into his mouth.

"Eleven more months."

Jackson nodded. "You still looking up places?"

"Yeah, whenever I have library privileges. Got it narrowed down to towns in California, Arizona, and Colorado."

"They all got a good art scene?"

Evan nuzzled his nose against Jackson's and pecked his lips. "They do." He wondered how he got so lucky. He'd spent his whole life fucking up, but somehow things were finally coming together. He was overcome with gratitude. The emotion that had once been so foreign to him now surged through him at the most unexpected times.

"Going to pimp your shit out," Jackson teased as Evan nibbled and tugged at Jack's lower lip. "Fucking talented bastard."

Evan smiled into the subsequent kisses, thinking that he finally knew what it felt like to have someone believe in him.

It made him believe in himself.

X

April

Jackson was aggravated when the bathrooms in C block were closed for maintenance. It was inconvenient to have to trek to D and the lines were incredibly long. The only bright spot was the fact that the COs had to loosen up shower time restrictions in order to ensure that every inmate had the opportunity to get clean. This meant, for two days, the D block bathroom was open all night.

It was a little after 11:00 p.m. when he passed Evan's door and glanced in. To his surprise his boyfriend was sitting up on his bed working on something in a notebook. They locked eyes for a moment and a sudden rush of energy coursed through Jackson's veins.

The bathroom was grosser than the one he typically used, but he didn't really mind because it was also empty. He walked into the stall and turned the knobs to release a weak spitting of water from the showerhead. Hanging his towel on the hook, he climbed in and began to lather his body up with soap. He didn't flinch when he felt arms wrap around the back of his waist and lips press against his shoulder. He knew those arms and lips as well as he knew his own. They didn't exchange any words, both too busy holding their breath. When he felt a finger covered in Vaseline make its way past his ass cheeks and press against his hole, Jackson sighed, leaning his forehead against the cold concrete wall. As Evan hastily opened him, Jack bit his wrist to hold back his moans, his whole body shaking from the pressure. He was tight. He knew that there was no way they had enough time for him to be prepped well enough. He grimaced and swallowed his cry when he felt his boyfriend's big dick inching inside of him, feeling like it was splitting him in half.

Evan went slow, given the circumstances, and tickled his fingers up and down Jackson's back while rolling his hips. Little moans escaped Evan's lips, causing Jackson to push past the pain to back up farther on him. His boyfriend took it as an invitation to grasp on to his hip bones and start thrusting harder. The warm water trickled over them as they fucked, bodies moving in the same rhythm, pleasured pants building. Random pangs of pain had Jackson dragging his hand down the stall, but he settled when he felt Evan's hand press on top of it, fingers intertwining. A familiar stutter in the redhead's breath caused Jack to drop his hand down to his dick and begin to pump it along with Evan's beat. The came together, both strangling the noises that were dying to escape their lips. Wordlessly, Evan turned him around, pressed his palms to his cheeks, and placed a tender kiss on Jack's lips.

When he came back the next day, Jackson shook his head and they held each other instead, the rips and tears too bad to push past.

Fuck prison.

X

October

As soon as Jackson entered the cafeteria his heart dropped. He knew Evan would be gone, but it didn't make it easier knowing. Jack went through the line and refused every item but an apple. Taking a seat at the same table he'd sat at for the past two years, he stared at the guy who was serving the hot meal and wished it was Evan.

Four lonely Thursdays and he'd never be away from him again.

39

It wasn't as though Evan hadn't spent time outside during his sentence. He'd made use of the yard whenever he'd had privileges. It was that it felt different to be outdoors when he was beyond the prison fence. The air was crisper, the sky bluer; the sun brighter. Everything beyond those walls was more vibrant and alive, except him.

Without Jackson, any light was dimmer, any happiness dulled.

Evan should have been elated as he exited the prison door and relieved when he saw Amy standing by the gate, but he was anything but. He'd left his heart behind in his small cell and the ghost ache in his chest was painful.

If he was on the inside, he'd be serving Jackson some inedible food, passing him a note, gazing into his eyes. Instead his boyfriend was in there without him. For twenty-eight days Evan wouldn't get to see Jackson's wonderful face, kiss his pouty lips, feel his hard body; a punishment significantly more brutal than the two years he spent in prison.

"Hey," Amy said, a half grin on her face as she hugged Evan. "You look good. Healthy."

"Thanks. Feel good, minus you know." He sniffed and gestured back to the building. "Left someone kinda important in there."

"One month," Amy reminded him, digging into her purse to pull out an envelope and cell phone. "Jack has the number. He's going to call you whenever he gets to use the phone, so keep the ringer on." She handed Evan the envelope and he peeked inside. "There's $1,000 in there."

"It's…wow. Thanks," he said, shaking his head in disbelief.

"I mean, it's not my money. Thank Jackson," she said with a shrug. "It should be enough for you to get a room at an extended-stay place that gives you breakfast." She paused to study Evan's face. "Just don't use it on drugs. You'll break his fucking heart."

Typically guilt didn't work on him. The idea of somebody putting their feelings in his hands and expecting a certain outcome was downright abhorrent, but he found it impossible to disregard his boyfriend's emotions. The thought of disappointing or hurting Jackson was harrowing. It was something he planned to avoid doing at any cost. "I won't. I'm done with that shit," he assured her, hoping it was a promise he was able to keep.

She nodded. "You have any idea of where you guys are going to go when he gets out?"

"Yeah, um, this place in Arizona. It's called Flagstaff." Evan looked down at his boot, not able to face her when asking a question that made him feel so vulnerable. "Do you think he really wants to go? I mean, he says he does, but I worry that he'll change his mind. That we'll get there and he'll want to come home or some shit."

She laughed lightly. "Jackson doesn't do anything that he doesn't want to do, and for you," she paused, "he'd do anything."

"But I want him to want to, you know. Not do it because he thinks he'll lose me, or whatever. I'd never leave him."

"As much as it sucks for me, I think this is what's best for him. I really believe it's what he wants, too. He worries about me, I know that, but being thousands of miles away from here and never looking back… He wants that," she promised. "Are you going to stay around here until the twelfth?"

Evan nodded, slipping the money and phone into his backpack. "Yeah, going to lay low, take hot showers, and eat shitty food that doesn't taste shitty."

"Sounds like a plan. I'll see you back here on the twelfth then. If you need anything else, you know my number."

"Three one two-two six seven-three one four two," Evan rattled off with a smirk.

"Good," Amy stated, pulling him in for a hug. "Don't hesitate to use it."

He hugged her back, thinking how strange it was that he felt close to her. Maybe it was because she was, in many ways, an extension of Jackson or that she never judged Evan even when she should have. She'd accepted him when he wasn't worthy of acceptance, something his family had never been able to do. And for that, he was grateful.

They parted ways with Amy making her way to the L and Evan heading toward the small town center a few miles away from the prison. He decided there wasn't much use in going farther because the closer he got to the South Side, the more chance he'd have of running into somebody he wanted to avoid.

He checked into a little shithole motel that charged him twenty-nine dollars a day, had a McDonald's across the street and a convenience store down the block. After paying for twenty-eight days upfront, he headed toward the golden arches and made love to a quarter pounder with cheese. It tasted really fucking good, but he figured it would've been even better if Jackson was sitting across from him. When Evan was done, he went to the store to buy toiletries, a notebook, and pencils. Though paper and pencil weren't his medium, it was better than nothing.

As soon as he opened the door to his room, his new cell phone began to ring. He picked it up as quickly as possible and threw the rest of his crap onto his bed. "Jackson?"

"You have a collect call from an inmate at Metropolitan Correctional Center. Please press one to accept the call."

Evan pressed with all his heart.

"Jack?" Evan repeated once the line clicked over.

"Hey," Jackson muttered, his tone more sullen than usual. He sounded a million miles away even though he was down the road. Evan tried to imagine where he was standing, thinking of the gray wall in front of him and the men in orange jumpsuits on either side. He never thought he'd long for the inside of a prison, but found that being on the outside felt like being locked down when his boyfriend wasn't with him.

"You a'ight?"

"Still in prison, so I've been better," Jack said with a wry laugh. He let out a labored sigh and spoke more softly into the phone. "Missing your goofy face."

"Miss you too," Evan replied sadly, picking the lint off the nearly threadbare comforter. "Wish we had the same amount of time."

"Don't do anything stupid and get your crazy ass thrown back in here," Jackson warned. "Just chill the fuck out and don't get into trouble."

"I'm good," Evan assured. "Just going to lie around, watch TV, draw, and eat McDonald's."

"Don't bring up McDonald's," Jackson groaned.

"Sorry." He thought of the disgusting food he'd been serving the day before and immediately regretted bringing up something even half edible to Jackson.

"Where are you?"

"At a piece-of-shit motel a few miles from the prison."

"And you're going to lay low, right?"

"Jackson," Evan said with an exasperated sigh, "I'm not going to fuck this up, a'ight? I want out of here. I'm not going to do anything to jeopardize that. Believe me."

"Just want this bullshit over with," Jackson admitted.

"I do too."

"Only got a few more minutes, but," he paused, "tell me more about it."

"About what?"

"Where we're going," he prompted.

Evan smiled, glad to hear the hopefulness and excitement in his boyfriend's voice. He'd been able to share only the same few facts every time Jackson had asked, but he hadn't seemed to mind the repetition. "It's the largest city in Northern Arizona, but it's kind of outdoorsy with like mountains and forests and shit."

"Never seen either of those," Jackson stated, just as he always had when they had the conversation.

"Yeah, me either. It's hot in the summer and cold in the winter. It snows and stuff but not as much as here."

"Don't sound bad."

"Nah, I think it will be pretty nice. It's got a good art scene, but we can get an apartment for way cheaper than we could in some of the places in California that are known to be creative or whatever," Evan reminded Jack. "And there's a university there, you know, so there's a lot of shit going on."

Jackson let out a labored sigh. "I can't fucking wait, baby."

"I can't either. Twenty-eight days, Jack. Twenty-eight days and we'll be on our way."

"Twenty-eight days," Jackson repeated.

X

There was no avoiding the fact that looking forward to something made his time in prison move impossibly slower than it had when he was in the drudges of his sentence. Jackson felt like he lived a year every day and hated that the only time the minutes flew by was when he was on the phone with Evan.

His boyfriend had proved to be down for him in ways Jack had never expected. He never missed one of his calls and spent most of his time checking shit out on the motel's computer so he could share something new or interesting about Flagstaff. The little details made it easier for Jackson's mind to escape the confines of the prison walls and daydream of what the future would hold.

As much as Jackson loved hearing about Evan's research, he loved the lucidness in his voice even more. Evan promised him that he was remaining clean, and his coherence acted as confirmation. Jackson had had a taste of what Evan was like when he wasn't inebriated, but never for long stretches of time. The prospect of a sober Evan excited Jack as much as the move.

Twenty-eight days after Evan had made this trek, Jackson walked down the hallway to the exterior doors, holding the items he'd arrived with twenty-six months earlier in his trembling hands. Anticipation was sparking through him like a live wire and he couldn't wait to get the fuck outside. The guard made some corny joke that Jackson barely comprehended, his mind too jumbled with the buzz of emotions. When the guard opened the door and gestured for Jackson to exit, he squinted into the sun, attempting to distinguish the figures in front of him.

A choked declaration of his name filled the air as strong arms wrapped around him. Dropping his shit, Jackson placed his palms on Evan's cheeks and accepted the kiss that Evan pressed onto Jack's lips in front of Amy and the guard. They kissed as if they were desperate to make up for twenty-six lost months and two decades of closeted years. They stayed connected until they were breathless, pulling back only when they needed to take in air.

Evan's arm remained around Jackson's waist as Amy pulled her brother in for a hug. "Here's your jacket," she said, handing him a coat so he wasn't left standing in his summer attire. He wasn't sure if it was the cold or adrenaline that had him feeling so goddamn shaky, but he was glad for the warmth either way.

"Thanks," he said with a grin, looking at his sister for what was sure to be the last time in a while.

"Nah. I'm the one that's supposed to thank you," she tsked, embracing him again. "Don't worry about me, okay? I'll be fine." Jackson nodded as she handed him his duffel back. "It's got everything you asked for plus your bank cards."

"You sure you're going to be all right?"

"Positive," she assured him. "Just get the fuck out of here before I start to cry like a bitch, okay?"

X

Amy watched as her brother and his boyfriend walked away hand in hand, bags slung over their shoulders, smiling lips stealing kisses as they made their way toward their forever.

They didn't look back.

EPILOGUE

Evan never had a concept of time. He wasn't sure if it was the chemicals he'd altered his body with that had caused him to live exclusively in the moment or if it was a consequence of a life he never found particularly worth living. Loving Jackson had altered so much, but the most jarring change had been an increased awareness of how fleeting an hour was, how fast a week could pass, and that even May had only thirty-one short days. It was strange how the years in prison had crawled by, forcing him to move like molasses through each day and wish the months away, while the year after had raced past him at a neck-breaking pace, full of moments he was unable to grasp on to even though he had desperately tried. Any amount of time with Jackson wasn't enough, each hour ephemeral.

"What're you thinking about?" his boyfriend asked, snapping him out of his thoughts and bringing him back to the present, another moment he wouldn't be able to keep.

"Painting," Evan replied, smiling at Jack before turning his attention back to the grouping of evergreen trees that stood proudly across from the balcony of their townhouse.

Jackson laughed and tapped the ash off his cigarette. "That ain't new. What about it?"

"I think it's the only way to freeze time." Evan paused and shook his head. "You paint a moment and all of a sudden it's yours. You can revisit it whenever you want."

Jack nodded and grinned at Evan when he caught his eyes.

"What?" Evan questioned, mirroring the look of amusement that was on his boyfriend's face.

"Like when you get like this," Jackson stated. "All philosophical and shit. Like you know what you're doing matters."

"Matters to me at least," Evan said, clarifying his statement when he saw Jackson bite his lip and lift his eyebrows. "And to you. It matters to you, too."

"And the motherfucker that bought your painting two days ago. Bet it matters to him, right?" Jack reminded him. "He liked it enough to pay for it and hang it in his house, so it probably does."

"To him too," Evan agreed, shaking his head in disbelief. "Still can't believe I sold one."

"Your first one," Jackson corrected. "First of many." He dropped his cigarette into the ashtray and patted his lap. "C'mere."

Evan obliged, climbing onto Jack, his legs straddled on either side of Jackson's hips, lips pressed against lips, stolen morning minutes before the start of their busy day. "I love you," Evan whispered as Jackson raked his fingers through Evan's hair and pulled him back in again for another kiss.

"Really fucking proud of you, man," Jackson told him, blue eyes earnest and full of emotion.

"Only paid for a month's rent, not that big of a deal," Evan said with a shrug.

"It's ain't about that and you know it," Jackson chided. "Going to have to get used to me complimenting you for something other than the way you fuck, Evan."

Evan rolled his eyes and laughed. "Don't act like that's not your favorite talent."

"Shut up." Jackson grinned when Evan leaned back in. Their tongues tangled languidly as they continued to push back their responsibilities. When the alarm on Jackson's cell phone chimed, they knew there was no more avoiding the inevitable. "Going to be late for class."

"My businessman," Evan flirted, grasping the fabric of Jackson's t-shirt in his fist and biting his lower lip. "Fucking hot-ass businessman."

"It's one class that I get for being a fucking slave to the university," Jackson replied with a laugh.

"But you clean that cafeteria like a stud," Evan teased, giving his boyfriend a peck.

"You wouldn't believe how entitled these motherfuckers are. They leave their trays on the table," Jack groused with a sigh. "I want to punch them in their fucking snot faces."

"Know how you feel," Evan sympathized, thinking of how snobbish the clientele at the gallery was, turning up their noses when he came through with the broom. He was thankful for the small corner Grant gave him to display his work, but cleaning the space wasn't Evan's dream.

Jackson always told Evan that it was a small step toward the greater good, and Evan did his best to remind his boyfriend of the same. "Going to be late tonight. First Friday Art Walk."

Jackson nodded. "Yeah, I was thinking of coming by."

"You were?" Evan felt light. "Thought it wasn't your scene."

"You'll be there, so I'll make it my scene," Jackson said matter-of-factly.

"Bet all the free drinks and food got nothing to do with it, huh?" Evan teased, nibbling on one of his favorite spots, Jackson's pouty lower lip.

"Not a thing," Jack deadpanned, unable to keep a straight face. "I'll see you after my shift, all right?" He spanked Evan's ass so he'd stand up.

"I'll walk out with you," Evan offered, following Jackson through the house. They grabbed their backpacks and locked the front door behind them. Pulling Jackson in for another kiss before he headed in the opposite direction, Evan said, "Ten hours."

"Ten hours," Jackson assured him, patting his cheek and looking softly into his eyes. "I'll call you after class and on my break, all right?"

Evan nodded wondering when he'd become so fucking codependent. He figured it was around the same time he started to feel like time was slipping away from them, no matter how hard he tried to hold on to it. "When we get home tonight I'm going to paint you."

"I like your other stuff though," Jackson chided, a pink hue crawling across his cheeks, ever the shy model.

"I like today." Evan sighed. "Going to hold on to it."

Jackson slotted his mouth against Evan's for one last kiss and then turned to head to the bus stop.

"That ass tho," Evan called with a grin, earning middle fingers and a laugh from his boyfriend.

Ten hours.

Six hundred minutes.

Thirty-six thousand seconds until he saw the love of his life.

ABOUT THE AUTHOR

Riley has always loved to write, believing that life has the possibility to be its most beautiful when it's portrayed on the pages of a book. Feeling the need to create and liberate in the midst of the political landscape, Riley writes novels that focus on LGBTQ protagonists, wanting to honor a community that deserves better representation depicting lives, loves and triumphs in all facets of fiction.

Did you enjoy this book? Drop us a line and say so. We love to hear from readers, and so do our authors. To connect, visit www.boroughspublishinggroup.com online, send comments directly to info@boroughspublishinggroup.com, or friend us on Facebook and follow us on Twitter and Instagram. Be sure to check back regularly for contests and new releases in your favorite subgenres of romance.

Are you an aspiring writer? Check out www.boroughspublishinggroup.com/submit and see if we can help you make your dreams come true.

Made in the USA
San Bernardino, CA
05 December 2017